The Tiger's Back

Also by Patrick C. Walsh

The Mac Maguire detective mysteries

The Body in the Boot

The Dead Squirrel

The Weeping Women

The Blackness

23 Cold Cases

Two Dogs

The Match of the Day Murders

The Chancer

Stories of the supernatural

13 Ghosts of Winter

The Black Vaults Experiment

All available in Amazon Books

Patrick C. Walsh

The Tiger's Back

The ninth 'Mac' Maguire mystery

Garden City Ink

A Garden City Ink book
www.gardencityink.com

First published in Great Britain in 2019

All rights reserved
Copyright © 2019 Patrick C. Walsh

The right of Patrick C. Walsh to be identified as the author of this work has been asserted in accordance with Section 77 of the Copyright, Designs and Patents Act 1988.

No part of this publication may be reproduced, stored in a retrieval system, or transmitted, in any form or means, electronic, mechanical, photocopying, recording or otherwise, without the prior permission of the copyright holder.

All characters in this publication are fictitious and any resemblance to real persons, living or dead, is purely co-incidental.

A CIP record for this title is available from the British Library

ISBN: 9781072651819

Cover art © Patrick C Walsh 2019

Photo credits - Erman Kayaalp (Tiger tattoo)
Michael Gaida (derelict building)

Garden City Ink Design

'Those who foolishly sought power by riding the back of the tiger ended up inside'

John F. Kennedy

For Jim who gave me the idea

It begins…

They'd been cruising the streets for two nights now and everyone was getting jumpy. This wasn't their turf. They all knew what would happen if they found members of another street gang in their area. It would be very short and very bloody. They watched every car that drove by just in case it started slowing down. This had already happened a few times and Skank had half-expected the windows to roll down and guns to be pointed at them. They'd been lucky so far but the ongoing tension had been draining and they were all tired and irritable.

They were beginning to know the area around the church quite well by now. They'd been told that this would be where they'd find their man. They parked up the black Mercedes SUV for a while. Each of them had a photograph of the man they were looking for.

'I don't get it,' one of them said. 'He's just an old man. Who is he and what's he done? It must be really something to get us this far off the Steele looking for him.'

'You don't need to get it,' Skank said with a snarl. 'You just need to do what you're told.'

'It's him,' the driver said pointing to the other side of the street.

An old man dressed in a dirty jacket and a woollen bobble hat walked straight past them. He was weaving from side to side and he had a glass bottle tucked into one pocket.

'He's right,' Skank said. 'Everyone out!'

Skank crossed the street.

'Hey bro, where you going?' Skank shouted at the man's back.

The man turned around and peered at Skank as if trying to focus his eyes. While he was doing this the driver came around behind him. He kicked the man's legs from under him and he fell to the floor. He, Skank and the other two started kicking the man as hard as they could. He let out a series of low moans as the kicks connected and then fell silent. Skank stopped.

'Kick him in the head a few times, make sure he's dead,' Skank said as he walked back to the car.

He opened up the boot and took out a large plastic bottle. He ambled back again. They stopped kicking as Skank looked down. He didn't even look like a man anymore, just a bloodied bundle of rags. He opened up the bottle and sprayed the contents on the man's body. He then took out a box of matches. He lit one up and dropped it. That's all it took.

The man's clothes caught fire easily. He watched as the flames grew brighter but the man didn't even twitch.

'Come on, let's go home,' Skank said.

They all got back into the car and drove off. Skank could still see the flames in the wing mirror. He smiled. He'd been worried about going off the estate but he'd got the job done.

Little Jools will be happy, he thought.

A young man had witnessed the attack. He'd hid and watched it all as tears rolled down his face.

The man who had been kicked to death was his friend, his only friend. A darkness descended on his mind. He didn't go towards the body but, instead, he started walking in the opposite direction. He walked south. He kept walking until he came to a small bridge over a lock gate. Beyond the bridge a small pier jutted out into the wide blackness of the River Thames. He climbed over the fence and walked towards the edge of the pier.

He didn't hesitate or look down he just kept on walking. The icy cold water made him gasp and the water flooded into his lungs. He was dead in seconds.

His body would be found three days later. It would be buried without a name.

Chapter One

Mac sat motionless in his office. It was quiet. It was still. It was boring. He sighed as he sat and waited for something to happen.

It was only a couple of days into the New Year and he'd decided that he might as well get back to work. He'd had a nice relaxing Christmas which he'd spent mostly with his best friend Tim. This was due to the fact that his daughter Bridget had been working at the hospital over most of the holiday season. Thankfully though, she did manage to get Christmas Day off. It was a good day and he had something of a full house for Christmas dinner as Tim was there as well as Bridget's boyfriend Tommy and his mother Annette. It had been the second Christmas since his wife Nora had died and a few moments of sadness had inevitably interrupted his enjoyment of the occasion. He hoped that he'd managed to disguise them though, he'd wanted his guests to have a good time.

This morning he'd decided that he'd relaxed enough. Tim had gone off for the day chasing down some antique furniture in one of the local New Year sales and he wouldn't be back until seven o'clock or so. He'd phoned and asked Mac if he wanted to go with him but Mac told him that he had some work to do. It was, of course, a lie. In truth, he'd felt a strange restlessness and he knew that he wouldn't be good company. He desperately needed a case. Even so, sitting alone in the silence of his office, he began to wonder if he'd done the right thing.

The last case he'd worked on had been over seven weeks ago and that had only lasted for three days. A solicitor had approached him and asked him if he could track down an heir to a will. It wasn't exactly a fortune, being just over twenty-five thousand pounds, but it was still a considerable amount of money. He'd enjoyed the puzzle that the case had provided and only wished that it could have lasted a bit longer.

He looked at his watch. It was only twelve fifteen. The eternity of a winter afternoon stretched out before him. He'd told Tim that he was going to spend the day doing some research. He'd opened up his laptop but after an hour or so he'd given up. He just couldn't get interested. So, he just sat there, silently waiting.

The silence was broken by his phone. He looked at the caller's number. It wasn't one he recognised. His hopes rose a fraction.

'Hello? Is that Mr. Maguire?' a woman's voice asked.

'Yes, it's Mac Maguire here. How can I help you?'

'I need to speak to you, somewhere private if possible.'

'Of course. When?'

'Right now, if you're free,' she said. 'I'm in Welwyn but I can be in Letchworth in about half an hour or so, if that's okay?'

Mac assured her that it was and gave her the address of his office. He finished the call and stood looking out of the window at the rain falling down on the car park that lay behind his office. It got heavier and made a drumming sound as the water hit the ground. He tried to remember if there was anything familiar about the woman's voice. He was fairly sure that there wasn't. He was more than curious but he'd just have to wait until she turned up to discover what it was all about.

A tentative knock on the door eventually announced her arrival.

'I'll hang your coat up if you like,' Mac said as he invited his guest in.

She'd obviously gotten caught in the worst of the rain as her black raincoat was heavy with the water it had absorbed. He hung it on the coat stand and placed her umbrella below it. A pool of water had already started to collect on the floor. He looked at her as she sat down. She was in her late thirties and wore a long black skirt and a dark grey twin set. Her hair was dark brown and cut efficiently short and she wore black rimmed glasses now streaked with rain and starting to mist over. He offered her a tissue which she gratefully accepted.

'Mr. Maguire, thank you for seeing me so quickly,' she said as she wiped her glasses.

'That's absolutely no problem,' he replied. 'What can I do for you?'

She put her glasses back on and looked at Mac. She hesitated for a moment before drawing a deep breath.

'I'd like you to look into a murder for me. I've tried everything else and I've gotten nowhere.'

'A murder? I take it that that the police already know about it?'

'Well, they say that they're looking into it but they've done nothing as far as I can see,' she said with some anger. 'They probably don't think it's worth their while.'

He could see that she was getting a little upset so he decided that they should first take a step back.

'Okay, we'll go into that in a moment. First of all, tell me a little about yourself and then we'll get back to why you want me to investigate this murder. Please take your time, I'm in no hurry,' Mac said.

She took a few seconds to calm herself down.

'My name is Marcia Notts and I'm training to be a solicitor with a law firm in Welwyn Garden City. It's mostly house and property related work, we don't do the criminal stuff. I should be fully qualified in another year or so.'

Mac thought that this probably explained her choice of clothes.

'I'm married, I have two children and we live in Old Welwyn. My husband's a vet, he's a partner in a practice here in Letchworth.'

Mac thought for a moment.

'Yes, it's on Norton Way, isn't it?'

'How on earth could you know that?' she asked looking suitably puzzled.

'I think I met your husband once. He likes wearing bow ties, doesn't he?'

'My God you really have met him, haven't you?' she said.

'Yes, I talked to him once about a dead squirrel but that's of no relevance here. Please go on.'

She flashed Mac a look of astonishment before carrying on.

'Well, just the week before Christmas I got a message to call the police in London,' she said getting visibly upset at the memory. 'They told me that my father had died, in fact that he'd been murdered. I thought that they needed me to formally identify the body but they said that there'd be no point.'

'Why was that?'

She took another deep breath before she answered.

'He'd been kicked to death and then his body had been sprayed with barbecue lighter fuel and set on fire. The police told me that there wasn't much left to identify.'

'So how were they able to identify him?' Mac asked.

'He had his RAF Retired Service Card in his trouser pocket. He always carried it with him and luckily the flames didn't get that. I was listed in his service record as a dependent and that's how they found me. I was able to confirm it was him by a birthmark he had on his back. I also described the tattoos he had on both arms. Even though his arms were badly burnt they could still make some of them out.'

Having said this, she seemed on the verge of tears. Mac quickly moved on.

'Where did the attack happen?'

'In London, Stepney to be exact.'

'Stepney? I take it that was where he lived?' Mac asked.

'He was born there Mr. Maguire and, although it was where he resided, I wouldn't call it living. My father was an alcoholic, he had been for years but we all coped with it somehow. He had a nice little house in Welwyn Garden City and, even with the drinking, he was doing okay. He was working and earning good money. Then my mum got ill and died. He became deeply depressed and just gave up on life. A couple of months later he disappeared from the house that he'd lived in for twenty five years and that was it, I never saw him again. I tried to find him but he obviously didn't want to be found. I heard about him every now and again from some relatives of ours who still live in Stepney. They told me that they'd seen him around the area but, beyond that, they knew nothing about how he lived. Then the police came and told me that he was dead.'

'Whereabouts in Stepney was he staying?'

Mac knew that, like most parts of London, Stepney had its good and bad parts.

'I'm not sure but I was told that he used to go to the soup kitchen at St. Philip's a lot.'

He knew exactly where St. Philip's Church was and it was definitely not in one of Stepney's better areas.

'So, what do you want me to do?' Mac asked.

'I don't know if you can do anything really but I can't bear to think that the animal who did such a terrible thing to my dad is still out there walking around. I know I must have sounded quite bitter about the police just now and, for all I know they might be doing everything they can, but the problem is I don't know that. Every time I try and speak to them I just get blanked. You're my last hope Mr. Maguire, if you can't help then I'll have no choice but to give up. But, if I don't find out what happened to my dad, I know that it will haunt me for the rest of my life.'

She did indeed look at the end of her tether.

'Okay, I'll do my best but I can't promise anything,' Mac said.

'I've looked you up on the internet Mr. Maguire and I'm sure that your best will do. I've copied everything I have about dad onto this stick including what little I've had from the police,' she said as she handed Mac a memory stick. 'I hope it helps. He was a good dad, even with the drink. He was funny and he really loved us. It was just our bad luck that he loved the drink even more.'

He fired up his laptop as soon as she'd left and spent the next few hours reading every detail about the case. He also managed to find some local newspaper reports of the crime. It was a brutal murder, a man beaten to death leaving a grieving daughter behind but it was a case and Mac was happy.

He was still reading when Tim appeared.

'I saw your light on. Come on you, it's pub time,' Tim said.

He looked at his watch and found that his friend was indeed right.

Chapter Two

The next morning Mac had finished reading everything that Mrs. Notts had given him for the second time and he was mulling it all over in his mind. It didn't really tell him very much and he was beginning to see why she'd felt so frustrated about the investigation. However, he could guess what had happened.

In such a high crime area and, with the ever dwindling resources that the police have to work with these days, he knew that they'd have to prioritise their case load. The murder of a homeless man might rank quite low in that situation. Mac had dealt with a few cases like this before and, even with the best will in the world, evidence had been almost impossible to find. This was due to fact that the victim, being homeless, usually moved around a fair bit and that most of the people who knew the victim moved around too. They were not only hard to find but, even when found, they were often unwilling to talk to the police who they sometimes saw as the enemy. With all the targets the police had to meet these days, if you had other cases that you stood a better chance of solving, then that's what you'd spend more time on.

Unfortunately, it was just the way it worked.

He rang Bethnal Green police station and asked for DI Janet Morris who was the officer that Mrs. Notts had last spoken to. She didn't sound too happy about it but she said that she could give him ten minutes at four o'clock. It was now nearly eleven so he decided to drive into London while the traffic wasn't too bad and spend some time having a looking around the area. It had been a while since he'd last been to Stepney.

It was clear and cold outside, his breath smoky white on the crisp January air. He had to scrape a thin layer of ice from his windscreen and side windows and then wait a while until his old Almera had warmed up enough to fully demist the windows. He recalled Toby from next door looking thoughtfully at his car and commenting on the fact that the garage down the road were doing some good deals. He'd bet that it wouldn't take those cars five minutes to defrost a windscreen but he immediately dismissed the thought and felt somewhat guilty at having had it in the first place. In reality he was quite attached to his little green car.

The traffic was heavy due to several stretches of road works within a few miles of each other and he didn't get into Central London until nearly one thirty. The sun was low in the sky and Mac had to drive with his sunglasses on. Even so the sun was blinding and it made for quite an uncomfortable trip. He remembered that he used to do this run nearly every day when he was working and wondered how on earth he'd managed it. He'd put St. Philips Church in his satnav and he decided to go there first.

The church looked impressively large as he drove towards it. It was a large Victorian grey stone gothic building with a high square castellated tower at the front. It was surrounded by greenery and graves and looked as if a prosperous country church had been dropped from the sky into the grey drab urban surroundings of tower blocks and council flats.

London had always puzzled Mac. Its so-called 'nice' areas were cheek by jowl with areas that basically weren't safe to walk about in the daytime never mind at night. Then magically, after someone had 'found' an area, 'nice' people started moving in and the area became 'nice' again. Except all the people who had lived there when it wasn't 'nice' had to go somewhere else and, priced out of the areas that they'd often been born and brought up in, they went where they could. Until some other wonder kid 'found' that area too he supposed.

Mac was glad that his wife had made the decision to live outside London. In his opinion it was an unmitigated madhouse.

He parked on a single yellow line and put his disabled badge on the dashboard. He looked again at his watch. He had an hour and a half to kill.

He took his crutch from the passenger seat and walked through the fancy wrought iron gates and into the church grounds. He guessed that this area had once been 'nice' during the Victorian era. This could be seen not only from the grandeur of the church but also from the gravestones that surrounded it. There were even statues including one of a very impressive angel. As Mac walked on it became a bit less impressive as he could see that one of its wings had been broken off. He could also see discarded chip papers, empty cans of high strength beer and cider as well as the odd empty bottle of cheap wine strewn between the gravestones.

As he passed by, he looked up at the angel who seemed to look down on him with a disapproving expression. Mac couldn't really blame him.

He stepped inside. The interior of the church was unexpectedly impressive. On either side of the building high Romanesque arches held up the lofty vaulted ceiling. The space was illuminated by several windows on either side, all with clear glass, but behind the ornate altar a huge stained-glass window depicted Christ's Ascension into Heaven dappled the space with coloured light.

A woman appeared from the left of the altar carrying a box full of white candles. She was in her thirties, had short hair and looked quite severe and very business-like. Mac walked towards her.

'Excuse me,' he said when he got closer, 'I wonder if...'

He was stopped by her putting her index finger to her lips. She pointed off to the left. Mac silently followed her feeling like a schoolboy who had been caught in the act. She took them into a little kitchen area.

She smiled at Mac as he walked in, a genuinely warm smile which changed Mac's initially negative impression of her immediately.

'I'm sorry but I never like to talk in there. People often pop in during the day for a bit of peace and quiet. How can I help?'

Mac gave her a business card.

'A private detective?' she said looking impressed. 'I've never met a real detective before.'

'A man was killed not far from here a week or so before Christmas and I'm looking into his murder for his daughter. He, unfortunately, was an alcoholic and he slept rough around the area. The only thing we know for certain is that he used to come here quite often for the soup kitchen. I was just wondering if there was anyone I could talk to who might have known him?'

'Poor woman, it must have been terrible for her to lose her father in such a way and at such a time as well. There is someone you can talk to but I'm afraid that you'll need to come back later this evening. The soup kitchen doesn't open until tonight. We open our doors at eight but the Reverend Smalley should be here a little earlier, around six thirty or so. If he's not here for any reason then his assistant might be worth talking to. Just ask for Callum, he's really nice.'

'Thanks, I'll do that,' Mac replied.

'Best of luck,' she said as Mac turned to go.

'Thanks.'

Mac walked back to the car and then rang Tim. It looked like their evening drink would have to be a bit later than planned. He then drove the short distance to Bethnal Green. The police station was a three storey Victorian pile that had been refurbished. It had a huge old-fashioned blue 'Police' light outside which made Mac smile. It reminded him quite a lot of the very first station he'd worked in. He found that the interior was a quite a bit brighter though as his old station had been all institutional dark greens and greys.

He was a bit early but he asked for DI Morris anyway and settled down in the lobby to wait. The chairs were highly uncomfortable so Mac was greatly relieved when DI Morris turned up a good twenty minutes before he'd expected and introduced herself.

She was possibly in her early forties with a stylish haircut, light make up and a black suit that had obviously been tailored to fit. She had high cheek bones and unwrinkled skin that made her age a little more difficult to guess.

'Please follow me, Mr. Maguire,' she said with a little smile.

She was being too nice and Mac couldn't help feeling as though the red carpet was being rolled out for him. He wondered why. She opened the door of a large office and sat down behind one of the desks. She gestured towards the seat opposite her. Thankfully it looked more comfortable than the ones in the lobby.

'So how can I help?' she asked.

'I've been asked to look into one of your cases by a relative.'

'What's the case?'

'It's the murder of a man named Bernard Bright,' Mac said. 'It happened two weeks or so ago. He was a homeless alcoholic who was beaten to death and then his body was set on fire.'

She thought for a moment and then consulted her computer.

'Oh yes, I remember now. He was found not far from St. Philips Church, wasn't he? Who did you say you're representing?'

'His daughter, Mrs. Marcia Notts,' he replied. 'She's anxious to know if there's been any progress with the case.'

'Okay, just let me have a look.'

She spent several minutes looking at the computer screen before saying, 'I'm sorry but there haven't been any developments logged recently.'

'Who's running the case?' Mac asked.

'Detective Inspector Patterson.'

'Can I speak to him?' Mac asked.

'Sure, I saw him not long ago. He should still be around,' she said with a smile.

Mac looked at her quizzically.

'Why?' he asked.

'Why what?' she asked looking puzzled.

'Why are you cooperating with me like this? I only arranged the interview with you as a long shot, I mean we're not known for cooperating with private detectives as a rule.'

'No, not normally but your name isn't unknown around here. My boss, DCI Ormesby, sends you his best.'

'Jim Ormesby's working here?' Mac asked in surprise.

'Yes, he says that he's sorry that he won't be around for a while as he's at a conference but he asked me to help you if I could.'

'Well, thank him for me then,' Mac said. 'When's he back at the station again?'

'In a couple of days, I think.'

'Good, I'll look forward to that.'

'Come on, let's look for DI Patterson. I think he was heading for the canteen for a coffee when I saw him last.'

The canteen! Mac suddenly felt hungry and wondered if they did sausage and egg sandwiches.

She led him down a corridor and Mac's nose told him that they weren't far away. They walked into a large room with basic tables and plastic chairs dotted around. It was almost empty except for a couple of uniforms chatting at one table and a man in a suit sitting at another. He was tapping away on his mobile phone.

'Just wait here a minute, please,' she asked

Mac waited a few yards away from the man's table while she went over and had a short conversation. The man glanced over at Mac with some interest. She soon returned.

'I'll leave you to it then Mr. Maguire. Here's my card, call me if you need anything.'

She smiled, handed him a card and left.

Mac turned and looked at the man more closely. He was in his early thirties and he had a dark grey suit on that looked like it had been slept in. His shirt collar was unbuttoned and, below it, a wrinkled blue tie was at half-mast. He looked tired and he had at least a day's worth of stubble on his chin. Mac guessed that he must be at the end of a very long shift.

'Mr. Maguire, please sit down,' he said. 'It's not often I get told to help a private detective, well never in fact.'

'I'd guess that the fact that your boss once worked for me might have something to do with that.'

'Really?' he said looking impressed. 'I was told that you're interested in the Bright case?'

'Yes, that's right. In fact, I'm representing his daughter. She was hoping that there might have been some progress with her father's case.'

He shook his head.

'My team are running four cases at the moment. We've given each case equal time at the start but, while the other three have given us some leads, we've gotten absolutely nowhere with the Bright case. So, inevitably it ended up on the back burner. No-one saw what happened, no-one seemed to know him, except for the people at the church, and we couldn't find any sort of motive for the crime. We can only assume that it's some sort of nutter who likes beating up homeless people. It's not unheard of around here, in fact we had a few cases three or four years back but, unless we catch them in the act, then we're stuck.'

It was just as Mac had anticipated.

'Yes, these cases can be difficult. I've been told about the church and I'm going there later on. There's nothing at all otherwise?' he asked more in hope than anything else.

DI Patterson shook his head.

'Look, I was about to go home and get some sleep but if you need me for anything I can hang around for a while.'

'No, that's okay. Thanks for talking to me anyway,' Mac said.

DI Patterson wrote down his mobile number and gave it to Mac.

'If you do come across something let me know. I'd really like to get whoever did this and, if it is a nutter, it's more than likely that he's going to do it again.'

Mac sat there thinking for a while after DI Patterson had left. This was soon interrupted by his stomach rumbling. He asked at the counter and apparently a sausage and egg sandwich could be cooked to order.

Mac smiled. It was definitely the best part of the day so far.

Chapter Three

Mac was early for his appointment at St. Philips. After all the running around he was quite happy to sit in the peace and quiet of the church and think while he waited. It was now dark outside and the soft yellow illumination inside the church reminded him of candlelight. He found it calming. Around six thirty a floppy haired man in his early thirties came and sat down beside Mac. He was wearing blue jeans, a fleece and a worn pair of trainers.

'I take it that you're Mr. Maguire?' he asked as he held his hand out.

Mac shook it.

'Yes.'

He didn't say anything else because he was trying to figure out whether this was the Reverend or his assistant Callum, who he'd been told was really nice. He decided that he must be the assistant.

'I'm Tom Smalley,' he said. 'Pam, our church warden, said that you were looking into a murder. I take it that you're talking about Bernie Bright then?'

Mac was surprised. It was the Reverend after all.

'Yes that's right. His daughter has hired me to see if I can find out who killed him.'

'I'm sorry but I wasn't aware that he had a daughter. The men rarely tell us anything about what they did before they ended up on the streets.'

'She told me that she'd tried to find her father several times but it appears that he didn't want to be found. Even so she's very upset about what happened to him,' Mac said.

'She's not the only one. I must admit that Bernie's death really shocked us all. We've still got no idea why it happened and that's got a lot of the men quite frightened. They're worried in case they might be next. Even so, we were told by a DI Patterson that most of the men wouldn't speak to the police on principle. So, he asked if Callum and myself could have a word with them. He was hoping that they might be able to tell us something about Bernie that they wouldn't say to the police. Bernie was a very popular man but it seems that no-one could shed any light on what happened to him on the night he died.'

'Why was Bernie so popular?' Mac asked.

The Reverend smiled.

'He was funny, no I mean really funny. He could make anyone laugh. As you can imagine, we get the odd flare up with the type of people who come here but, if Bernie was around, he could defuse the situation with just a couple of jokes. Believe me, laughter is a valuable commodity when you're down on your luck. He was well liked by just about everyone.'

'Did anyone see Bernie on the night he was killed?' Mac asked.

'Oh yes, in fact I think most of us did. He was in the queue that night when we opened the kitchen up. I opened the door myself and, when I heard the laughter, I knew that Bernie was there. He came in with a friend, a younger man, and ate.'

'What was his friend's name?'

'I'm afraid that I never learned his name but Callum, my assistant, might know,' the Reverend replied. 'He's gotten to know a lot of the men quite well.'

'And after that?' Mac asked.

'I was told that after that he was seen outside with a couple of other regulars sharing a bottle of cider.'

'Who were the regulars?'

'Like most of the people who come here they just have nicknames. They're known as Polish Pete and Wee Jackie.'

'Would it possible to speak to them?' Mac asked.

The Reverend shrugged.

'You can try but I can never predict when they might come in next or if they'd speak to you even if they did turn up. I know that the police have already had a word but I don't think they got much out of them.'

'I'd like to try anyway.'

The Reverend shrugged.

'Okay, tonight's not usually one of their nights to come here but if they do come they'll be in the queue at eight o'clock. Jackie and Pete always come together so, if they do turn up, you'll get to speak to both of them.'

'Where do they eat then if they don't eat here?' Mac asked.

'The nearest other kitchen is well over a mile away, it's run by a homeless charity. The men often go from one to the other depending on where they end up sleeping and, sometimes, they get so drunk that they just forget to eat. That's why, when we're finished here, my assistant Callum goes out and takes what food is left to some of the more popular outdoor drinking spots. You should really have a word with him. He knew Bernie as well as anyone, I think. He might also have some ideas about where Jackie and Pete might be hanging out.'

'Thanks, I will. Is he around now?' Mac asked.

'I'm sorry but he's usually not around until eight and then he's out for most of the night after that,' the Reverend said.

Mac looked at his watch. It was now twenty to seven.

'If you can't wait, I can always ask him to meet you here early tomorrow evening, if you like?' the Reverend said.

Mac decided that this might be the best option. He thanked the Reverend and headed back towards his car. As he walked outside he could see that a couple of men were already hanging around even though it had started to turn really chilly. They were sitting on a tombstone and passing a bottle of Buckfast around.

Mac thought that it had been a good start on the whole and his head was full of the case as he walked into the street. He was about to open his car door when he heard a voice speak from behind him.

'DCS Maguire, we meet again at last.'

The voice was deep and deeply Glaswegian. It came from somewhere around a foot and a half above his head. Mac knew immediately who it was. It was a voice from the past and one he'd hoped that he'd never have to hear again. He glanced down the street, it was unfortunately totally devoid of life. As he turned around he wondered if his will was up to date.

He felt scared, as scared as he'd ever felt in his life. He looked up at the man standing before him. He was six feet four inches of hard muscle covered in tattoos. His hair was tied back in a ponytail and his square rock-hewn face had a stubbly beard.

It was him, the Tiger, the most violent and feared criminal that Mac had ever met. Mac had put him behind bars nearly ten years ago but he was now back on the streets and, in all probability, looking for revenge.

Mac's stomach turned to water. He'd seen what the Tiger had done to people who he'd had a grudge against and he knew that his luck had run out at last.

He just hoped that it would be quick.

Chapter Four

'Would you like a coffee?' the Tiger said. 'We can go inside, it's a bit parky out here.'

Mac looked at him as though he'd just spoken in a foreign language. He had to play it back a few times in his head before he was sure that was actually what he'd said.

'A coffee, well yes, why not?' Mac replied.

He looked up and saw no flying pigs in the dark skies above. Mac had the strange notion that he'd suddenly slipped into a surreal alternative universe. He followed the big man back towards the church and through a side door that led into a large room crammed with assorted tables and benches. At the far end there was a kitchen behind a high counter and the appetising smell of food drifted towards them.

'Sit down and I'll bring them over,' Tiger said pointing at a table.

To say that Mac was in a state of shock was to put it lightly. He was totally adrift and felt as if he was in one of his medication inspired lucid dreams. He overheard Tiger talking to someone who was working in the kitchen and then laughing. That was new too. He'd spent quite a lot of time with Tiger after his arrest and he didn't seem as if he was the laughing type.

'Here you go,' Tiger said as he handed him a steaming mug.

Mac looked at him as he sipped his drink. He looked different, something about the eyes.

'You look surprised to see me here,' Tiger said with a smile.

'Not surprised, flabbergasted maybe.'

'Yes, well I can understand that. It's not exactly the type of place I used to hang out in before I went into prison. I've been working here since I got out, seven months ago now.'

'Why?' Mac asked.

He was still totally bemused by the fact that he was sitting next to a man who had once bitten a friend's ear clean off after disagreeing about an offside decision while watching a football match. He didn't even support either of the teams.

'Well, I suppose it is a bit of a change. You know when I was arrested, I thought that it was the worst thing that could have happened to me but it turned out to have been the best in the end.'

'How was that?' Mac asked.

He knew he'd be a little late for Tim but this was one story he just had to hear.

'Well, prison was easy enough I suppose. Nobody messed with me, not more than once anyway. If you did the right people favours you could get just about anything you wanted. Even so after seven years inside I went a bit mental, stir crazy I suppose. I ended up doing five consecutive stretches in solitary after being involved in fights, fights I'd provoked. If anyone looked at me the wrong way I'd go after them and believe me nothing could stop me once I'd kicked off.'

Mac knew all too well what Tiger was like when he 'kicked off'.

'So, I sat there all by myself while the anger roared within me. I started banging my head off the walls and even cutting myself to try and satisfy my anger but nothing worked. It hurt Mr. Maguire and it was the worst pain I'd ever felt. Then one day, someone came into my cell and sat down beside me. He was a priest, a small man with glasses. He didn't do or say anything, he just sat there quietly and then after a while he went away. I'll be honest, I just didn't know what to make of him. I could have easily torn his head off and there were times when I was really tempted to do just that but I suppose he intrigued me. I think I respected him a little too. He had balls, unlike the warders who would only come into my cell six at a time. For five visits he just sat there and said nothing but on the sixth visit he spoke. He told me a story of all things.

A man had a son, he said, who he loved dearly. He'd worked hard to build up a business to hand on to his son and he had great plans for him. He was going to get married, have lots of children and found a dynasty. However, the son had other ideas. He was a thoughtful, spiritual boy and he decided that he wanted give up everything and become a monk. So, he climbed to the top of the mountain and asked the Lord Buddha if he could become a monk and spend the rest of his life in quiet contemplation.

Well, you might have thought that by now I would have done him some violence but there was something in the way he spoke that was almost hypnotic. I couldn't help but listen.

So anyway, this man, when he heard that his son had been accepted as a monk, went absolutely apeshit. It meant that he could never marry or take over the family business as he'd planned. So, he decided that he was going to climb up the mountain to give the Lord Buddha a piece of his mind and then make his son see some sense. With every step up the mountain his anger grew and he was pretty much at boiling point by the time he came across the Lord Buddha sitting under a tree.

The man let him have it. He shouted and screamed and cursed at the top of his voice but the Lord Buddha just sat there unmoved.

When the man had run out of things to say he looked at the Lord Buddha and said, 'Haven't you got anything to say to me?'

The Lord Buddha said, 'If you had brought me a present of a box of mangoes all the way up the mountain and I said that I couldn't accept them then what would you do?'

The man thought about this and said, 'Well, I suppose that I'd just have to bring them back home with me.'

The Lord Buddha smiled and said, 'I do not accept your anger.'

He then smiled, closed his eyes and went back to his meditations.'

Mac thought that this was a highly unusual story for a priest to tell but Tiger was right, it was intriguing.

'It was strange but afterwards I thought so much about that story that I forgot about everything else, you know the head-banging and the self-harm. I finally figured out what it meant, or at least I thought I did, and I told the priest next time I saw him. I said that anger could be transmitted from person to person but it was up to you if you accepted it, if you took it on and became angry too.

Father Andrew, that's the priest's name as I found out, just asked me where I got my anger from.

That one kept me going for ages. I finally realised that it had been beaten into me by my father. He'd wanted me to be tough but I just ended up being mean. His anger came from the fact that a promising football career had ended at the age of eighteen with a knee injury and then my mother had died young. He took to the bottle big time and it just made his anger worse. He ended up hating everyone and getting his retaliation in first as he used to put it. I ended up being just like him.

When I told this to Father Andrew, he just asked me why I was still nurturing my father's anger long after he was dead?

Now that one had me stumped.

I was lying awake that night thinking about what he'd said and, now I don't know if it was a dream or not, but for a short time, half an hour perhaps, all my anger left me. It was the most wonderful feeling that I'd ever experienced in my life. It was as if a ton weight had been lifted from me and I felt as if I could have floated up to the ceiling. The anger was back when I woke up in the morning but I now knew it for what it was. With Father Andrew's help, I started to fight it and I'm fighting it still. He helped me with the parole board and I got out early after a couple of years of good behaviour. Tom's a friend of his and he asked him for a favour and so here I am. I help out in the kitchen and do a bit of bouncing when the men play up. Then I do outreach every night, not just food but taking the men to the hospital if they're ill and helping them with their benefits and medicines and so on.'

Mac was finding it hard to take in. Callum McEachan, AKA 'The Tiger', the most feared enforcer in the criminal world had found God.

'No, it's not quite God, at least not yet, but it's something. I prayed for the anger to leave me and it did. You know I love it here, I love the people and what Tom's trying to do. In fact, the time I've spent helping out here have been the happiest days of my life.'

Callum's face lit up with a smile.

'You really have changed, haven't you?' Mac said in wonder.

'I have, oh and by the way I'm sorry for your troubles. I heard about your wife passing.'

'Thanks Callum. Has Tom told you why I'm here?'

'No, he just mentioned that a Mac Maguire had been visiting and I ran straight out to catch you.'

'It's about Bernie Bright,' Mac said.

He told him the whole story.

'I never knew that Bernie had a daughter but then again most of the men don't talk about their former lives. It's like they don't want to remember because they're so ashamed of the people they've become. He was a nice man, a funny man. His jokes meant that I didn't have to bang quite so many heads together at times.'

'So, you've not totally given up violence?'

'No, but I only use it when I have to and only for the right reasons. Even then it's minimum damage only, not like the old days. I wish I'd seen who did that to Bernie though, I might well have broken that particular rule.'

'Look I have to go but I could do with some help. I'm looking for Polish Pete and Wee Jackie,' Mac said. 'It looks like they were the last people to see Bernie alive. They've already talked to the police but, apparently, they didn't say much. I was hoping that they might tell me a little more.'

Callum thought for a while.

'Okay, I've no idea where they are right now but I'm pretty sure where they'll be tomorrow evening. If you want to meet me here around nine tomorrow you can come out with me when I'm doing my rounds if you like.'

'Now that sounds like a plan. Okay then, I'll see you here tomorrow,' Mac said offering Callum his hand.

Callum's hand was so big that it made Mac's hand look like it belonged to a child.

'Who'd have thought that we'd end up working together?' Callum said with a smile.

Who indeed? Mac thought as he walked out of the door.

He looked back at the church and shook his head. He still felt as if he'd just stepped out of an absurdly surrealistic dream. He rang Tim as he walked to the car and, as he was still finishing off a piece of furniture, he was happy to meet up a bit later than planned.

It was nearly nine when he sat down at table thirteen in the Magnets and sipped his first pint of the night. He told Tim all about his day.

'Did you really think that your number was up when this Callum spoke to you?'

'Absolutely. He was the one of the biggest challenges I'd ever had to face as a policeman for quite a number of reasons. We only got him by a bit of luck in the end and it's quite a story.'

'Well, we've got all night or what's left of it,' Tim said.

'True and I certainly don't have to get up early tomorrow, in fact a lie-in would be a good idea as I'll probably be staying up quite late tomorrow night. Okay, I'll get another round in and then I'll tell you all about Tiger McEachan.'

Mac told Tim the story -

'Around ten years or so ago there was a major turf war over drugs in North London between two major gangs. One of them was a well-established Irish gang that had been around for quite a while and the other was a gang from one of the estates. This gang, who were called 'The Steeley Boys' as they lived on the Steele Estate, had gotten bigger over time and they were now attempting to take over part of the Irish gang's territory. They reckoned that, with all the manpower they had, they easily outgunned their rivals. The leader of the Irish gang was a man called Johnny McInerney. He'd been around for quite a while too and the fact that he'd lasted that long wasn't down to luck. He knew that the Steeley Boys were growing in numbers and that they were going to be a problem so he called in some favours and got some help in.'

'What did he do? Get a gang of lads over from the old country?' Tim asked.

'No, he contacted an Irish gang in Glasgow and got just one man, Tiger McEachan. As you'll see that was all he needed. There'd been a sort of simmering cold war going on between the two gangs until a cousin of Johnny McInerney's was found beaten to death. The Steeley Boys were sending a message and so Johnny sent them an answer. He set the Tiger loose on them. The next night one of their members disappeared, not the foot soldiers who sell the stuff on the streets and who were basically expendable, but a fairly important long-standing gang member. The morning after some of his body parts were found strewn around the Steele Estate. Not a nice sight for the kids walking to school I dare say. That morning a war started but it didn't last long. The Irish gang, fearing reprisals, had suspended operations and they were in lock down. So, the Steeley Boys were frustrated as they couldn't find anyone to take their revenge on.

Then the next night, even though they were being careful, two more Steeley Boys disappeared. Just as before bits of them were found distributed around the estate and, apparently, one gang member's head was found impaled on a set of railings right outside one of the gang's meeting places. No-one in the gang had a clue who was carrying out the killings but they had a fair idea that Johnny McInerney must be the man behind them. So, they decided to up the ante and threw a bomb into a pub where they'd been told that some of the Irish gang had been drinking. They ended up blowing up a few of the gang's elderly relatives instead and Johnny McInerney decided that it was time to end the war once and for all.

So it was that the morning afterwards everyone on the Steele Estate woke up to see a naked body nailed to a tree right in the centre of the estate. The body belonged to Brian Sangredo, the leader of the Steeley Boys. He'd been cut over a hundred times and had literally had salt rubbed into his wounds. His eyes were then gouged out and his ears cut off. He was then nailed to the tree while he was still alive. His balls had been cut off and were nailed to a nearby branch. A six-inch nail right in the centre of his forehead finally finished him off. After that an equitable settlement between the two gangs was reached. However, we heard that Johnny kept the Tiger around for a while just in case.'

'My God, he sounds like he was some sort of ultra-evil super hero or something. How did you manage to arrest him?' Tim asked.

'It was just by sheer luck in the end. A member of the Irish gang called Little Benny was caught ferrying a pallet full of money in a van. The van had broken down and the police stopped to help as he was blocking the road. From the way he was behaving they suspected that he might have something in the van that he didn't want them to see. When they looked what they found that at the back of the van, hidden behind a load of cardboard boxes, there was a shrink-wrapped pallet of banknotes about four feet high. We knew that it was drug money but we couldn't prove anything beyond that. Little Benny, however, wasn't all that bright and when we said that he'd get ten to fifteen years if he didn't cooperate, he cut a deal and gave us Tiger McEachan. It was him that told us that Tiger had been behind the killings on the Steele Estate, in fact he almost boasted about it. He figured that the Tiger, not being an actual gang member, might not matter all that much. It turned out that he was wrong about that as he was found dead in prison a few days later. He'd been stabbed with a shiv fifteen times.

Anyway, we went to where Benny said that the Tiger would be and, sure enough, there he was. He had a man tied to a chair. He'd already broken both the man's kneecaps and some of his fingers with a hammer and he was in the process of pulling his fingernails out when we interrupted him. It took eight of the Police Rugby Team and three tasers before we finally restrained him. He really was like a cornered tiger. However, we couldn't charge him for the killings because we never found any evidence to back up Bennie's story. So, we did him for kidnapping and Grievous Bodily Harm for which he got the absolute maximum the judge could give him. He never said the words as such but he gave me a look when he left the court that reminded me of something.'

'What words?' Tim asked.

'Oh you know the usual threats, 'I'll get even', 'Wait until I get out' and so on. He never said a word though, he just looked at me. Have you ever been to the Dublin Zoo, Tim?'

'I have, I went there many times when I was a kid.'

'Then you'll remember the big cats' house that they used to have there. I only visited it once when I was six or so. My mother was staying with one of her sisters for a few days before travelling on to Donegal. Anyway, the zoo was okay but it was the big cats that I remembered most vividly, especially the tigers. There was this one tiger in particular. He was a large male and he was pacing up and down inside the cage. You could see the muscles flow and sense the immense power in his body. He growled and showed me his sharp yellow teeth. In those days they didn't have glass separating you from the animals but thick iron bars. I felt that I could somehow smell the anger and hatred coming from that tiger.

Then the scariest thing of all happened.

The tiger stopped and looked right at me and I mean right at me. I'll never forget those eyes, they were golden with a black dot in the middle. As he looked at me the dot grew larger and I knew what he was thinking. He was thinking that, if only the bars would disappear, then he could spring out and sink those sharp yellow teeth into me and then tear me to pieces. He'd enjoy doing it too. For a second, in my imagination, the bars started to dissolve and I got so scared that I nearly wet myself. Well, when Tiger McEachan looked at me I saw those eyes again and I knew exactly what that look meant. When I heard his voice tonight I honestly thought that was it.'

'Is that why he's called 'The Tiger' then, because he's so fierce?' Tim asked.

'I guess so but he's also got this tattoo that covers his whole back. It's of a tiger's head. The tiger is snarling and showing its teeth. It's quite lifelike really.'

'And you reckon he's changed?' Tim asked.

'Oh yes, he's nothing like the Tiger I knew before.'

'Well, I hope you're right as you're going to be driving around with him on your own tomorrow. There'll be no bars between the two of you then.'

Later that night, Mac thought about his friend's misgivings as he tried to get some sleep. He dismissed the thought. The Tiger had changed, of that he was sure.

Well almost sure.

Chapter Five

Leigh half woke up. It was still dark and she hoped that there would be enough time for her to turn over and have another sleep. She sighed when she finally dared to look at the clock and realised that she had all of five minutes. She turned the alarm off and reluctantly got out of bed. Perhaps the shower would help to wake her up.

As she let the water wash some of the tiredness away, she thought about the case that her boss Dan Carter had handed her and her partner the afternoon before. They'd only had time to have a quick read though the case file before they'd finished for the day.

It was either a case of murder or a hit and run accident. From what she'd read so far it could easily have been either. Just two days ago a body had been found in a field by a farmer. It was the body of someone the farmer had known fairly well. The dead man's name was Eric Braithwaite and he'd been a Professor at the Cambridge History Faculty. The investigation team that had attended the accident reckoned that he'd been walking back down a country road to where his car had been parked when he'd been hit by a vehicle. The vehicle must have been going at speed as the Professor ended up going right over a six foot hedge. Just about every bone in his body was broken by the impact. He had been on the correct side of the road, walking towards the oncoming traffic, and the only brake marks on the road were well after the point of impact.

That's what made murder a real possibility.

If the vehicle had swerved to avoid an animal or if there was some loss of control then you'd expect to see tyre marks during the swerve. There weren't any. So today she was going to meet her partner, DI Jo Dugdale, at the station and they were going to drive to Cambridge to start asking people who knew the Professor some questions. They needed to establish if it was indeed some weird sort of accident or if there was anyone who might have had a good enough motive for the Professor's murder.

She was still thinking about the case as she dressed. She checked herself in the mirror and smiled. She'd just had her hair cut and she thought that it really suited her. She worried about her figure though. Was she getting too thin? She thought of Jo with her curvy fuller figure and envied her a little.

Maybe she should start eating more, she thought.

As she locked the door behind her, she realised that she'd been living in her little flat for just over six months now. She loved living there. It was quiet and the neighbours were really nice too. As she walked out onto the pavement, she looked down the street at the neatly rendered white Letchworth cottages and once again marvelled at where she'd ended up.

Her last station had been in a very urban and quite scruffy part of Watford. Even the dark clouds and icy rain didn't dampen her spirits. She hadn't really known what she'd been letting herself in for when she applied for the post in Letchworth, she just knew that she hated where she was working and she had to get away. For once in her life she'd gotten lucky.

She was lucky with her partner too, she thought as she drove the short distance to the police station.

Jo Dugdale had been one of two sergeants attached to the Major Crime Unit when Leigh had joined the team. When one of the Detective Inspectors recently left the team, Jo had applied for his post. Only two others in the team could have applied but DS Kate Grimsson not only made it clear that she wouldn't be applying but that, in her opinion, DS Adil Thakkar or Jo would both make great Detective Inspectors. It was then all down to the decision of their boss Dan Carter and he eventually decided on Jo which surprised a lot of people, mostly people who didn't know Dan all that well. Adil took it with good grace even though he must have been disappointed.

When she got to the station Jo was sitting by herself in the Major Crime Unit's room. Dan was in his office talking to Andy Reid about something.

After exchanging their usual greetings Leigh asked Jo where they were going to start their investigation.

'I've contacted the Cambridge History Faculty and I've managed to have a word with Professor

Braithwaite's assistant,' Jo replied. 'She's agreed to see us this morning. She's at the Political History Research Centre just off West Road so it shouldn't take us long to get there.'

'What's the assistant's name?' Leigh asked.

'It's Ms. Elinor Grayem-Weiss.'

'Why do they have to have these double-barrelled names? I mean I don't go around calling myself Leigh McAllen-Marston, do I? Not that I ever would...God it sounds like a firm of solicitors, doesn't it?' she said.

Jo started laughing and Leigh suddenly remembered Jo's decision not to keep her maiden name after calling herself Jo Thibonais-Dugdale for all of two weeks after she came back from her honeymoon.

'Oh, I'm sorry Jo, you had one for a while, didn't you?' she said with an embarrassed smile.

'I thought it would be so cool but I got fed up of it pretty quickly. Anyway, Jo Dugdale sounds just fine to me. Come on then, Ms. Grayem-Weiss won't interview herself.'

Leigh had been expecting a crumbling old Victorian pile but, from where they parked, all she could see were brand new four storied office blocks. The History Faculty was one of them and, as it was hidden behind several other buildings, they had to park on the road and go down a wide walkway to reach it. Jo asked for Ms. Grayem-Weiss at reception. They only had to wait a few minutes before she came down to meet them. She was probably only a year or two older than Leigh but she dressed as if she was in her fifties. She wore flat shoes, a tweed skirt topped off with a sensible twin set and she had her hair tied in a severe bun. She wore thick black rimmed glasses.

Jo wondered if she was trying to make herself look unattractive on purpose for some reason.

'I'm so glad that the police are taking this seriously,' Ms. Grayem-Weiss said as she walked towards the lift. 'I hope you catch whoever did this although...'

Jo and Leigh never got to hear what she was going to say as the lift doors opened and some people got out. She pressed the button for the third floor and didn't say anything further until she sat them down in an empty office and shut the door behind her.

'Ms. Grayem-Weiss...' Jo said as they all sat down.

'Oh, please call me Elinor,' she said.

As it was somewhat shorter Jo was quite happy to do just that.

'Okay, Elinor first of all tell us what you were to the Professor.'

'Well, I was his assistant which meant that I helped him with his research, looked after his diary, made sure that he got things done on time, made his travel arrangements when he needed me to and so on. He also let me proof read his papers and articles before they were published.'

Jo noticed that this last part was said as though the Professor had done her a great favour rather than it just being part of her work.

'What was he like?' she asked.

'He's brilliant, in my eyes he's the best historian there is...or was, I suppose I should say,' she said with frown. 'He was kind too, at least kind to me.'

'Was he kind to everyone?' Jo asked.

'Well almost everyone, everyone except for Cruella de Vil of course,' she said with a snarl.

'Cruella De Vil?' Jo asked in some puzzlement.

'Sorry, it's just what I call her. Her real name is Caroline Ormonde De Gray. She's a Professor too but she's on the other side.'

'The other side?'

'Well, the Professor always referred to the period that he specialised in as The English Revolution. You might know it better as the English Civil War, however, in fact there were actually three wars not one and calling it a revolution is being much more accurate. It was a failed revolution of course but a revolution nonetheless,' she said in a tumble of words.

'So, Roundheads and Cavaliers then,' Leigh said trying to be helpful.

The expression seemed to physically hurt Miss Grayem-Weiss.

'That's a vast over-simplification of the period but broadly yes, I suppose. Anyway, the other Professor always referred to it as 'a spot of local bother' between the reigns of two kings. I heard her say once that it was 'just the local oiks kicking up a fuss'. But it was important, it led to the French Revolution and the creation of the United States but she could never see that. She hated him, I overheard her saying once that she'd like to see him dead.'

'When was this?' Jo asked getting more interested.

'It was after a debate at one of the seminars for the Historical Research Society. He'd wiped the floor with her and she was practically frothing at the mouth. She said that she'd like to throttle him with her own hands.'

Jo sighed. Unfortunately, it was just the type of non-specific threat that people make every day, she thought. Now if the Professor had actually been strangled then that might have been something.

'So, are you saying that Professor Braithwaite might have been murdered?' Jo asked.

Elinor nodded her head vigorously.

'Tell me why,' Jo asked.

'Well, the Professor was run over while walking back to his car after he'd gone for a stroll around Thriplow. It was something he often did when he needed to think. He was putting together an important presentation for a talk at the Institute of Historical Research in London in a couple of weeks and I think he was trying to finalise exactly what he was going to say. He was a brilliant man, he used to think his way through presentations and lectures in such detail that he rarely needed to do much editing when he wrote it all down.'

'Why Thriplow?' Jo asked.

She had a vague idea that Thriplow was somewhere between Letchworth and Cambridge but beyond that she knew nothing about it.

'Oh, it's famous. Thriplow Heath is where the New Model Army encamped in 1647 when it refused to disband as ordered by Parliament. If they'd have marched on London, as some of the agitators wanted them to, the course of history would have been changed forever and not only that...'

'Yes, that's very interesting but can we get back to the Professor?' Jo interrupted fearing a lecture.

'Yes of course, I'm sorry. Well, the Professor used to always park his car at the Green Man pub and then walk down the lane as far as the church in Fowlmere and then walk back again.'

'Was he well known in Thriplow?' Jo asked.

'Yes, I'd say so. He was always quite happy to stop and chat when he was out walking and he also gave quite a few talks around the area on the English Revolution. That started after one of the local farmers, who owns some of the land that borders the lane, got to know the Professor quite well. The first time they met some years ago he told Mr. Gardiner what had happened right there on that very spot and that seemed to have sparked a real interest in the subject. I was with the Professor once when he went walking and we bumped into Mr. Gardiner. He'd obviously been reading about the period and he was quite proud of the part his land had played in the history of our country,' she replied.

She looked down at the floor for a few seconds before looking up at Jo again.

'It was Mr. Gardiner who found the Professor's body, wasn't it?' she said looking quite upset and more than a little tearful. 'Anyway, it was something he did quite regularly and he always parked his car at the pub. Anyone would know that, if his car was at the pub, then he'd be out on the lane somewhere.'

Jo had to admit that this was a very good point.

'And you think that this Professor De Gray ran him over?'

'Possibly, she was rich so perhaps she hired someone else to do it for her,' Elinor said as she dabbed at her tears with a tissue. 'She's the only person I know who had any motive to harm the Professor. I've seen a look in her eyes sometimes when she was with the Professor, she really hated him.'

'Where does she work?

'She's got an office at Clare College in the town.'

'Is she anything to do with Dominic De Gray?' Leigh asked.

'Why yes, they're brother and sister. I think he dropped the 'Ormonde' bit of his name when he went into politics to make him sound a little less upper class. I don't know why he bothered though, all he has to do is open his mouth,' she said in an accent that sounded quite upper class to Leigh.

Jo looked at Leigh with some respect. She'd never have linked the two.

Dominic De Gray was in all the papers at the moment as the Government were in their usual crisis. While half the party supported the current Prime Minister, the other half were urging Mr. De Gray to challenge her for the leadership. They talked about him as if he were some sort of saviour who would ride in and magically solve all their problems. Jo had seen him on TV, he was in his forties but he dressed as if he was eighty something and when he spoke it always sounded to her as if he was putting it on. No-one could really be that upper class.

'Did the Professor have any relatives?' Jo asked.

'As far as I know he only had a sister. She still lives in London, that's where the Professor's from. She's older than him but they were quite close. He rang her every week and went to see her every second week. He always made sure that it was in his diary,' Elinor replied.

'Could I have a copy of his diary before we leave and his sister's address and phone number too please?' Jo asked. Elinor nodded. 'Was there anything else that the Professor got involved with besides his work?'

'Well he really liked his darts. He went every second Wednesday to the Air Force Club. He's in a team there and afterwards he always stayed the night with a friend of his.'

'A friend?' Jo asked.

'Yes, he's something or other at the base, I forget what.'

'So, what's the Professor's connection to the Air Force?'

'Oh, he was in it when he was young, for nearly seven years I think.'

'He was a pilot then?' Jo asked.

'No chance!' Elinor said with a shake of her head. 'He was an engine technician and he worked on the jet fighters. He always said that you had to be born with a silver spoon to qualify as a pilot.'

'Where's the Air Force Club?'

'At Witterlow, it's just outside Peterborough.'

'Did he ever take you with him to this club?' Jo asked.

Elinor shook her head again.

'I must admit that I was curious and I asked him more than once if he'd take me but he said that only serving and ex-members were allowed on the grounds. He also said that quite a bit of drinking went on.'

'Did he drink much normally?'

'No, not normally, just on every other Wednesday when he went there.'

'So, is there anything else you can tell us that might help?' Jo asked.

Elinor shrugged.

'Apart from his darts night the Professor just worked, that's all he ever did.'

Jo gave her a card and made sure that she got a copy of the diary and the Professor's sister's details before they left.

'So, what do you think?' Jo asked as they walked back to the car.

'Well, there's not much to go on is there?' Leigh replied. 'Just this other Professor by the look of it.'

'Well, I know we've only just started but I'd like to have a closer look at Ms. Grayem-Weiss too.'

Leigh gave her a puzzled look.

'I was watching her while she spoke and she was genuinely upset,' Jo continued. 'Then there's the way she dresses, like she's thirty years older than she actually is. I think there might be a better than even chance that she was in love with the Professor.'

'And where there's love there's sometimes hate as well, isn't there?' Leigh said.

Chapter Six

It didn't take them long to get to Clare College. They had to park on the main road and then walk through an ornate wrought iron gate. They walked along a path that had gardens on both sides.

Leigh thought it must be quite nice in the summer when everything would be in bloom. It was still quite pretty in a way as all the plants were covered with a thick white frosting that glinted in the rays of the low winter sun.

They crossed over the River Cam by way of an old bridge with stone balustrades. As cold out as it was, a punt went through the bridge as they crossed over and the sound of laughter echoed from underneath their feet. The view down the river to some other ancient college buildings was exquisite.

The college stood right in front of them. It was so old that Leigh found it really hard to put a date on it. The front of the building was huge, made of grey weathered stone that was three stories high and topped with towers and ornate stone chimneys. They headed for an arched entrance that was just wide enough to drive a carriage through.

They quickly found the porter's lodge where a middle-aged man with long sideburns stood in attendance. He was dressed in an old-fashioned black suit, a white shirt with a black tie, a black waistcoat and black boots. Jo thought that he looked like an extra who had just escaped from a Dickens film. He mistook them for visitors at first until she showed him her warrant card.

'I'm looking for Professor De Gray,' Jo asked.

'Of course, just let me check and see if she's in,' the porter said.

He consulted a signing in book and then looked quite puzzled.

'Well, she signed in yesterday afternoon and she's not signed out since,' he said. 'While it's frowned upon, some of the academic staff do occasionally sleep over in their chambers especially after the feasts. However, I've never known Professor De Gray to do so before. She's probably forgotten to sign out I should think. I'll take you to her office anyway, if you like, just in case she's still there.'

He took them through the archway and Leigh could see that the building was even bigger than she'd thought. She was now standing in a large open square intersected by cobbled walkways and large rectangular sections of grass that were a very pale green under their frosted coating. The building ran right around the square and even more towers and chimneys could be seen. She couldn't help thinking of Harry Potter and Hogwarts School for some reason. The porter took them to the opposite corner of the square and through a small door. The ceiling was quite low and the walls were panelled in dark wood. He took them up some polished wooden stairs and then stopped outside a door. A brass plate informed them that this was the chambers of Professor Caroline Ormonde De Gray.

The porter tapped quietly at the door. Then he tapped a little louder. Then he gave up.

'I'm sorry but she obviously isn't in,' the porter said giving them a helpless look.

'She might be asleep or something,' Jo said.

'I doubt it but if she is then it's probably best not to wake her up. She can be a bit tetchy at times if you know what I mean.'

'Are you saying that you can't open the door for us to even check whether she's in there or not?'

'Yes, that's right. You see I'd need the Professor's permission to...'

Jo had had enough.

'Look, we're conducting a possible murder enquiry here and I need to see the Professor.' She took her phone out. 'If you prefer it, I can call for some police officers who will have that door down in a matter of seconds. There won't be much of it left afterwards though.'

'Oh, it's most irregular,' the porter fretted. 'Just a look you say?'

Jo nodded.

She could see the wheels going around in the porter's head.

'Okay, I'll go and get the keys,' he eventually said before he scurried off back down the stairs.

'You're very forceful today,' Leigh said.

'Sorry, I suppose I could have been more diplomatic but I've got a funny feeling about this one,' Jo said with a frown.

The porter came scurrying back up the stairs with a huge bunch of keys in his hand. It must have taken him a full minute to find the right one.

'Just a look you say?' he asked again before he inserted the key. 'You'll not touch anything?'

Jo assured him that they wouldn't.

He unlocked the door and they stepped into a large wood panelled room that was illuminated by two long ornate diamond-leaded windows that overlooked the square. There were lots of maps and framed documents on the walls, a large old-fashioned desk and an even larger table both groaning under the weight of books, files and documents. In the far corner there a small sofa, an armchair and a coffee table. Under the window there was a long window seat with red cushions on it and long heavy curtains were furled up on both sides and held back by red satin ties.

Jo only noticed all of this sometime afterwards. The first thing that caught her attention as she stepped into the room was the middle-aged woman who was hanging from the light fitting.

The porter stood frozen at the sight with his hand covering his mouth. Jo had to walk around him to get a good look at the woman's face. Her mouth was open and her skin was pale. The head was inclined to one side and she noticed that saliva had trickled down one side of her chin. She touched her hand, it was icy cold, and then checked for a pulse at her wrist. There wasn't one.

'She's dead. Leigh can you call it in?' Jo asked.

Leigh nodded and went into the hallway to make the call.

The porter hadn't moved a muscle.

'I take it that this is the Professor?' Jo asked.

The porter nodded his head while still keeping his hand over his mouth.

'I want you lock the door to this part of the building please and then give the keys to the police when they arrive,' Jo said. 'And don't allow anyone into the college until my colleagues arrive.'

He looked from the hanging body to her and back again. He then seemed to wake up.

'Oh yes, of course, of course,' he said before he scurried off again.

Jo looked at the woman again. The Professor was dressed all in black; a black silk blouse, black skirt, black tights and black court shoes, one of which had fallen to the floor. It looked strange, as though she'd been in mourning or something. A small stool was also on the floor. It was on its side and she guessed that the Professor has used it to stand on while she put the noose around her neck. She had a quick look around the room while she waited. Everything seemed to be related to Kings named James or Charles. Kings and Queens hadn't exactly been Jo's strong point at school so she supposed that she'd have to ask Elinor if she wanted to know why she'd been so interested in them.

'I've called Dan and he's on his way. I told him who was dead and also who her brother is,' Leigh said.

'I'll bet he loved that, the possible next Prime Minister of Great Britain's sister topping herself. The press will be all over it like flies.'

'I actually heard him groan when I told him. He's contacting the local police and getting them to send someone over straight away to secure the scene. He'll also get a forensics team over too as soon as he can. What do you think then? Suicide?'

'Yes, I've seen a couple before and this definitely looks like one to me,' Jo replied. 'Have a look at the ligature, you can see that it's been cut from one of the ropes that are used to open and close the curtains. There's also a half empty bottle of gin on the desk and just the one glass. Yes, I'd be really surprised if it isn't called as suicide. Why though, that's the question, and what does it have to do with Professor Braithwaite's death? We've now got two dead history professors on our hands. There surely has to be some connection.'

Chapter Seven

The local police arrived a few minutes later so Jo and Leigh left them in charge of the crime scene. They waited by the porter's lodge for Dan Carter and the rest of Major Crime Unit to turn up. Two uniformed policemen were already on guard stopping people from entering the college grounds. A few people were hanging around and looking at the police activity with some interest. Jo turned and noticed that the porter was sitting down in his little office. His hand shook as he poured a large slug of whisky into a mug of tea.

A few minutes later two members of the local detective team turned up. One of them was tall, slim and going somewhat bald. Jo knew him very well indeed.

'Chris!' she said as she gave him a big hug.

Leigh gave him a hug too.

Chris Skorupski had been part of the Major Crime Unit until fairly recently when he'd accepted a job as head of the Cambridge detective team. Indeed, it was Chris leaving that had allowed Jo to become a DI. Jo had the feeling that he'd been reluctant to leave the team but his wife was expecting their first child and, as they lived in Cambridge, he'd decided that he wanted to be as close to home as possible.

'How's Maja doing?' Jo asked.

'She's doing really well. We've just another month to go and she's finally taking it easy at last, not that she has much choice. By the way this is DS Kohli,' Chris said gesturing towards his partner, a slightly older man who was not quite so slim. 'Dan rang and asked if someone from the local detective team could attend so we came straight away. What have we got?'

'It looks like suicide to me but it's not so much what as who in this case. You've heard of Dominic De Gray?'

'Of course, he's the Defence Secretary. I only saw him on breakfast TV this morning. He's likely to be the next Prime Minister or so they were saying. It's not him in there is it?' he asked.

'No, it's his sister,' Jo said. 'She's a Professor here or was a Professor I should say.'

'His sister? The press will have a field day with that alright. What have you found so far?' Chris asked.

Jo briefly told them about Professor Braithwaite and how investigating that case had led them to finding Professor De Gray hanging from a rope.

'Two dead history Professors,' DI Kohli said with a shake of the head. 'That sounds like something off the telly, Morse perhaps.'

'Morse? I remember watching him with my mum when I was young. She loved that series but I don't think I understood much of what was going on at the time. I liked the music though,' Jo replied. 'Have you ever had any reason to come here before?'

'What Clare College?' Chris replied. 'It's the first time I've been near the place. What about you, Govinder?'

DS Kohli shook his head.

'It's not exactly a high crime area, is it?'

They were interrupted by the sight of Detective Superintendent Dan Carter striding purposefully towards them. He was closely followed by DI Andy Reid and DS Adil Thakkar.

'So, we've recently had to deal with a soap actress, a rock musician and a football star so I guess a politician just had to be next,' Dan said with a scowl. 'So, what have we got?'

Jo told Dan everything she knew.

'So, you think that it might be a straight forward suicide then?' he asked hopefully.

'Yes, that's what I think,' Jo replied.

'Well, I really hope you're right. If it is suicide then that means that our involvement should be minimal. I've had more than enough of being hounded by the press,' Dan said with feeling.

'The problem is I've got a strong feeling that Professor De Gray's suicide is somehow linked to the case you gave us yesterday, Professor Braithwaite,' Jo said.

'Have you found anything specific that links the two deaths yet?' Dan said looking worried.

'No, but what she wore was, in itself, suggestive. She was dressed all in black as though she'd been going to a funeral. I'd guess that she killed herself not too long after she'd gotten the news about Professor Braithwaite's death. It might just be a coincidence but I'd still like to follow it up just in case. I'd like to talk to her brother too if that's possible.'

'Well, I'll wish you luck with that one. My guess is that, if it happens at all, it will be the Chief Constable who'll be doing that interview and he'll be wearing his softest kid gloves when he does. You'd be better off doing something else for now. If I can get you a few minutes with De Gray I'll let you know but I wouldn't hold my breath if I were you,' Dan said.

They were interrupted by the arrival of the forensics team. Three white suited figures made their way over the bridge towards them.

'Well we'd better get on with it then. It's a big place so probably lots of people to interview,' Dan said.

'Do you want me and Leigh to stay and help?' Jo asked.

Dan gave this some thought.

'I think it might be better if you and Leigh follow up on this connection to the other dead professor just in case there's something to it. I've got a feeling we might be stuck here for some time,' he said with an audible sigh.

Dan followed the forensics team into the courtyard leaving Jo and Leigh in the company of the two uniformed police who were guarding the entrance. The people hanging about outside the entrance had now grown into a small crowd.

DS Kohli tapped Jo on the shoulder.

'By the way I'd watch out for him if I were you,' he told her as he pointed at a man in the crowd. 'That's Ted Curtis, he's a reporter from the local rag and he misses nothing. Tell him anything and it'll be on the front page of every national newspaper tomorrow.'

Jo thanked him for the tip.

'So, what now?' Leigh asked.

'I'm not sure, if I'm honest.'

'Well, I was just wondering if the Professor De Gray had an assistant too, you know, someone like Elinor Grayem-Weiss,' Leigh said.

For the second time that day Jo looked at Leigh with some respect.

'Now that's a very good thought indeed.'

She looked around and her eye caught the porter again. He was still sitting at his desk and looking somewhat stunned. Jo went over to him.

'Excuse me,' she said.

The porter didn't move. He looked as if he was in a trance.

'Excuse me!' Jo said a little louder.

The porter suddenly woke up.

'Oh I'm sorry, I was…well I don't know what I was really,' he said looking flustered.

'Do you know if the Professor had an assistant or someone who helped her with her day to day work?' Jo asked.

'Oh yes, that would be Ms. Eckersley. She and the Professor were together most of the time.'

'Do you know where I can find this Ms. Eckersley?'

'Oh yes,' the porter replied. 'Follow me.'

He led Jo and Leigh out of the entrance and looked over the growing crowd milling around outside.

'That's her over there,' he said, 'the woman smoking a cigarette. I saw her trying to get in a few minutes ago.'

He pointed towards a woman in her late thirties who was leaning against a wall. She was anxiously watching the comings and goings while puffing furiously at a cigarette. She was dressed in faded blue denims and a black T shirt worn underneath a camouflage jacket. Her long black hair was bundled up in a brightly coloured head scarf. Kate would have expected the assistant of someone called Professor Ormonde De Gray to be a bit more like Elinor. She obviously wasn't.

She stood up straight when Jo and Leigh started walking towards her. Jo showed her warrant card.

'You're Professor De Gray's assistant?' Jo asked.

'Yes, is it true what Robbie's just told me?' she asked anxiously.

Her accent identified her as being from the Newcastle area.

'Who's Robbie?' Jo asked.

'The porter, Robbie Edmonds.'

Jo looked around. The reporter from the local paper was hovering within earshot and he looked more than interested in what they were saying.

'Can we talk in the car?' Jo asked.

'Sure,' Ms. Eckersley replied as she threw her cigarette on the ground. It had been smoked right down to the filter. 'First one of those I've had in five years. I don't suppose you smoke?' she asked hopefully.

Jo and Leigh both shook their heads.

They walked through the growing crowd and back over the bridge. Jo sat in the back of the car with Ms. Eckersley.

'Ms. Eckersley, what exactly did Robbie tell you?' Jo asked.

'Oh, please call me Jan. He could only speak for a few seconds but he told me that the prof was dead, that she'd killed herself. Is that true?'

'Yes Jan, I'm afraid it is, the bit about her being dead anyway. It looks like it might have been suicide but we still need to confirm that. Have you any idea why she might have done such a thing?' Jo asked.

'No, I was thinking about that when you arrived but I couldn't come up with anything. She was full of life the day before yesterday. She was getting her presentation ready for the Institute of Historical Research meeting in a couple of weeks or so and I'd just read through the first draft for her. It was brilliant and I told her so. She seemed to be in an excellent mood.'

'Is this the same meeting that Professor Braithwaite was going to attend?'

'Oh yes, it was due to be another double header. The tickets all sold out within a week, the Prof versus Red Eric was always going to be a big draw.'

'How did she find out about Professor Braithwaite's death?' Jo asked.

'Oh, I told her. I got it straight from Robbie yesterday afternoon. The prof was working from home so I rang her as soon as I found out and told her the good news.'

'And did she think that it was good news?'

Jan gave it some thought.

'You know, I'm not so sure that she did and, if I'm being honest, I was a bit puzzled by that. I told her about how he'd been run over while walking back to his car after doing that stupid walk of his at Thriplow but she didn't say anything. There was just this silence that seemed to go on forever. Eventually she just said 'Thanks' and then put the phone down.'

'Did you speak to her again after that?'

'No, we were due to meet later that afternoon in her chambers when I got a text from her calling it off.'

'What time was that?' Jo asked.

'Here I can show you,' Jan said as she produced her phone.

She tapped through and found the message. It was timed at two ten in the afternoon.

Jan sorry but have to cancel our 4pm. There's something I need to do goodbye Caro

Jo passed the phone to Leigh before she asked, 'Did she normally say goodbye when she texted you?'

'Goodbye? No, never,' Jan said with a shake of her head. 'Did she really say that?'

Leigh handed her back her phone.

'You know, I never noticed that,' she said.

She looked like she was about to start crying so Jo quickly asked her next question.

'Did she often wear black?'

'Black? She was dressed in black?' Jan asked looking more than puzzled.

'Yes, everything she wore was black.'

'No, she hated black, the colour of death she used to call it. Red was her colour. Christ, she really did kill herself, didn't she?'

This time the tears did come. All Jo could do was hold her hand and wait until she stopped.

'Are you okay now?' Jo asked.

Jan nodded.

'Do you think that the reason the Professor might have wanted to kill herself had anything to do with Professor Braithwaite's death?' Jo continued.

'Who Red Eric?' Jan said shaking her head. 'No way! I'd have guessed that the first thing she'd have done when she heard the news was to get the bubbly out. They hated each other, just ask Elinor.'

'That's Elinor Grayem-Weiss? You're on first name terms with her?'

'Yes of course, just because the profs were at war with each other didn't mean that we had to be. When we were at conferences together, we always had quite a bit of hanging around to do. She's quite good fun really.'

Jo had a bit if a hard time assimilating the fact that the buttoned-down person she'd met might be 'fun'.

'Do you have a copy of the Professor's diary?'

'Yes sure, but it's on my laptop in there,' Jan said pointing towards the college. 'But I do have a cut down version on my phone if that would help.'

Jo assured her that it would. Jan sent over the diary via email. She'd have a look at it later.

'Is there anything else that you can think of that might be relevant?' Jo asked.

Jan shrugged.

'I'm sorry, I'm not thinking very straight at the moment.'

'That's understandable, it must have been quite a shock. What you'll need to do now is to go back to the college and tell one of the policemen on guard who you are and that you need to have your statement taken. If you think of anything else please include it in your statement or, if you think of anything later on, call me at any time,' Jo said as she gave her a card.

Jo sat there for a while thinking after Jan had gone.

'So, what do you think?' she asked as she eventually joined Leigh in the front of the car.

'It looks more and more like suicide, doesn't it?' Leigh replied. 'But why were you asking about whether there was anything between the two Professors? From what their assistants have told us it looks like they hated each other.'

'It's the black clothes, the colour of death,' Jo replied. 'I still think that there might have been more between the two Professors than their assistants might have been aware of. I've nothing to back my little theory up as yet so we'll see.'

'What's next?' Leigh asked.

'Let's drive to Thriplow. It might be interesting to see the scene of the crime,' Jo suggested.

They drove out of town on the main road towards Royston through the flat fields of Cambridgeshire. They soon turned left onto a narrow country road and headed for Fowlmere. Jo realised when they pulled up outside the Green

Man pub that they'd just driven down at least part of the walk that the Professor regularly used to take. They parked their car where the Professor would have done and got out.

From the outside 'The Green Man' looked like a nice country pub and it was even nicer inside. The food smelt heavenly and Jo made a mental note. It would make for a nice drive out one Sunday for her and Gerry when the weather was warmer. They bought two coffees from the woman behind the bar. Jo showed her warrant card after getting her change.

'We're investigating the recent death of Professor Eric Braithwaite. Did you know him?'

'Of course, he used to come in here at least once a week and two or three times when he was working on something. He'd always park his car outside and then walk off down the lane towards Fowlmere. He'd turn up back here an hour or two later, buy a pint of our best bitter and then spend some time writing in his notebook,' she replied. 'Once he'd finished writing he'd always have a bit of a chat with whoever was in.'

'He was quite sociable then?' Jo asked.

'Oh yes, he'd talk to anyone. I'd say he was quite well liked in the area.'

'So, you wouldn't know of anyone who might have wanted the Professor dead then?'

The landlady gave Jo a puzzled look before it dawned on her what she'd actually been asked.

'Do you really think that someone might have run him over on purpose?' she said with a disbelieving look on her face.

'No, we're still investigating and, while it looks more than likely that it was just an accident, we still have to keep an open mind,' Jo said.

'That never occurred to me, you know, that it might be murder,' the landlady said. 'But no, I honestly can't think of anyone around here who would wish him any harm at all.'

After a few more questions that got her nowhere Jo gave up. They drank their coffees and went outside. A spitefully cold wind gusted into their faces and made Jo shiver. They walked up the lane on the side facing the traffic coming towards them. There wasn't any. Jo took out a tablet and had a look at the photos taken at the point of impact.

'It must be just there I'd guess,' Jo said as she pointed to the hedge a little further up the road.

They walked on and stood at the very spot that the Professor had been standing on just before he died. Jo looked up the lane. It curved towards a corner that wasn't visible from where she stood.

'So, the investigators reckoned that the car came from that direction,' Jo said pointing towards the corner, 'and hit the Professor sending him over the hedge. It's taller than I thought it would be, so it must have hit him very hard. They also thought that an SUV type of vehicle might have been involved, didn't they?'

'Yes, they said that from the impact injuries it was likely to be something other than a car and that an SUV would be the most likely candidate. That would make sense to me for another reason,' Leigh replied. 'I had a case like this when I was in uniform. There was a collision when a car ran off the road onto the pavement and the man it hit ended up on the other side of a fence that was all of seven feet high. He was badly injured but he survived. The car involved was a Land Rover and apparently the victim had been thrown up onto the bonnet and then bounced off the windscreen and rolled up and over the roof. The height of the car was over six feet so it wouldn't have taken much extra force to propel him over the fence which was only a foot or so higher.'

Jo gave this some thought.

'Yes, that makes absolute sense when you put it like that. That's a fact worth remembering.'

They walked on a little further until they came to a gate and they could see what lay on the other side of the hedge. The land had a light growth of green that had been turned frosty white in the areas that had been shaded from the sun. The view seemed cold and desolate to Jo. It made her shiver again.

She definitely wasn't a winter person, she thought. What she wouldn't give right now for a hot summer's day, lying on her sun lounger with a cold drink close at hand.

She was still deep in thought when a large drop of icy cold rain hit her on the top of her head. This was quickly followed by several more.

'Come on let's get back to the car,' she said with some urgency.

They started walking but ended up running as the rain gained in intensity. They were both fairly wet by the time they made it to the car.

'My God, don't you just love the English weather,' Jo said with a scowl. 'We might as well go back to the station and look these diaries over while we dry out. You never know but our murderer might be in there somewhere. If there really is one that is.'

Leigh turned the heater up a notch and had to keep the window wipers going at full speed most of the way back. The sound of the rain on the car roof went from loud to louder.

Back at the station Jo took out her phone and looked through Professor De Gray's diary while Leigh started on Professor Braithwaite's. Something struck her almost straight away. She showed it to Leigh and together they checked both diaries going back as far as they could. Jo then called Jan Eckersley and had a short conversation with her. She smiled to herself afterwards.

She now knew exactly what they'd be doing tomorrow morning.

Chapter Eight

Mac found himself once again sitting in the silence of St. Philips Church. He'd slept for as long as he could and then had a late and leisurely breakfast. He'd driven into London at a reasonable pace but, even so, he was still early. It was only seven thirty and he wasn't due to meet with Callum until nine.

'You just can't keep away Mr. Maguire, can you?' a deep Scottish voice said from behind him.

'Good evening Callum,' Mac said with a smile as he turned around. 'I was just enjoying the peace and quiet.'

'Aye, I like coming here myself sometimes. I find that I can think a little more clearly somehow. Well, as you're early, do you want to come and see what we get up to?'

Mac did. He followed Callum outside and then into a side entrance that led into the same large room that they'd drank coffee in the evening before. The smell of cooking hit him once again as soon as the door opened. It was some sort of stew and its aroma was tempting. Callum walked towards the kitchen area in the corner of the room where, behind a long 'L' shaped counter, four women and two men were attending to several massive cooking pots. One of the men turned at waved at Mac. It was the Reverend Smalley.

'Need anything doing?' Callum asked.

A short rotund lady in her fifties turned around and gave Callum a big smile. Her grey hair was bunched into a ponytail and she was covered up with a long white apron.

'As you're such as big lovely lad I'm sure I could think of something,' she said with a wicked glint in her eye.

Unless he was mistaken Callum actually blushed a little which was a sight that Mac thought he'd never see.

'Aw, come on, Francie!' Callum protested.

He turned to Mac.

'This is Francie, she's our head hash slinger.'

'Head chef to you cheeky,' she said. 'Who's your friend?'

'Oh, this is Mr. Maguire, he's a policeman, well he used to be a policeman. He's looking into Bernie's death.'

Francie's demeanour changed on hearing this. The smile disappeared and was replaced by an angry look.

'Well, may God forgive me for swearing but I hope you get the bastard who did that to our Bernie. That was cruel that was.' She shook her head as if to clear it and the smile quickly returned. 'Anyway, Callum you've just turned up in time to mash the potatoes.'

'Aye, now that's a job I can do alright,' Callum said with a smile.

He lifted a flap and went behind the counter. He picked up the biggest steel pot that Mac had ever seen and started mashing away.

'That'll take him a while but he does the smoothest mash you've ever tasted. I was just going to have a quick cuppa. Do you want one?'

He did. She returned a minute later with two steaming cups of tea and they sat down at a nearby table.

'The calm before the storm, love,' she said. 'This place will be packed out in a few minutes.'

'Did you know Bernie Bright well?' Mac asked.

'I don't think you can ever say that you really know anyone who comes here but I liked Bernie. We had the same sense of humour. There was no harm in him at all so why would anyone want to do that to him?'

'That's what I'm trying to find out. Unfortunately, we do get incidents like this from time to time. These men are just so vulnerable living where and how they do.'

'Callum said that you were an ex-policeman is that right?' Francie asked.

'Yes, but I work as a private detective these days. Bernie's daughter has asked me to see what I can find out about his death.'

'Bernie had a daughter? That surprises me somehow although I don't suppose that it should. Did she ever get in contact with him at all in the weeks before he died?'

'Not as far as I know,' Mac said. 'Why do you ask?'

'Well Bernie was broke. He'd had some trouble with his benefits and they wouldn't pay him anything for ages. For weeks he'd been scrounging off his friends and I heard that even they were getting a bit fed up of it. Then suddenly he had cash again, it must have been a fair bit too as he paid everyone back what he owed them. It wasn't from his benefits either, Callum was still trying to get that sorted out when he died.'

'Now that's interesting,' Mac said.

And it was. It gave him something concrete to go after.

Francie glanced up at the clock.

'Oh well, nearly time to open up,' she said as she stood up. 'It's been nice meeting you Mr. Maguire and the best of luck with finding Bernie's killer. I'll say a little prayer for you.'

'Thanks,' Mac said.

'Action stations!' she said loudly as she walked back towards the kitchen area. 'Callum can you do the door? Oh, and do me a favour and give anyone who's playing up a smack and tell them that it's from me.'

'Aye, no problem,' he said with a smile.

Mac sat and watched as Callum opened up the door. The men poured in and started queueing at the counter. They were mostly men although he thought that he could see the odd woman in the crowd. Sometimes it was hard to tell. They must all have been hungry yet they mostly formed an orderly line. Many of them were smiling at the prospect of a hot meal. Two men at the back of the line weren't so orderly and started a drunken fight. Callum pulled them out and held them up by the collars of their coats. For all the world it looked like a dad telling off his two small children.

'Keep that up and I'll tek ye both outside and skelp ye's,' Callum said loudly.

Mac noticed that Callum's Glasgow tones came to the fore when he was angry. He glared a warning at the rest of the queue as they went by. There were no more altercations.

Callum came over, 'Sorry Mr. Maguire but there's no sign of Polish Pete or Wee Jackie as yet.'

'Thanks, oh and please just call me Mac,' he replied.

'Okay,' Callum said with a smile. 'I'd better go and give them a hand.'

As the men shuffled by Mac's nose picked up the scent of unwashed bodies, damp clothing and strong alcohol. Some were dressed in little more than rags while others just looked normal.

Recent arrivals on the streets, Mac guessed. He could see from their faces that most of these were ashamed to be seen at a soup kitchen.

What made his heart really sink was the number of young men waiting to be fed and he wondered what had led them to this. One especially caught Mac's eye. He was wearing an old woollen hat and a scruffy jumper. He couldn't have been any more than twenty yet his face looked drawn and older. His eyes were hollow and were fixed on the floor as he slowly moved forward in the queue. His body language spoke eloquently of his hopelessness. Mac wondered what his story was.

The tables had started to fill up and the room was full of the clatter of cutlery on plates as the food was wolfed down. After all the meals had been eaten there was the pleasant hubbub of conversation and, if he closed his eyes, Mac could almost imagine himself in a pub or restaurant somewhere. Many of the conversations seemed quite animated and were punctuated by peals of laughter from here and there about the room.

Callum came and sat by him.

'Aye, it's not just the food. We'll be open until ten thirty so it gives them a chance to have a chat and catch up with friends in a safe space.'

'So many of them are so young, aren't they?' Mac said. 'In my day most of the down and outs seemed to be old, too old to work I suppose, but what's the story with these youngsters?'

'I've had to bone up on benefits and all that and I've learned quite a bit. I was told that there used to be a sort of 'safety net' years ago which meant that if you lost your job then you'd be covered by benefits until you got another one. Nowadays that's all changed, you can lose your job and not get a penny for months. With so many people in low paid work and having little or no savings that means that for some they've no option left but the streets,' Callum said with a sad shake of his head. 'It's too easy to end up somewhere like here these days and, with the drink and the drugs, there's not that many that manage to claw their way back into some sort of normal life.'

Mac looked around and he remembered walking past the Food Bank in Letchworth a few weeks before when he'd been walking his dog. Living in such a prosperous town he'd been surprised to see people waiting for it to open up. He began to wonder what sort of a country he was living in.

'Anyway, Francie's putting the takeaways together now. As soon as they're ready we'll be on our way,' Callum said.

Mac found that he would be glad to get going. He was finding his visit to the soup kitchen more than a little depressing.

'Okay big man!' Francie shouted. 'They're ready.'

'I'll see you outside. The van's white and it's got the name of the church on the side,' Callum said.

Mac went out and took a big gulp of fresh air. It wasn't the smell of their unwashed bodies that had bothered him as much as the smell of desperation. He spotted the van and, as he walked towards it, he could see that, cold as it was, little groups of men were dotted around the graveyard, all passing cigarettes or bottles around.

Callum came out a few minutes later holding four huge insulated bags in each hand. Mac would have had a problem with just one. He opened up the van, placed the bags carefully inside and went back to the church. He returned with four more bags in one hand and a small laptop in the other.

'Right, we're set then. I've established a sort of route that I go along starting with the places that are the most used. The first one's a car park just off Stepney Way,' Callum explained.

'I take it that the car park is only used during the day,' Mac said as he climbed into the van.

'It's not used at all actually. It was owned by the council until they shut down the local housing office but I've no idea who owns it now. The men use it because no-one bothers them there plus that fact that it's quite sheltered in one corner as there are walls all around it. They've put up an old tarpaulin to keep out the rain,' Callum replied. 'By the way you won't find Pete or Jackie at this one but you might stand a better chance at the next place we'll be visiting.'

Callum couldn't pull into the car park as the entrance was closed off by two large concrete blocks so he parked on the street as close as he could. Mac followed him out. Callum walked in between the concrete blocks and headed towards a light in the far corner of the car park. As Mac got closer, he could see that a group of nine or ten men were sitting in a circle around the fire and a bottle was being passed from hand to hand. The men's faces were illuminated by the glow of a fire that was contained in an old oil drum that had holes pierced into the sides. The sound of laughing faded away as they drew nearer and the faces turned to look at them.

'Look, it's the big man!' one of the men said loudly. 'I hope you've got some of Francie's stew with you.'

Mac could see the men relax although a few of them still looked at him with some interest. The walls did their job in keeping the worst of the wind at bay but it was still very cold out. Even colder weather was predicted for the near future. He could tell from their bulky appearance that the men must be wearing several layers of clothing but he still wondered at their hardiness.

'Oh aye Dougie, I never come empty handed,' Callum said. 'Anyone else got room for some of Francie's best stew?'

All the men's hands shot up. Callum counted them.

'Before I go and get your food, I'd like to introduce you to someone. This is Mac, he's looking into the murder of Bernie Bright. Any help you can give him would be really appreciated,' Callum said.

He nodded to Mac before he headed back to the van.

'Police?' Dougie asked as the men eyed him sceptically.

Dougie was obviously the leader of this band of merry men. Mac knew he'd have to convince him if was going to get any answers.

'No, I'm a friend of his daughter's. She's asked me to find out what I could about her father's death,' Mac lied.

A small lie but it seemed to have worked. He could see the men relax a little when he said this.

'I never knew Bernie had a daughter. He was a nice man. Oh well, if you're not police and Callum thinks you're okay then you must be okay. Take a seat,' Dougie said.

They made room for Mac on an improvised bench made out of plastic boxes and a wide plank of wood. In truth he was happy to take the pressure off his back for a while. The bottle came around to him. He didn't wipe the top or hesitate, he took a swallow and passed it on. It was some sort of fortified wine and he had to admit that it was warming on such a cold night.

He looked around at his companions. They were mostly old, with a couple of them being in their late thirties perhaps, and they were all bundled up in thick jackets or coats. All of them wore a hat of some sort. Mac had his fedora on and so he fitted right in with them.

The talk started off again and he had to admit that, as low as these men had sunk in most people's eyes, and, as much as they'd lost in life, it seemed that they still had each other. Even he felt a sort of comfort as he watched the flames flicker and let the talk wash over him as the bottle made its way around. Mac didn't drink any more though, he needed to keep his wits about him, but no-one made any comment. He'd taken a drink with them and had accepted their hospitality so that was okay.

Callum returned and started passing out plastic tubs and spoons. As they opened the tubs the smell of Francie's stew spread around the fire like fragrant smoke. The men's faces broke into smiles. Even Mac had to admit that he felt a little of the excitement of camping out that he'd experienced when he was a child. Callum sat next to Mac and watched the men eat. Not a word was said until the last man had finished.

'My compliments to Francie,' a tall thin man sitting opposite Mac said as he returned the tub to Callum. 'An excellent repast as always and even better eaten al fresco.'

His voice matched his flowery words. He sounded as if he should be eating in a superior London restaurant rather than being crouched around a fire in the corner of a Stepney car park. Mac was intrigued.

'Thanks Alfred, I'll let Francie know,' Callum said. 'I know some of you need to talk about your benefits but before we get into that I'd like you to listen to Mac for a minute or two.'

Mac knew that this was his chance. The men were fed and in a good mood and hopefully not too drunk as yet. He'd keep it as brief as possible.

'Bernie's daughter is called Marcia and she loved her father. Bernie was born here in Stepney but he'd lived in Welwyn Garden City for the last twenty-five years or more. When Bernie's wife died it seems like he gave up and he ended up back here, where he grew up.'

Mac could see a number of men nodding at this. It must have been a familiar story for them.

'She wants to know what happened to her father, why he died and who killed him. So, if you know anything at all about what Bernie was doing before he was killed, I'd be glad to hear it.'

Mac looked hopefully around the group.

'He was broke for a while, I know that,' a short man in a bright blue puffer jacket said. 'A few weeks before he died, he came here and he literally hadn't got a penny. Luckily a few of us had just picked up our money so we managed.'

They managed. Mac supposed that was what it was all about, just making it through the night.

'Aye Danny, I never was able to sort his benefits out,' Callum said.

'Then a couple of nights before he died he turned up here with a crate of Thunderbird,' a man with a Newcastle accent said. 'We had a good night that night, didn't we lads?'

The men all nodded and smiled at the memory.

'Did he tell anyone where he'd gotten the money from?' Mac asked.

All the men looked at each other and shook their heads. All except for one man sitting to Mac's left. He was a large man with a round face from which sprouted a magnificently long beard. He had a red baseball hat on his head which had the slogan 'Make America Great Again' on the crown in yellow letters.

Mac hadn't been the only one to notice.

'Zee-Zee, did Bernie tell you anything?' Callum asked.

The bearded man looked up.

'Well, not really,' he replied.

Mac had been half expecting an American accent for some reason but, although he definitely came from the West, Zee-Zee's accent was from somewhere nearer Bristol.

'I did ask him,' Zee-Zee continued, 'but he just winked and said that he'd been to see an old friend that afternoon.'

'He didn't say who this old friend was?' Mac asked.

Zee-Zee shook his head.

'Was it someone he'd been to school with or someone he'd worked with perhaps?' Mac asked hopefully.

From the way he was screwing up his face Mac could see that he was giving it his best shot so he waited while Zee-Zee thought.

'Sorry but he didn't say,' he said eventually.

'Thanks anyway, Zee-Zee,' Mac said.

He watched on as Callum asked about the men's health and then made sure that they were all getting their benefits. He opened up the small laptop he'd brought with him and started making notes. This new caring Tiger McEachan was still a thing of wonder to him. There was sort of a gentleness about him as he talked to the men. They obviously respected him, respect was one thing that Callum had always had, but Mac could see that the men really liked him too.

'Okay then, take care you lot and, as I've said before, don't go around by yourself if you can help it. If it was a nutter who killed Bernie then he might still be out there looking for another victim. If you see anyone suspicious hanging around just get a word to me and I'll see to it.'

The men all shouted out their goodbyes as Mac followed Callum back to the van. He looked back at the group of men who were making happy sounds.

'Where do they sleep, Callum?'

'Did you notice the pile of cardboard boxes in the corner?' Mac nodded. 'Well, that's what they sleep in. They slide themselves inside and then fill in any extra space with newspaper or the like.'

As Callum said this an icy breeze chilled Mac's face.

'My God but they must be freezing in this weather.'

'Most of them still prefer the streets even when there's snow on the ground. I remember I asked one man I met, not long after I started doing this, whether he wouldn't sooner be inside somewhere warm and in a proper bed. He just shook his head.

He said he liked his independence and that he was afraid that he'd lose his 'street skin' as he called it. He'd get too used to being indoors and wouldn't be able to sleep outside any more. I've heard that by quite a few of them.'

'What's the story with Alfred?' Mac asked.

'Alfred? Much the same as Bernie's really. His full name is Alfred Tennyson Feycourt believe it or not. He used to be an English teacher, private schools mostly from what he told me. He was quite well off at one time I suppose. He said that he'd always liked a drink but, when his partner died, he took to it in a big way. It didn't take him long before he lost everything and ended up here. Alcoholism isn't any respecter of class.'

Mac stood and looked back at the illuminated faces around the fire.

'Are they okay for a drink?' Mac asked unsure of the etiquette involved.

'You want to buy them one, do you?' Callum asked with surprise as he put the bags with the empty containers in the back of the van.

'Well they were helpful and it is starting to get a bit cold.'

'Aye, it is that. Winter's here and it will take a good few of them away. I noticed that was their last bottle so I guess another one won't kill them.'

Mac took out his wallet and at that moment the wind picked up sending a shiver down Mac's spine. He gave Callum three ten-pound notes.

'Get them a couple.'

Callum walked down the street to a corner shop and returned with two bottles of Thunderbird. He could hear the loud cheers from the men as Callum handed them over.

'Well that went down well,' Callum said with a smile as he got back into the van. 'Next stop is just down the road. It's a pub.'

Mac wondered at that until they pulled up outside. The pub looked as if it had been built in the fifties and he guessed that the original, like so many buildings in this part of London, might have been bombed out during the war. It was quite big and had the unusual feature of having a balcony above a large bow window. The bow window, like all the others, was boarded up and weeds were growing from every crevice in the paved courtyard. The pub's sign was still there although it had been faded by time. It said 'The Old Beetroot' and had quite a realistic picture of a purplish beetroot with green leaves sprouting from it.

'Around this way,' Callum said.

Mac followed him as he walked around the side of the pub. There was a substantial brick garage with wooden double doors that were held shut by a robust looking padlock. Callum walked down the side of the garage where Mac could see that there was a sort of path where the wild vegetation had been trodden down. He stopped outside a door at the back and knocked. A few seconds later the door opened a fraction and an eyeball peeked out. It then opened fully.

'It's just the big man,' a voice announced in an Irish accent.

Mac followed Callum inside and was quite staggered at what he found there. While it reeked of cheap tobacco and body odour it was well lit and was warmed by a couple of old electric fan heaters. Stained mattresses with sleeping bags lined one wall while the other had a couple of wooden picnic tables pushed together around which eight men were seated. They were passing the inevitable bottle around. He noticed that a microwave oven stood on a little table in the corner.

Quite a little home from home, Mac thought.

'Mac, you're in luck,' Callum said softly. 'That's Pete and Jackie sitting at the far end of the table.'

Chapter Nine

They all looked at Callum hungrily so he went and brought the food in first. Each man was given a plastic box and they began wolfing down Francie's stew. Callum waited until they had all eaten before he introduced Mac and told them that he was looking into Bernie Bright's murder on behalf of his daughter. Mac gave them the same little speech that he'd given the previous group.

'So, Bernie had a daughter then,' the man with the Irish accent said. Mac had learned that his name was, inevitably, Paddy. 'It's a shame he died. He was always welcome here. We were always willing to trade a few drinks for a good laugh, now weren't we lads?'

All the men nodded.

'And did you have to do that a lot with Bernie?' Mac asked.

'Aye, he was broke for quite a time as he was having trouble with his benefits. Then one night he turned up with six bottles of the best. That was a night and a half.'

The men all smiled with the memory of it.

'Has anyone any idea how Bernie came into his money?' Mac asked.

They all looked at each other and shook their heads, everyone that is except for a gaunt-faced bearded man wearing a beanie hat who could have been anything from forty to seventy.

'Excuse me, what's your name?' Mac asked.

The man looked to those either side of him before realising that Mac was talking to him.

'It's Baz,' he said in a near whisper.

'Don't be worried Baz, we're just chatting. Do you know where Bernie got his money from?'

'I saw him, I saw him in the Blue Boar about three weeks ago,' he replied as he nervously scratched at his beard.

'That's a pub not far from here,' Callum explained.

'Were you in the pub too?' Mac asked.

Baz grinned and shook his head.

'No, the gaffer wouldn't let the likes of us in there and it's too bloody expensive anyway.'

'So how did you get to see him?'

'He was sitting near the window.'

'Was there anyone with him?'

'Yes, he was with a man,' Baz said.

Interviewing Baz was a bit like pulling teeth but Mac persevered.

'What was the man like?'

'He wasn't one of us that's for sure. He was getting on a bit and he had a nice suit and tie on. I remember that he had this lovely coat hanging on the back of his chair. It was so nice and warm looking that I'd have nicked that coat if I could have. If the gaffer would have ever let me in that is.'

'Did you see anything happen between Bernie and this man?'

Baz shrugged.

'They just talked. Bernie laughed a few times, he looked like he was enjoying himself. Then I saw the man give Bernie some money.'

'How much did he give him, could you tell?' Mac asked.

'Not really, I only caught a glimpse as he put it in Bernie's hand. The top note was a twenty though.'

'What happened after that?' Mac asked.

'They just talked some more and then they left. Bernie saw me when he came out and he came over to me. He said that he'd come into some money so we went down to the supermarket and he bought a couple of bottles.'

'And he never said who the man was?'

'Dunno really. He might have but, after a couple of bottles, I wouldn't have remembered anyway,' he said with a smile.

'Thank you, Baz. You've been really helpful,' Mac said. 'Has anyone else remembered anything about Bernie that might help?'

They all looked at each other but no-one else came forward. Mac went to where Pete and Jackie were sitting.

'What about you Pete and Jackie? It looks like you were the last people who saw Bernie before he was killed.'

They gave each other an uncertain look.

They looked an odd couple indeed, Mac thought. Pete was a large bald man with a round moon face while Jackie was 'wee' indeed and looked like a child sitting next to him. Jackie was as thin as Pete was round and he was thin faced with it. Mac couldn't help wondering if he'd had an accident and had gotten squashed between two buses or something. It was Pete who answered his question.

'We met him at the church after we had something to eat and we shared a bottle, that's all,' Pete said in a pure East End accent.

'He didn't say anything about the man he'd met in the pub or how he'd gotten his money?'

Mac noticed Jackie pause for thought and then screw up his face in concentration. He gave him some time.

'Didn't he say something about there being plenty more on the way?' he asked in a high-pitched Scottish accent.

Pete had to think deeply before the memory surfaced.

'Oh yes, I remember now. He said he'd be going west soon and he'd be picking up his wage packet.'

'That's what he said? 'Picking up his wage packet'?' Mac asked.

'I think so, something like that anyway,' Pete replied with a shrug.

Jackie nodded in agreement.

'Did he say anything more about exactly where he was going?' Mac asked.

'No, 'west' was all he said,' Pete confirmed.

Mac wished that Bernie could have found it in him to be a bit more specific. There was an awful lot of London west of where they were sitting.

'And that was all Bernie told you?' Mac asked.

'I asked but he wouldn't tell us any more,' Pete said. 'I really wanted to know how he got the money too. I was wondering if he was fiddling his benefits or something and, if he was, I was going to have a go at doing it myself.'

Mac asked a few more questions but it looked like that was all he was going to get out of them. Nonetheless, what they'd told him was intriguing to say the least.

Before he left he took his wallet out and handed Pete a twenty pound note.

'Buy you and the lads a drink on me.'

'Thanks, I'll do that,' Pete said with a toothless smile as he held up the note for all to see.

Mac got the thumbs up from them all.

'By the way why do they call you Polish Pete? You don't sound that Polish to me,' Mac asked.

Pete smiled, 'I get asked that a lot. I started off being called Pete the Polisher as I used to do French polishing and the like for a living before I took to the bottle. Then it became 'Poll-ish Pete' and finally 'Polish Pete'. I still get some of the Polish guys who are new to the street come up and speak to me and it's embarrassing as I can't understand a bloody word of their lingo. I suppose I could always change my name.'

'Or learn how to speak Polish,' Jackie said in a sly voice.

This got a round of laughter from them all.

They were still laughing when Callum closed the door behind them. The cold outside felt even more bitter after the warmth of the men's snug little den. Mac shivered, he definitely didn't have his 'street skin' yet and he hoped that he'd never need it.

'How do they get their electricity?' Mac asked as they walked back to the van.

'One of the lads used to be an electrician and, when they shut the pub down they didn't bother disconnecting the supply just turned it all off at the breaker box. So, he turned on one of the power points and then ran a lead from the pub into the garage.'

'Didn't the people who own the pub notice?'

'Well the lads said that someone came down to have a look at the pub last year. They reckon he must have noticed them but he obviously didn't say anything,' Callum replied.

'What are they going to do with it then?'

'The pub? From what I've heard they're leaving it as it is until gentrification hits this part of London a few years from now. They've already got the plans approved to build luxury flats on the land from what I've been told.'

Mac wondered what would happen to 'the lads' then. He hoped that, if it had to happen, then it might happen in the summer and not when it was freezing outside. They were all too used to being in the warm. He was quiet as they drove to their next stop which Callum said wasn't too far from the tube station. They drove past low blocks of flats that were built in the thirties. They were now showing their age.

'I'm only taking you to this next one on the off chance that a guy called Jamie might be sleeping it off there. He's a young guy who Bernie took under his wing for a while. They seemed to get on really well but then Jamie disappeared around the same time that Bernie was killed.'

This intrigued Mac too. People who disappear after a crime usually do so for a good reason.

'What's this Jamie like?'

'He's in his early twenties, a shy lad really,' Callum replied. 'It's my guess that he'd been abused when he was a kid. He certainly had some mental health issues but being with Bernie seemed to cheer him up.'

'Do you think that this Jamie could have had anything to do with Bernie's death?' Mac asked.

'No, I doubt it. I don't think he'd have it in him to kill anyone but, as he spent a lot of time with Bernie recently, there's a chance that he might have seen something.'

Mac hoped that Callum was right.

They turned right and drove alongside an elevated railway bridge. The bridge was Victorian and built with black engineering bricks. Underneath the railway line there was a series of large arches. Mac knew that there was a lot of space in those arches and that was why they were quite popular with many small businesses who couldn't afford the exorbitant rents now being asked in most areas of London. All of the arches here were boarded up.

The street came to a dead end and Callum pulled up just before the road ran out at the railway tracks. He retrieved a couple of food bags and a large torch from the van and walked towards the arch.

'Stay behind me Mac. Some of them can be a bit edgy at times, shall we say,' Callum warned.

Mac had every intention of following his advice. He could see that someone had broken the boarding away on one side creating enough room for a person to get through. Callum had to contort his body somewhat to get inside but Mac found it easy enough.

It was quiet inside the arch and dark too. Mac could hear the sound of dripping water. Callum turned the torch on and shone it on himself.

'It's alright, it's only me, Callum from St. Philips. Does anyone want any food? It's Francie's best stew,' Callum said in as light a tone as he could muster.

He shone the torch out into the darkness. It was so cold that his breath was white. People were strewn across the floor. Most were in sleeping bags but Mac noticed a couple of people sleeping in or on cardboard boxes. One man was lying on the cold floor in just his clothes. They were mostly young, some very young indeed. One couple sharing a sleeping bag held each other tight and gave them a scared look. They couldn't have been any older than fifteen. Some were obviously high. They sat with their backs against the wall, eyes wide open but their minds were clearly on another planet.

A few stirred themselves and moved slowly towards Callum. Their joints were so cold that moving was almost painful. Callum handed out the meals and had a word with each recipient to see if they needed any help. He handed out cards inviting them to an advice session at the church the next day. It was all he could do. He left some food for those who were sleeping or high just in case.

Before they left Callum went around all of the sleepers and made sure they really were just sleeping. Mac then followed Callum outside.

'I always check now because a few months back I noticed that there was this guy who was still in exactly the same position he'd been in when I'd seen him a few nights before. That was because he was dead. He'd been lying there for five days would you believe. I'm sorry that Jamie wasn't there, Mac.'

'Thanks for trying anyway. Do you know Jamie's surname?'

Callum shrugged, 'Sorry Mac, the only time I ever get to know people's surnames is if they have any problems with their benefits but he never came to me for that. All I know is that he had a Scottish accent, not Glasgow more Edinburgh perhaps.'

A young man from Edinburgh called Jamie, Mac thought. It didn't really narrow it down very much. He thought about the man lying on the ground in just his clothes.

'What are they using nowadays?' Mac asked as they made their way back to the car.

'Spice seems to be the drug of choice at the moment,' Callum replied.

Mac had heard about the drug but had rarely come across it when he'd been in the force. It was a fairly new synthetic drug that was sprayed onto plant material to make it look like marijuana. It was far more powerful though and far more addictive. The users of the drug had often been referred to in the media as 'zombies' because it often caused them to freeze in peculiar positions for hours or they'd just curl up on the floor as if they were dead. Once awake they'd be so disoriented that they were often quite aggressive. Mac guessed that's why Callum had warned him to stay close.

'Most of them are so young. What's the story with them?' Mac asked.

'It's quite simple really, they bunk off school because they think it's the cool thing to do. Then they find that when they leave school and go out into the real world, they can only get minimum wage or zero-hour contract work. They're literally living hand to mouth. With the new government benefit rules, if they can't get work, then they can't claim anything for six weeks and sometimes it's even longer. So, they get kicked out by their landlords, or sometimes it's their parents, and they find themselves on the street. They do whatever they can to get money and then spend that money on getting zonked out of their brains so that they can forget how bad life is for a while. The only trouble is that they have to wake up sometime, although there's always a few who never do.'

It was no shock to Mac. He'd seen it all before but it still made him feel sad. The scene underneath the railway arch was like something out of a Dickens novel and yet, a short walk from where they stood, there were people sitting inside expensive restaurants and gastro-pubs who would think nothing of spending three hundred pounds on a dinner for two.

Something was wrong with the world, Mac decided.

'I'm going over the other side of the parish now and I doubt we'll find anyone who would have known Bernie there. Shall I drop you off at your car?' Callum asked.

Mac was feeling tired and his bed was where he needed to be. He thanked Callum and headed back out of London for home and some sleep. It started snowing as he neared Letchworth and he was grateful that he hadn't got far to go.

Later, as he lay back in his warm and comfortable bed, he thought of those young unfortunates lying on the cold floor underneath a railway arch.

It was dark in Mac's bedroom, he thought as he drifted off to sleep, but it was much, much darker where they were.

Chapter Ten

Leigh turned off the alarm and lay back for a moment. She noticed that a bright pearly-white light was seeping in around the edges of her curtains. She got up and pulled the curtains wide to reveal a street that had a pure white covering of snow. It looked like a cake that had been covered with a dusting of icing sugar. She smiled. Seeing snow on the ground still gave her the same thrill of excitement that she'd felt as a child. She stood there for a while just looking until she realised that she needed to get going. It was going to be a busy day.

The air was icy cold when she stepped outside and it made her gasp. She guessed that the snow wouldn't be going anywhere if it stayed as cold as this. Luckily, there was only a light covering at the moment. She knew that it wouldn't take much more snow to fall before the usual chaos on the roads took place. She kept her fingers crossed as she knew that they had some driving to do.

At the station she sat and had a welcome coffee with Jo as they discussed what they should do next. They settled on visiting the Royal Air Force base at Witterlow first. Luckily it was fairly easy driving as all the main roads had been salted and, for now at least, they were more or less free of snow. It didn't take long before they were turning off the main road and into the air base's main entrance. They had to show their warrant cards at the check point and were then told that they'd have to wait in a little room until an airman turned up. He came a few minutes later and introduced himself as Sergeant Thomas of the RAF Police. He asked how he could help them.

'We're looking for information about someone called Eric Braithwaite,' Jo explained. 'He served in the RAF some years ago and we've been told that he used to come here every second Wednesday to a club for a darts evening.'

'A darts evening?' the sergeant said looking puzzled. 'I don't think we've had one of those for quite a few years. If it's about an ex-member then Old Fred might be the best person to speak to. He's been at the base for as long as any of us can remember. He should be over at the officers' mess. Please follow me.'

They followed him to a blue Land Rover. Jo and Leigh got in the back and they sped off. The base was far larger than they'd imagined and it took over five minutes before they pulled up outside a group of buildings. They walked down a lengthy corridor that was lined with paintings and photographs, all of which featured an aircraft of some sort. They came to a small sign on a door that said 'Officers' Mess.' The Sergeant held the door open for them. A few officers in blue uniforms were sitting around having a drink.

'That's Fred there,' he said pointing at an old bald-headed man in a crisp white jacket and bow tie who was standing behind the bar.

The Sergeant went over and explained the situation to him. Fred handed the bar over to another, somewhat younger man, who was also wearing a crisp white jacket and bow tie and joined Jo and Leigh at a table.

Jo asked him about the darts nights.

'Darts nights?' he said with a bemused expression. 'I remember that we used to have darts nights many years ago. They were quite popular back then but no-one seems interested in them these days which is a pity. I used to like a nice game of darts, not that I was ever any good at it.'

Jo and Leigh exchanged puzzled looks.

'Have you ever heard of a man called Eric Braithwaite?' Jo asked. 'He used to be in the RAF many years ago.'

'I joined the RAF as a young man on my eighteenth birthday and I'm still involved nearly sixty years later,' Fred said with some pride. 'I always try and keep in touch with as many of the old hands as I can. Now Eric Braithwaite? That name seems familiar but why?'

Jo gave him some time to locate the memory.

'Oh yes, I remember now where I saw it,' Fred said with a smile. 'Follow me.'

They followed Fred outside into the hallway and watched him as he looked at some of the photographs displayed on the walls. He checked a number of them out before stopping in front of one. He smiled widely.

'Yes, I knew I was right. Here you are,' he said pointing to some text under the photo.

The photo showed a pilot dressed in a flight suit. He was holding a helmet in one hand as he stood proudly in front of a jet aircraft. He was smiling as were the three men in overalls who were standing in the background.

Jo read the text below –

'Flt Lt Jack Caulderdale standing in front of the first Hawker Siddeley Harrier GR1 jet received at RAF Witterlow. Behind him are members of the technical crew Chf Tech Joseph Myers, Sgt Bernard Bright and Cpl Eric Braithwaite.'

Jo looked closely at the young man on the left. It was definitely the Professor. He was quite handsome in those days, she thought.

'The reason I remembered his name was because this became something of an iconic photo,' Fred explained. 'It was the very first time that a Harrier jet flew out of Witterlow. Jack Caulderdale was the pilot and he later became Commander of the base. Of course, that was all a long, long time ago.'

'And you've never heard of Eric Braithwaite in any other context since?' Jo asked. 'Perhaps he might have visited some of the bars or messes?'

'I think I would have known if he had. I always try to make sure I meet all our old hands if they ever visit,' Fred said apologetically.

The Sergeant gave them a lift back to the check point. Before they left, he checked and ensured them that no visitor called Braithwaite had ever been logged into the system.

As they walked back to the car Leigh said, 'Well whatever it was the Professor was doing every second Wednesday it certainly wasn't playing darts with his RAF friends.'

'So, what was he doing then?' Jo said. 'Let's go and check out Professor De Gray's diary entry. She was supposed to have been having a girl's night out in St. Neots every second Wednesday and staying with a friend.'

'So, what do we do, start checking every pub and restaurant in the area?' Leigh asked.

Jo was thoughtful for a moment and remembered her theory.

'No, let's start with the hotels.'

Leigh looked surprised but said nothing. As Jo drove them to St. Neots, she got her phone out and started looking at hotels in the area. Luckily St. Neots wasn't that big and so it wouldn't take them long to go around them all. It was still bright out but, as they drove back down the motorway, she could see some dark grey clouds on the horizon that looked quite ominous.

They showed photographs of the two Professors at the first hotel and drew a blank. It was the same at the second one. At the third hotel, however, they struck lucky. It was one of a nationwide chain of hotels that was situated near a motorway junction. It had a steak restaurant attached. The receptionist, a large woman in her late thirties with purple glasses, introduced herself as Mandy.

Jo showed her the photographs of the two Professors and she recognised them instantly.

'Oh yes, that's Mr. and Mrs. Winstanley,' Mandy replied. 'Everyone here knows them. They've been coming here for years, every other Wednesday at seven o'clock without fail.'

'What did they do here?' Jo asked.

'Well, you know,' Mandy replied pulling a face that said far more than words ever could.

Jo and Leigh exchanged surprised looks.

'They were a very loving couple and very generous with their tips too. All the staff really liked them,' Mandy continued. 'They always arrived separately and they always had the same room, number thirteen. They'd put their bags in the room first and then they'd come down and have a meal in the restaurant. They always had wine with their meal and then they'd take a bottle of something bubbly back up to their room.'

'And you say that they were very loving?' Jo asked.

'I'll say. I was told that they were originally put in room thirteen because it's the end room and there's only a store room on the other side so it wouldn't matter too much if they were a bit noisy.'

'And were they noisy?'

'Yes, they could be. I mean they were both getting on a bit but it seemed as if they had plenty of energy, if you know what I mean,' Mandy said with a knowing smile.

Jo did.

'Did they ever say anything about themselves, what they did for a living for instance?'

'Not that I can ever remember,' Mandy replied. She gave Jo and Leigh a serious look. 'I hope that they haven't done anything wrong. We all reckoned that they were both married and having an affair. Their other halves haven't found out or anything, have they?'

'No, they weren't married,' Jo said, 'except possibly to their work.'

'Well, that's a real surprise then. So why are the police looking for them then?' Mandy asked.

'We're not looking for them,' Jo replied. 'We're trying to find out something about their last movements. They're both dead I'm afraid.'

'Dead?' Mandy said in disbelief. 'Really? I only saw them the week before last and you say that they're both dead?'

'Yes, I'm afraid to say they are,' Jo replied. She didn't want to go into details so she went straight on. 'Are there any other members of the staff here who might have had contact with the Winstanleys?'

'Just about all of them I'd have thought at one time or another.'

'Do you have a room free that we can use to interview them?' Jo asked.

Mandy set them up in one of the hotel rooms on the ground floor and sent the members of her staff in one by one. Everyone they talked to knew Mr. and Mrs. Winstanley and seemed to have a good opinion of them. However, it seemed that the Professors had been very close-lipped about their real lives during their visits to the hotel. The only clue they got was from a young chambermaid called Jasmine who'd overheard them talking the last time they'd been at the hotel.

'I was finishing off the room opposite one morning a few weeks ago. They had their door open and their bags packed and they were talking to each other.'

'What did they say?' Jo asked.

'I can't remember the exact words but Mr. Winstanley was talking to Mrs. Winstanley and he said something about meeting an old friend who he hadn't seen for years. He said that he'd met him by accident when he was leaving his sister's house and then said something about how sad he felt. That's it really,' she said.

Back at reception Jo gave Mandy some cards.

'If any of the other members of staff who aren't here today remember anything, please get them to call me straight away. It's really important.'

Mandy assured her that she would.

As they walked to the car Leigh said, 'Well, that was a surprise. The two Professors, who appeared to all the world to be rabid enemies, appeared to have had a truce every other Wednesday night.'

'And it also explains why Professor De Gray killed herself, doesn't it?' Jo said picturing her body dressed in black dangling from the rope. 'I think she really loved him.'

'I don't get it though,' Leigh said as she climbed into the car. 'Why the pretence of hating each other then? I mean they weren't married or anything.'

'I think they were. I wasn't being light when I said that they were married to their work. I think they absolutely believed that their versions of history were the right ones and, while they hated each other's views, that didn't mean that they had to hate each other. They were both at the top of their profession and I'd be surprised if they didn't at least respect each other's work. I'd bet that they often stayed at the same hotels when they were attending events so, perhaps they had few drinks afterwards one night and ended up in bed together.'

'But why keep it a secret though?' Leigh asked.

'Maybe it added to the fun of it, who knows?'

Jo was silent for a moment.

'I need to make a call.'

Jo patiently held the phone to her ear but obviously whoever she was calling wasn't picking up. Jo then phoned Professor Braithwaite's assistant, Elinor.

'I know you gave us the Professor's sister's landline number but she isn't picking up. I was wondering if you had a mobile phone number for her?'

'Oh yes, of course. I'll get it for you,' Elinor replied.

A few seconds later she read it out.

'Thanks. Oh, by the way I was just wondering if the name Winstanley meant anything to you?' Jo asked.

'I should say so!' Elinor replied with some enthusiasm. 'Gerard Winstanley was one of the Professor's heroes. In the seventeenth century he was the leader of a movement called the 'Diggers' who also called themselves the 'True Levellers'. They were against the ownership of land and he founded a colony in Surrey where...'

Not wanting the complete lecture Jo cut her short and said her goodbyes. She phoned the Professor's sister on the mobile number and arranged to meet her in an hour and a half.

'So, we're off to Stepney then,' Leigh said.

'It might be worth a try. After all we've still got no real idea if the Professor's death was a murder or just an accident. Let's hope that his sister knows something.'

As they drove towards the capital Jo rang Dan Carter and updated him with what they'd found. This new information made it even more certain that Professor De Gray's death was suicide. She couldn't help noticing that Dan sounded much happier at the end of their conversation than he had at the start.

Chapter Eleven

Although it was now mid-afternoon Mac was sipping his first coffee of the day as he looked out over the back garden and watched the birds line up at the feeders. Having taken one of his little blue pills, he'd slept well except for a dream that had woken him up around six o'clock or so.

He'd been dreaming that he was in an echoing dark space somewhere. It was icy cold and all he could hear was the sound of water dripping and his own teeth chattering. He was afraid. He could sense that something was slowly shuffling towards him through the darkness. He didn't know what it was, just that it was something nameless, something terrible. It came closer. He shut his eyes but he could still feel its hot breath on his face. He tried but he couldn't help himself. He was just about to open his eyes and see what horror was waiting for him when he woke up. The sounds and images slipped away but the feeling of dread stayed with him. He got up, went to the toilet and then went back to bed in the hope of returning to sleep. Luckily, he had no more dreams and slept on until nearly one o'clock.

Although the sun shone brightly it had been a cold night and the grass and plants were still covered with a light dusting of snow. More snow had been forecast for later in the day and the temperature was once again going to plummet overnight.

He thought of the poor young people sleeping in the railway arch again and found that he had to push such dark thoughts out of his head. He still had a case to solve and he needed to think. So, what had he learned so far?

Bernie had been well liked by just about everyone it seemed; he'd been penniless and then he'd met a well-dressed man in a pub who had given him some money; he'd talked of going 'west' to pick up his 'wage packet', whatever that meant, and he used to be friends with a young man called Jamie. Not much to go on really. However, he reminded himself that he'd solved many cases where he'd started off with a lot less than that.

Who was the man who gave Bernie money? Who was going to give him his 'wage packet'? Was it the same man as the one in the pub or somebody else? He knew that the money was probably going to be the key to solving the mystery around Bernie Bright's death. So, what to do next?

Mac's first reaction was to go back to the case file. He poured himself a second cup of coffee, settled down on the sofa and opened up the file. He knew that in many cases it was often some key event in the past that had finally caught up with the murder victim. As he read on, he thought back to a case he'd recently been involved with where a death from thirty years earlier had led to a murder. A large part of Bernie's life had been spent in the RAF, so Mac concluded that he should start with that. He looked at the clock, it was nearly three. As the Royal Air Force base was less than an hour away, Mac decided that he just had time to pay them a visit.

He presented himself at the check point, gave the receptionist one of his 'Garden City Detective Agency' cards and asked if there was anyone who he could talk to about an ex-RAF technician.

'That's strange,' the young corporal said. 'We've had the police here not long ago asking about an ex-member too. As you're not with the police I'm not sure if we can help you but I'll give someone a ring anyway. You never know.'

Mac had to wait for nearly fifteen minutes before a blue Land Rover pulled up outside and a sergeant got out.

'Mr. Maguire? My name's Sergeant Thomas of the RAF Police. You're not enquiring into someone called Eric Braithwaite by any chance?' he asked.

'Eric Braithwaite? No. Why do you ask?'

'Oh, I just thought...well, it's unusual that we get two enquiries about ex-members on the same day. So, how can I help?'

'I'm looking into the murder of a man called Bernard Bright on behalf of his daughter. As he spent a large part of his younger life working on this base, I thought that it might be a good place to start.'

'Have you any identification that you can show me?' the sergeant asked.

As Mac took his driving license out of his wallet his police warrant card fell out with it. The Sergeant picked it up, looked at it and handed it back to him.

'You're with the police?' the Sergeant asked. 'I thought you said you were a private detective?'

'I've been a policeman for most of my life but I'm retired now. I still work with the police from time to time as a consultant and that's why I've got the warrant card,' Mac explained.

'Oh, I see,' the Sergeant said.

He was thoughtful for a while.

'Yes, Bernard Bright. I think I've seen that name earlier today. Follow me,' the Sergeant ordered.

Mac got into a blue Land Rover and they drove a surprising distance before stopping outside of a group of buildings. They entered one of the buildings and walked down a long corridor. The Sergeant started slowing down to look at the photographs. He finally came to a halt in front of one of them.

'This is the photo that we showed the police when they came earlier,' the Sergeant said.

Mac read the text underneath and then looked at the photo carefully. It was definitely Bernie Bright. He looked happy in the photo.

'And you say that the police were asking about this man here?' Mac said pointing to the young man on the left.

'Yes, they said that he was a Professor and that he'd recently been killed in some sort of accident.'

Mac felt his pulse speeding up. It surely couldn't be a coincidence, could it?

'Is there anyone still around who might have known Bernard Bright?' Mac asked more in hope than anything else.

'I might just have the man,' the Sergeant said with a smile. 'Just wait here.'

He returned a minute later with an old man dressed in a white jacket and bow tie.

'This is Fred Bassett. Fred this is Mr. Maguire and he's looking into another death. This man here,' the Sergeant said pointing to Bernie in the photo.

Fred looked at Mac with a puzzled expression and then looked at the photograph.

'Oh yes, I remember him,' he said with a smile. 'Bernie the Bolt they used to call him for some reason. He was a real character. He used to do a little comedy act at some of the social nights and he was very funny. I'm sorry to hear that he's dead.'

'Is there anything else you can tell me about him?'

Mac was beginning to get the feeling that he might be finally onto something.

'Well, I didn't have much to do with him really as he worked over in the Harrier stores. He was an expert too and I think that he knew the proper name and identification number of just about every part that went into the plane. I remember that they used to bring bits of the aircraft to the club and challenge him to give the identification number and where it went on the aircraft. He never failed once as far as I can remember. I've heard him boast that he could build a plane himself from all the bits he kept in the stores. Oh yes, that was another thing about Bernie, he really liked a pint but then again so did most of the men at the time.'

Mac thanked Fred and then took a photo before he left.

As they drove back to the check point Mac asked the sergeant, 'Who were the policemen who came here earlier?'

'They were policewomen actually, a DI Dugdale and DC Marston. Do you know them?'

'Yes, yes I do. Thank you so much for your help.'

Before he left he got the phone number of someone who might be able to supply both men's service records.

Mac smiled to himself as he drove off.

It surely couldn't be a coincidence that two men in the same photo had died in mysterious circumstances within a few weeks of each other. He then told himself not to get his hopes up as he knew that such coincidences happen a lot more often than people might think.

However, this didn't dent his good spirits one little bit. At last he had a lead!

It had started snowing again as he drove back to Letchworth and the traffic was very slow. Luckily, he had plenty of time as Jo and Leigh were also struggling back through the London traffic.

He waited patiently in the empty Major Crime Unit's room at Letchworth Police Station letting the case simmer gently in his mind as he sipped at a welcome coffee. The room was empty because it was now six forty. Jo and Leigh had been going to head straight home after interviewing Professor Braithwaite's sister in Stepney but that was before Mac had called them. He was still deep in thought when they arrived.

'Hello Mac, we haven't seen you for a while,' Jo said just before she gave him a big hug. 'How have you been keeping?'

'Oh, keeping busy…well trying to anyway,' he replied.

'Hi Mac,' Leigh said giving him a shy wave of her hand.

'You were being very mysterious when you called,' Jo said. 'You said that you might have something that could help us with our case.'

Mac took his phone out and brought up the photo that he'd taken at the air base. He showed it to Jo and Leigh.

'We were just looking at that exact same photo earlier today. How on earth did you know about that?' Jo asked in amazement.

'I didn't until I was told by an RAF Police Sergeant a short while ago. I'm looking into a death too. It was of this man here, the one standing next to Mr. Braithwaite,' he said pointing to Bernie in the photo. 'He was murdered two weeks ago in Stepney.'

Jo and Leigh looked very interested at this. Mac told them everything that he'd unearthed.

'And you think that there's a connection?' Jo asked.

'Well, I don't know for certain but it would be quite a coincidence, wouldn't it? Did you discover anything in Stepney?'

'No, not really,' Jo replied. 'The Professor's sister, Mrs. Darnley, was a lovely woman but she didn't tell us anything that might help.'

'She never said anything about the Professor meeting up with an old friend?'

Jo shook her head but then she remembered what the hotel chambermaid had told her.

'No, she didn't but the Professor was overheard talking to someone else about meeting an old friend on the street after he'd left his sister's house. He said that it had made him feel sad.'

'Now that's interesting. I wonder if your Professor might have been the mysterious man that Bernie Bright met in the pub. Have you got a photo of him that I could have?'

Leigh emailed him a photo of the Professor.

'So, what now?' Jo asked.

'Nothing really, at least not until I've shown this to the man who saw Bernie in the pub. If I can get him to confirm that it was the Professor then we might just have a double murder on our hands.'

They agreed to work as a team for now and to meet the next morning at nine to discuss what they should do next.

A few minutes after he'd finished talking to Jo and Leigh, Mac was back on the motorway and heading towards London. He was lucky as the snow had held off and he seemed to have just missed the worst of the rush hour. He made it just in time to catch Callum before he set out on his rounds. He explained that he needed to show Baz a photo to see if he could identify the man that he'd seen Bernie with in the pub.

'So, I take it that you're making some progress then?' Callum asked as they once again drove towards the Old Beetroot pub.

'That might well depend on what Baz says,' Mac replied.

'Who's the man in the photo then?'

'He's someone who would have known Bernie quite a long time ago when they were both in the RAF together. Did Bernie ever mention being in the RAF?'

Callum shook his head.

'Not that I ever remember but perhaps the lads might know something about that.'

As Mac followed Callum once again inside the garage his eyes sought out Baz. He noticed that both Polish Pete and Wee Jackie were there but he couldn't see anyone in a beanie hat. He relaxed when he spotted Baz who had swapped his beanie for a stylish flat cap. Mac wasn't going to ask where he got it from.

Mac waited patiently until everyone had eaten and Callum had returned all the empty containers to his bags before he spoke. As there were a couple of new faces Mac went over what he'd said the evening before about why he was looking into the death of Bernie Bright.

'Has anyone had any thoughts since I spoke to you yesterday?' Mac asked.

They all looked at each other and then looked nonplussed.

'Baz you said that you saw Bernie in the pub with a man,' Mac said. He could see that Baz was having problems remembering so he added, 'You said that he had a nice coat, one you admired a lot.'

Mac breathed a sigh of relief as the penny finally dropped.

'Oh yes, I remember now,' Baz said. 'The man Bernie was drinking with in the Blue Boar.'

'Can you tell me if this was the man you saw in the pub with Bernie?' Mac asked as he showed him a photo of Eric Brathwaite.

'Yes, that's him,' Baz said. 'I wish I had friends like that with nice coats and twenty pound notes. All I've got is this lot.'

It was said with a smile though and Baz received some good-natured banter back which just made his smile wider.

Mac turned to the two new men. They introduced themselves as Del and Scouser. Del was a short round man who precariously wore a pair of glasses that only had one arm. Scouser was taller and thinner and had long hair and a wispy beard. It was hard to tell either of their ages.

'Is there anything you can tell me about Bernie?' Mac asked hopefully. 'Even the smallest detail might help.'

They looked at each other before Scouser spoke in a Liverpool accent.

'Well he knew his planes.'

'What do you mean?' Mac asked.

'I think it was sometime in the spring and we were sitting outside the shop just down the road when there was some sort of...I don't know. What do you call it when loads of planes fly over?'

'A fly past?' Mac suggested.

'Yes, that's it. Anyway, loads of planes flew over, all different types they were, and Bernie knew just about all of them.'

Mac vaguely remembered the RAF having some sort of anniversary earlier in the year and wondered if the fly past was something to do with that.

'Anything else?' Mac asked.

Scouser shrugged but Del was still deep in thought.

'Del?' Mac prompted.

'What?' he said looking a little apprehensive.

'Do you remember anything about Bernie?' Mac asked softly.

'Well, I doubt that it's going to be of much help but I remember that he had this bee in his bonnet about the London Eye,' Del replied. 'In fact, he got quite angry about it.'

The London Eye was a massive Ferris wheel that stood on the south bank of the Thames. It was a major tourist attraction these days.

'Go on,' Mac said although he wasn't sure exactly where this might be going.

'Well, he said he'd just got his hands on some money... remember that time Scouse when he bought us some bottles?' Del said.

'Oh yes, at least I think I do. I was already a bit pissed so I'm afraid that it's all a bit of a blur now,' Scouser replied.

'How long ago was this?' Mac asked.

'Not long, four or five weeks ago perhaps,' Del replied.

'So, what was it about the London Eye that made him so angry?'

'He saw it on the other side of the river and fancied having a go but, when he went over there, they told him that he couldn't buy a ticket as it had to be booked in advance. He didn't believe them. He said that if he'd have been dressed in a smart suit they'd have took his money no problem,' Del said.

'And he didn't say where he'd been before that?' Del's answer was a shrug.

'But he definitely said that he'd just got some money?' Mac asked.

'That's what he said. He even showed it to me. He'd bought a few bottles but he must have still had at least a hundred left,' Del said. 'I had to tell him to put it away. There's some right robbing bastards around here.'

Mac asked everyone again before he left if they'd thought of anything but no-one had. Before he left Baz tugged at his sleeve.

'What happened to that man in the photo?' he asked.

'He's dead, he was run over,' Mac replied.

Baz thought this over for a moment.

'You don't know what happened to his coat do you?' he asked. 'That was a really nice coat that was. I hope he wasn't wearing it when he was run over.'

Mac assured Baz that if he heard anything about the coat then he'd let him know. This seemed to satisfy him.

As he drove back the snow had started falling quite heavily and he had to take his time as the roads were getting quite slippery. As he tentatively made progress down the motorway, he thought about what he'd just learned. He was more than intrigued and wondered if the investigation, unlike his car, was finally gaining some real traction.

Chapter Twelve

Mac had arrived at the police station in Letchworth far earlier than he needed to that morning. He'd been hoping to catch Dan Carter, the Major Crime Unit's leader, and run a few things past him. He was in luck and he caught Dan just as he was on his way out. He didn't look a happy man and Mac guessed that he was finding the De Gray case, and all the attention it was getting from the press, to be more than a little wearing.

Mac was deep in conversation with Martin Selby, the team's computer and data specialist, when Jo and Leigh turned up within a few seconds of each other.

'Jo, Leigh, good morning,' Mac said with a smile. 'I think it's safe to say that there have been a few developments.'

They gathered around Jo's desk.

'I take it from the look on your face that this Baz has identified the Professor,' Jo said.

'Yes, he did but I've learned even more than that. By the way I've had a quick chat with Dan and he's happy for us to start treating the two deaths as part of a single investigation for now,' Mac said.

'How's he getting on with Professor De Gray's case?' Leigh asked. 'He was as grumpy as hell the last time I saw him.'

'Well, if I'm honest, he was still a bit grumpy but he was also hopeful of closing the case out fairly quickly,' Mac said. 'Of course, everything's still pointing towards it being a suicide but he's also aware that, with a De Gray being involved, he needs to make sure that everything's been investigated to death before he closes the file.'

'Okay then, what have you found?' Jo asked cutting to the chase.

Mac told them what Del had said about the London Eye.

'So, what are you thinking?' Jo asked looking puzzled.

'Well, Bernie had come into some money and shortly afterwards, according to Del, saw the Eye on the other side of the river. If that's the case then there's only one place that he could have been standing, isn't there?'

Jo and Leigh exchanged blank looks.

'As far as I remember there's only the Houses of Parliament...' Seeing Mac's smile widen Jo continued, 'Are you really thinking that Bernie Bright went to see someone at the Houses of Parliament?'

'I think there's a chance,' Mac replied. 'He got money from someone on that visit and then talked about it being a 'wage packet' to someone else so, at least in his mind, it wasn't going to be a one-off payment.'

'Do you think that he might have been blackmailing someone?' Leigh asked.

'That was my initial thought and it's not exactly unheard of in political circles, is it? Anyway, that's all it is at the moment, a thought. Luckily, I know one of the police commanders who works there. I've already called and asked him if he can check the visitor logs to see if anyone called Bernard Bright has paid them a visit in the past three months or so. If he has, he'll also try and find out who he was visiting. He said he'll get back to me later today.'

'Have you got any idea who he might have been visiting or why?' Jo asked.

Mac shook his head.

'I wish I had. Bernie used to work in the RAF and I've got a sneaking feeling that his visit might be related to that in some way but that's all I've got at the moment. Martin is checking out his work history to see if that sheds any light on matters.'

'So, what do we do next then?' Jo asked.

'For now, I'd suggest that we all relax, have a coffee and wait to see what comes in,' Mac said. 'Dan said that we should give it a week and, if we haven't found any hard evidence in that time, then he'll review the case and make a decision on what happens next.'

'That sounds logical,' Jo said. 'Okay, so we've got a week to find some evidence that links the possible murder by vehicle of a history Professor in Cambridge and the violent killing of a down and out in Stepney. I don't know Mac, any link between the two still sounds a bit far-fetched when I put it like that.'

Mac shrugged.

'Sometimes life can be far-fetched. However, one thing we do know is that the Professor and Bernie met and, less than two weeks after that, they were both dead. It might just be a coincidence but we still need to check it out.'

'Well, I like the bit about relaxing and coffee,' Leigh said. 'I overslept a little and missed breakfast. I'll go and get them.'

'So, how's married life suiting you?' Mac asked as Leigh disappeared through the door.

Jo had married her police colleague Gerry Dugdale the summer before and it turned out to be one of the best weddings that Mac had ever been to.

'Oh, it's great, better than great actually. I come from a very big family that lived in a small house and I had to sleep with one of my sisters for years. I was so glad when I got my own place and a bed that would be all mine. Yet, if I'm being honest, I never really got used to sleeping by myself. It's so nice to wake up next to someone in the morning plus there are other advantages too when it's a man,' she said with a wicked smile which left Mac in doubt as to what she was referring to.

Mac thought with some sadness of his own bed. It was far too big now that his Nora had gone.

Noticing his expression Jo put her hand on Mac's and said softly, 'Would you ever try again? It's been well over a year now.'

'What marry again?'

'Well you don't have to get married,' Jo replied with just a hint of that wicked smile.

This made Mac smile too.

'No, I don't think so. I still live in the same house that we spent thirty years as a couple in, I visit her grave every chance I get and I still talk to her believe it or not. When I'm in the house I often hold conversations with thin air and, if anyone was watching, I suppose they'd think I was mad. Thankfully the only witness is my dog and he won't snitch on me. Nora may be physically gone but she's still in here,' Mac said as he tapped the side of his head.

'And you're happy with that?' Jo asked.

'No, I'm not happy. When I go to bed it's cold and when I wake up in the middle of the night there's only the sound of my own breathing. But, if she wasn't there in my head, then she'd be truly dead and I honestly don't know if I could cope with that.'

Jo gripped his hand.

Leigh, seeing their sombre expressions, said as she handed out the coffees, 'Have we had some bad news about the case or something?'

'No, we were just talking about something else,' Mac said. He needed to change the subject. 'Another thing, we're going to have to get the detective team at Bethnal Green involved, after all Bernie Bright is their case. Luckily, I know their boss. I'll have a word with him after we hopefully get something to go on.'

'Yes, of course,' Jo said. 'I hadn't thought of that but, if it is a double murder, we could probably do with some help anyway.'

While they waited Mac asked Jo and Leigh to tell him everything that they'd learned so far about the death of Eric Braithwaite.

'I agree with you that the lack of skid marks looks suspicious but I suppose we'd better keep an open mind anyway,' Mac said. 'I was once told about a case where there were multiple collisions with parked cars and everyone thought that a drunk or a madman must have been on the loose. It turned out to be an old woman who'd forgotten to take her reading glasses off when she started driving...'

'Something's come through for you from the Houses of Parliament,' Martin interrupted. 'I'll print it off.'

'Keep your fingers crossed,' Mac said as he got up.

Jo and Leigh looked closely at Mac's face as he slowly walked back towards them while reading the print-off. When his face broke into a smile, they both knew that they might be on to something. Then he looked really puzzled and they weren't so sure.

'What is it?' Jo asked anxiously.

'According to my contact Bernie did indeed visit the Houses of Parliament, in fact he attended a debate about the 'Future of the Armed Forces' in Westminster Hall,' Mac replied.

'What had you looking so puzzled then?' Leigh asked.

'I've heard about these debates before. It's where an individual MP can arrange to have a debate on an issue that's important to them. What had me puzzled was the name of the MP who was holding the debate,' Mac said as he handed Jo the sheet.

Jo read the name out loud, 'Julian Sangredo MP, Minister for Defence Procurement.'

'Oh, I've seen him on Question Time on the TV,' Leigh said with a smile. 'He's quite fit actually.'

'Sangredo? I've come across that name before,' Mac said. 'Jo could you do me a favour and look up his bio on Wikipedia?'

Jo got it up on her computer screen.

'Well, it says here that he was born in one of those sink estates in North London but, instead of becoming a gang member like his brother, he got himself off to university...'

'Was his brother's name Brian by any chance?' Mac asked.

'Why yes. How did you know that?' Jo asked.

'Brian Sangredo used to be the leader of the Steeley Boys gang some years ago,' Mac explained. 'He was honestly one of coldest, most vicious people I've ever come across. Unfortunately for him, he eventually came across someone who was even more vicious than he was and he ended up being tortured and then nailed to a tree. I didn't know that he had a little brother though.'

'He was crucified? Who on earth did that to him?' Jo asked.

'Well, you know the man I told you about who works at the soup kitchen?'

'What that nice man Callum who drove you around and who helps all the homeless people out?' Jo said.

'Yes, that's right. We think it was him but please keep that to yourselves,' Mac said.

Jo and Leigh exchanged looks of astonishment.

'My God and you drive around with him at night?' Jo said.

'He's changed,' Mac said. On seeing Jo's look of disbelief, he continued, 'No, he really has. I think he's found God or something, anyway I trust him.'

'I should think that you'd need to,' Jo said still looking unconvinced.

'Anyway, Julian Sangredo has become the Tory party's poster boy,' Leigh chipped in. 'He's got it all really. He came from a bad area but he pulled himself up by his own bootstraps and got through university, a double first no less, plus he talks well and he's really good looking. All the old dears swoon over him.'

'And how do you know all that?' Mac asked.

'Oh, I never miss Question Time on the TV if I can help it and he's on the programme a lot. I've got to admit that I quite fancy him myself,' she replied with a near giggle.

'So, what's the connection between Julian Sangredo and Bernie Bright then?' Jo asked.

'The obvious one is the Armed Forces, isn't it?' Mac replied. 'Bernie used to serve in the RAF and Sangredo is at the Ministry of Defence but, beyond that, I haven't got a clue. Let's wait and see if Martin can come up with something.'

A half an hour later Martin handed Mac another print-off.

'So, according to the Ministry of Works and Pensions, Bernie Bright worked in the RAF from the age of eighteen until he retired over thirty years later. He then did nothing for a year or so before getting himself some work in a warehouse but that only lasted a few years. He then got another job in a warehouse before he finally started work at an aeronautical museum in Duxford near Cambridge as a technical consultant, whatever that is. He was employed at the museum for just over three years and that was his last job,' Mac said. He was thoughtful for a while before he continued, 'Yes, the leaving date for the job at the museum wasn't long after his wife died. After that he went back to Stepney and disappeared.'

'Was it the British War Museum?' Leigh asked. 'My brother used to take me there when we were young. He loves planes.'

'No, it's called the Museum of Modern Air Warfare,' Mac replied.

'My brother took me to just about every museum in the area but I've never heard of that one,' Leigh said.

'Well, it might be a fairly new one I suppose...'

Mac was interrupted by his phone going off.

'Jim!' Mac said into the phone, 'I was just about to call you...' He then listened for quite a while before saying, 'Okay, I'll be right there.'

'I'm going to have to go,' Mac said with a worried expression as he stood up. 'That was DCI Jim Ormesby at Bethnal Green.'

'What's happened?' Jo asked.

'They've just arrested Callum McEachan.'

'Why? What's he done?' Jo asked.

'According to one of the victims, he attacked two men without any warning and hospitalised them both. One of them has had an elbow and knee joint shattered while the other requires facial reconstruction after Callum head-butted him.'

'Okay,' Jo said exchanging a nervous glance with Leigh. 'What do you want us to do?'

'Do you fancy checking out this museum in Duxford?' Mac suggested. 'I'll call you later if I find anything.'

'Yes, we'll do just that,' Jo said.

Mac rushed out of the door.

'Well, in the short time I've known Mac I've found his instincts to be pretty much on the button,' Jo said. 'However, it looks like he might have gotten it wrong this time.'

'Yes, perhaps this Callum hasn't changed as much as Mac thought he had,' Leigh said as she gave Jo a worried look.

Chapter Thirteen

Mac couldn't help feeling worried as he drove into London. It had started snowing again and the dark clouds made it look more like early evening than morning. It somehow suited his mood. A question burned in his brain.

Had Callum really gone back to his bad old ways?

He said a little prayer that it wasn't so. Although he'd been surprised at first by the new Callum, he found that he was beginning to like him. However, Mac knew that it was about much more than his feelings. As he thought about Callum the word 'redemption' swirled through his brain. People are so often written off as lost causes but Callum had given Mac some hope for the world. If the most violent, rabid and fearsome criminal he'd ever encountered in his career could find redemption and build a new life then there was hope for everyone.

At Bethnal Green Police Station, he found himself standing outside a door that had a brass plate screwed to it that said 'Detective Chief Inspector James Ormesby'. He hesitated before knocking as a memory came back to him.

Jim Ormesby had only just become a detective when he'd applied to work on Mac's team. He was twenty-four at the time and looked younger. He'd been nervous at that first interview and probably with good cause as Mac had already gotten a reputation for 'moving on' detectives who he felt didn't fit into his team. However, Mac saw something in that first interview and he quickly became convinced that Jim would make a good copper. He'd been right too. Jim had progressed from detective constable to sergeant in less than five years and six years after that he was an Inspector. He remembered Jim talking to him about leaving the Murder Squad for another job some years ago. It was a promotion and Mac had advised him to go for it. He hoped that his advice had been right.

He knocked on the door.

'Come in,' a familiar voice said.

Mac did. A man jumped up from behind the desk and ran to meet him. They shook hands firmly and with feeling.

'It's so good to see you!' Jim exclaimed. 'You're looking well.'

Mac thought Jim looked well too. His hair was receding slightly and there was a hint of weight around his middle but, in most respects, he hadn't changed much since that first interview. He supposed that, while looking younger than your years might be a pain when you're young, it certainly pays dividends when you get older.

After a few minutes of small talk and catching up Mac cut to the chase.

'What happened with Callum McEachan?' he asked anxiously.

'I'm sorry for calling you but it was at Mr. McEachan's request. I'll take you to see him in a minute. We got a call from the hospital just after three o'clock this morning. The ambulance service had responded to an anonymous call and they found two men lying on the street just down the road from St. Philip's Church. One of the men was unconscious after having most of his face flattened and the other probably wished he was unconscious as his right elbow and left knee joints were both shattered. He swore a complaint out saying that a man had attacked them without any warning. He was a big white man they said and gave us a description of someone who could only be Callum McEachan. They said that the attack was racially motivated and that he'd used racist language, including the 'N' word, as he attacked them.'

'That doesn't sound right to me,' Mac said with a shake of his head. 'Even when he was at his most violent I don't think he was ever racist about it. He'd dish it out equally whatever your skin colour was.'

'Well, as it was reported as a hate crime, we've got to investigate it thoroughly, so we picked up Mr. McEachan and interviewed him.'

'Did he resist arrest?' Mac asked.

'No, not at all, in fact he was more than happy to come with my men from what I've been told. Anyway, he told us a different story, one I'm more inclined to believe if I'm honest. He said that he'd finished his rounds delivering food and he was on his way back to the church when he saw a group of four men. He slowed down and saw that they were gathered around a man who was lying on the floor. They were kicking him. He got out and recognised the man on the floor. He said that his name was Alfred Feycourt.'

Mac remembered a tall slim gentle man sitting around a fire and thanking Callum in fine words for the food he'd brought. He was old and frail and looked as if a gust of wind might have knocked him over.

'He said that he approached the men and two of them pulled machetes on him. There were two other men there, one was still kicking the man before starting to spray barbecue lighter fuel over him, while the other was filming it all on his phone. Mr. McEachan said that he felt he had to intervene when the man who was spraying the fuel started throwing matches at Mr. Feycourt in an effort to set him on fire. After crippling one of the men with the machetes and ruining the good looks of the other, the other two assailants ran off which was probably a wise decision on their part. Mr. McEachan said that he rang for an ambulance for the men and then picked up Mr. Feycourt and took him straight to hospital. We've confirmed that they do indeed have someone of that name at the local hospital. He's got a broken arm, broken kneecap, several cracked ribs and severe bruising just about everywhere.'

'That attack sounds very similar to the one on Bernard Bright a few weeks back,' Mac said.

'Yes, DI Patterson told me about that. He's gone to interview the men in hospital and he's taken some uniforms with him to make sure that they don't disappear on us. He should be back soon.'

'Can I see Callum?' Mac asked.

'Yes, of course,' Jim replied.

He took Mac down in the lift and into the bowels of the station. The sergeant in charge of the lock-up opened the cell door for them. He wasn't sure exactly what he expected to see when the door opened but it certainly wasn't the relaxed smiling Callum that greeted him.

'I'll leave you to it then Mac,' Jim said. 'I'll make sure the sergeant here keeps an eye on you. Come and see me in my office when you're finished.'

Mac said his thanks before turning to look at Callum.

'And there was me thinking that you didn't like cells,' Mac said as he sat down on the bed beside him.

'It only a cell if you think it's a cell,' Callum replied. 'I'm actually enjoying the peace and quiet if I'm honest.'

Mac couldn't help smiling.

'So, what happened?' he asked as he sat on the bed beside the big man.

'I was on my way back to the church when I saw these wee bastards kicking seven bells out of poor Alfred. And then, to top it all, they started trying to set fire to him, I mean I couldn't let that happen, could I?' Callum replied. 'I went as easy on them as I could.'

While shattered elbow and knee joints and a face that needed reconstructing might not be deemed as being especially 'easy', Mac knew what he meant. In his former life he'd have broken every bone in their bodies one by one before dispatching them with a six inch nail into their skulls.

'Who were they?' Mac asked.

'I've no idea. I've certainly not seen them around the area before. Do you think that they might have been the ones who killed Bernie?'

'It's a possibility and certainly the MO seems the same. Why do you think they did it? Was it just for kicks or was there something else behind it?'

Callum shrugged, 'I've no idea but I do know that there are some really sick bastards out there so I wouldn't be surprised if it was just for kicks.'

Mac didn't say anything. He was beginning to get the feeling that there might be more to it than that.

'If I'm stuck in here for a while can you tell the Rev and Francie what's happened? Someone will need to do the rounds, a lot of the men rely on the food deliveries now.'

'Don't worry I will. However, I'm hoping that you won't be in here that long. Just sit tight,' Mac advised.

It took him a while to find the lift again and by the time he reached Jim's office he saw that the door was open and that he and DI Janet Morris were looking at something on a computer monitor with great interest.

'Mac, come and look at this!' Jim said with a smile. 'It's quite something.'

He joined them around the computer screen as Janet started the video off again. Whoever took the video was well above the action so Mac guessed that they must have been on the first floor of a nearby building. Four men were on the street below. Three of them were shouting as they kicked something on the floor while one of them filmed it all on a phone. Callum came on the scene from the left of the shot. Two of the men pulled out big machetes and waved them menacingly at him. Callum raised his hands, palms facing outwards, and he sounded as if he was trying to calm them down. When one of the men sprayed something out of a plastic bottle over the man on the floor and started throwing matches, Callum's body shape changed.

He made a feint towards the nearest man who then held his machete out in a threatening manner. That turned out to be a big mistake. At lightning speed Callum caught him by the wrist, pulled his arm straight and then smashed the heel of his hand into the locked elbow joint. A split second after that his left foot flew out and impacted on the man's knee joint. The whole leg flexed inwards in an unnatural and quite sickening way. He fell to the floor screaming. The other one slashed out and tried to cut Callum with his machete but he nimbly moved out of the way and hit the man's wrist hard with the side of his hand. The machete fell to the floor as Callum gripped the man's jacket with both hands and pulled him briskly forward as his head came at speed from the other direction. There was an audible crunch as the top of Callum's head hit the bridge of the man's nose. He fell to the floor as though dead.

The two other men looked at Callum and froze for a moment before taking to their heels and disappearing out of frame at speed. The camera stayed on Callum as he picked up Alfred and carried him away. The video ended.

'Wow!' Janet said. 'That was better than a lot of the action movies I've seen recently.'

'Well, it certainly backs up Mr. McEachan's story that's for sure,' Jim said. 'I'd better ring DI Patterson and let him know that he's got two criminals not victims in the hospital.'

While he was doing this Mac asked Janet where the video had come from.

'It was uploaded anonymously onto our 'Report a Crime' website a few hours ago. The timestamp on the video confirms the time and date of the incident.'

'That was lucky for Callum, otherwise it might have just been their word against his.'

As he said this, he noticed that Jim's expression had gotten somewhat more serious. Both he and Janet didn't say a word until he'd put the phone down.

'That was Patterson. He wasn't surprised when I told him about the video. He said that he had an inkling that their account of things might have been somewhat suspect from the first moment he saw them.'

'Why was that?' Janet asked.

'They were covered in tattoos and, having only hospital gowns on, most of them were visible,' Jim said. 'Patterson recognised one of the tattoos. It had a snake in the form of an 'S' intertwined with a 'B' with a knife in the background.'

'Steeley Boys? They were both gang members?' Mac asked in something like amazement.

'That's right,' Jim replied. 'Apparently, Patterson grew up not too far from that estate and so he knows the tattoo well.'

Mac still looked puzzled.

'What on earth were four members of the Steeley Boys doing in Stepney? They were well off their patch and I guess that they'd have had to go through the territories of several other gangs to get here. That's taking a real chance.'

'You're right there,' Jim said looking puzzled too. 'We've never seen any Steeley Boys on our patch before so you have to wonder what could have been so important that it would bring them all this way?'

That indeed was the question, Mac thought. They'd risked their very lives in coming to Stepney and Mac was determined to find out why.

Chapter Fourteen

The investigation into the 'Museum of Modern Air Warfare' wasn't going at all well. Jo and Leigh had expected to find lots of information about it on the internet but, apart from a single page that said that the website was 'under construction', they found exactly nothing. In desperation they turned to Martin for help. They decided to have another coffee while they waited to see what he came up with.

'That's strange though, us not finding anything,' Jo said. 'You'd think that a museum would want to get as much information about itself out there as it could.'

'That's true but then again I suppose it might take some time to build it and to gather all the exhibits,' Leigh replied.

'Bernie Bright worked there for over three years though. Would it have taken that long?'

Leigh could only shrug as she replied, 'Yes, that does seem like a long time I suppose...'

They were interrupted by Martin who walked towards them with a deeply puzzled expression on his face.

'Have you found something?' Jo asked more in hope than anything else.

'No, I've found nothing and that's what's really strange,' Martin replied with a shrug. 'The only thing we've got is the page that you found. I've tried to find out who owns the domain name but unfortunately the information's private. All I can say is that the page was put up some four years ago and it hasn't been amended since.'

'That is strange,' Jo said.

'I've had a look at the museum on Google Earth and I found a picture of the site from six years ago and one that was taken more recently.'

They both peered at the two aerial photos on Martin's monitor screen. They were both absolutely identical.

'Well, it doesn't look like they've done much building work in the last few years then, have they?' Jo said.

'No,' Martin said. 'They've also not done much in the way of promotions, press conferences, ads or being featured in any news stories. I can only think that they're trying to keep a low profile on purpose.'

'Yes, and that makes me think that they might just have something to hide,' Jo said. 'Well, as the internet's failed us, let's go old school and go and knock on their front door.'

It took them just over half an hour to drive to Duxford. The flat countryside was frosted white but thankfully the roads had been heavily salted overnight and traffic was moving freely. They passed by the British War Museum and then found themselves once again in the countryside.

Where was the museum then? Jo asked herself.

She knew they were in the right area but she hadn't seen any signs to indicate that the museum existed.

'Why do they have air museums around here anyway?' Jo asked as she went right around the next roundabout and drove back towards the British War Museum.

'I think it's because there's been an aerodrome here at Duxford since the First World War. Apparently, it also played an important part in the Battle of Britain or so my brother told me,' Leigh replied.

'I suppose that makes sense then,' Jo said.

She was still looking on the other side of the road for something that looked like a museum and failed. The only entrance she could see was a long gate embedded into a high hedge. It was directly opposite a petrol station.

'That's got to be it,' Jo said as she pointed towards the gate. 'There's nothing else around here.'

She drove around the traffic island and went back on herself, once again passing the air museum before pulling up in front of the gate. She and Leigh got out and had a look. The gate was electric, at least ten feet high and made up of sturdy looking steel bars. There was a roll of barbed wire on top of the gate as well as the usual dire warning signs about security guards, dogs and CCTV. There was also a small sign that said, 'MOMAW – Ring bell for deliveries'.

'Well, the initials match so this must be it then,' Jo said as she peered between the metal bars of the gate. 'It doesn't look like there's much is going on in there though, does it?'

Leigh could only agree. All she could see was a road that veered away to the left and out of sight and beyond that the very tops of some buildings. She noticed that some potholes in the road had recently been filled.

'They've been repairing the road,' she said.

'Yes, so I suppose that something must be happening in there,' Jo said. 'Let's try the intercom.'

She pressed the button several times but there was no sound from the intercom and no-one came to the gate.

'Well, if anyone's in there, they know that we're out here anyway,' Leigh said pointing to the CCTV cameras that stood on poles peeking over the hedge on either side.

After waiting several minutes Jo gave up and went back to the car. Before she got in, she stopped and looked across the road at the petrol station.

'I wonder if they might have seen something,' she said.

So, once again she drove up the road to the next traffic island and then turned back on herself. Jo parked well away from the petrol pumps and Leigh followed her into the shop. A man in dusty overalls was being served by a short middle-aged woman dressed in a bright flowery top. He paid for his petrol, sandwich, crisps, Mars bar and coffee and then left. Jo showed the woman her warrant card.

'Can we speak?' Jo asked.

'Oh, nothing's happened to Larry, has it?' she said as she gave them a frightened glance.

'No, this has nothing to do with you or the petrol station.'

'Oh, thank God for that. I always worry about him when he's away,' she said.

'Who's Larry?'

'He's my son. He's flew out yesterday for a few days in Barcelona with a gang of his friends and I do worry. Some of them are a bit wild so who knows what they'll get up to.'

'What's your name?' Jo asked.

'Annie, Annie Gosling,' she replied.

'Who else works here?'

'Well, I do days from Monday to Friday and my niece does the weekends. Then my husband does some evenings and my nephew helps out too,' she said.

'I take it that you own the petrol station then?' Jo asked.

'Yes, well my husband does. He also owns a car dealership in Royston so that's why he can't do days.'

'How long is the station usually open for?'

'We open at seven in the morning and then close around eleven o'clock in the evening depending on what's happening. Why do you want to know all this anyway?' she asked.

As she said this another customer walked in. Mrs. Gosling took his money and, after the door had closed again, Jo gave her the answer.

'We're interested in the museum over the road.'

The woman gave her a very puzzled look.

'What the British War Museum?' she asked.

'No, the Museum of Modern Air Warfare. It's just over the road there,' Jo said pointing to the gate on the other side of the road.

'Really?' she said as she peered out of the window. 'Is that what it is? I'd never have guessed, nothing much seems to happen over there.'

'Have you seen anything at all? Any traffic coming in and out for instance?' Jo asked hopefully.

'Well, sometimes a few cars go through the gate in the morning and then come out in the evening but that's not every day. They certainly don't seem to have that many people working over there. Other than that, we've seen vans and sometime lorries come and go but never that often. My husband told me that he's seen a couple of big low loaders go inside but that's always been quite late at night.'

'And that's all you can tell us?' Jo asked.

She had to wait for her answer as yet another customer came in and paid for their petrol.

'I'm sorry but that's it really. I've been wondering myself about that place. All I do is sit here when it's quiet and look out of the window. I'd never have believed that it was a museum though. Where are all the visitors?'

Indeed, Jo thought as she walked back to the car. She'd given Mrs. Gosling a card in case her niece or nephew had noticed anything. She'd also gotten the address of her husband's car dealership. She wanted to know a bit more about these low loaders.

It took them less than ten minutes to drive to the small town of Royston and they found Gosling's Motors just down the road from the police station. It wasn't the largest dealership Jo had even seen but she noticed that the cars were all from the more expensive end of the market. She noticed Leigh stop in front of a gleaming Audi TT sports car.

'I've always fancied one of these,' she explained with a look of longing. 'I don't like the big sports cars so much but, for some reason, I've always pictured myself behind the wheel of one of these driving around somewhere romantic.'

'I've never been that bothered about cars personally,' Jo said. 'There's only one type of car I really like and that's the type that doesn't break down. So long as it gets me there and back safely then I'm happy.'

'I know you're probably right still...' Leigh said as she caressed the bright red paintwork with her hand.

A tall balding man with a salesman's grin greeted them as they walked in. The grin disappeared when Jo produced her warrant card. He looked a little nervous until Jo explained exactly why they were there.

'So, you're interested in that place over the road from the garage then?' he said as he visibly relaxed. 'I never could make out what was going on in there.'

'I believe that you saw some low loaders delivering there. Is that right?' Jo asked.

'Yes, that was a surprise. I mean I've seen vans and the odd lorry going in and out but nothing quite that big.'

'What time was it when you saw them?'

'It was after two in the morning both times.'

'Why were you at the garage so late?' Jo asked. 'I thought that the station closed at eleven.'

'It does but we've had the odd occasion when we've started to run a bit short of petrol and I've had to get an extra delivery in. They slot them in whenever they can but, unfortunately for me, it's usually in the middle of the night.'

'Could you make out what was on these low loaders?'

Mr. Gosling thought about this for some time.

'It was all boxed in but I thought that it could have been an aircraft of some sort, it was certainly the right shape. Not the wings of course, just the fuselage. I can't be certain about that though.'

'Did you think it was unusual in being so late at night?' Jo asked.

'Not really, I know a lot of these large lorries prefer to travel at night when there's less traffic,' he replied.

While that certainly sounded plausible Jo couldn't help wondering if there was another reason for the lateness of the deliveries.

'So, what now?' Leigh asked as they climbed back into the car.

'Well, if anyone would know what the people at the museum were up to, it might just be another museum. What do you think?' Jo asked.

'I think that's an excellent idea,' Leigh replied.

They parked as close to the British War Museum's visitor centre as they could and went inside. They were met by the din of several school parties, some of whom were on their way out while others had just arrived. They went to the head of the queue and got hostile stares while they explained to the receptionist that they needed to speak to someone in the management team. They waited for over fifteen minutes until a confident looking woman in her forties introduced herself as Angela Raynes, Assistant to the Director of the Museum. Leigh had been hoping to see something of the exhibits but, unfortunately for her, Angela led them down a corridor and into a small office.

'How can I help the police?' she asked as she sat down behind her desk.

'It's nothing to do with the museum as such. The Museum of Modern Air Warfare just down the road has cropped up in a case that we've been working on and we were wondering if you could tell us anything about it,' Jo said.

Angela raised her eyebrows in surprise.

'That lot! We'd like to know what they're up to as well. We've been trying to get some of the Harriers that are just going out of service. We've already got a few of the older ones in our exhibits but some of the latest ones would have been nice for events and so on. They're very popular with the public.'

'And they've managed to get some?' Jo asked.

'Yes and it's puzzled the hell out of us. My boss has tried to get some idea as to why from the Ministry of Defence but he got nowhere. He concluded that there must be some sort of hush-hush operation going on down there.'

'What? An intelligence operation?' Jo asked.

She hadn't thought of that as an option.

'Anyway, he told me that he decided to stop asking questions about it after seeing someone at the Ministry of Defence,' Angela said.

'What's the name of your boss?'

'Sir Joseph Adamson.'

'Is he around?' Jo asked.

'No, I'm afraid he's at the main museum in London at the moment. He won't be here until sometime next week.'

A few more questions helped to convince Jo that she'd squeezed this particular lemon dry. As they walked back towards the car, she thought about what they should do next and there was only one thing that came to mind.

She needed to speak to Mac.

Chapter Fifteen

Mac was thinking about his conversation with Jo as he made his way west through the London mid-day traffic. It was snowing and the traffic was even slower than usual. He was going to call in at the MI5 headquarters in Millbank before heading over the river to Lambeth and the War Museum. As he drove past the Houses of Parliament, he thought about Julian Sangredo M.P.

He was the only link they had at the moment between the Steeley Boys and Bernie Bright. Members of the gang had been responsible for beating up and trying to set on fire one homeless old man and Mac was fairly certain that they must have been involved in Bernie Bright's death too. Was it just a coincidence that Sangredo grew up on the Steele Estate and now represented the area in Parliament? He couldn't imagine that Bernie would really be all that interested in a debate on 'The Future of the Armed Forces' when he was so down on his luck. So, what was he doing there?

He left his car in a nearby car park and was still mulling over the case in his head during the short walk to the MI5 building. He walked through the high arched entrance into the lobby and asked for Sir Philip Suskind. A smartly dressed and quite muscular young man appeared a few minutes later and escorted him down a maze of corridors to a plain door that gave no indication as to what might be inside. He tapped on the door and Mac heard a familiar voice say 'Enter'.

The young man opened the door and then stood outside as Mac shut the door behind him.

'Mac!' said a beaming man in his fifties dressed in an immaculate pinstripe suit, crisp white shirt and, literally, an old school tie. 'It's been quite a while. I thought they'd put you out to grass and all that.'

'They did, I'm just helping the police out with a few cases these days.'

'Sit down,' Sir Philip said as he pointed to an old leather sofa in the corner. 'So how can I help?'

Mac told him the story so far and his part in it.

'As the Director of the British War Museum at Duxford seems to think that this might be one of your little scams, I thought that I'd ask you first and perhaps save ourselves a lot of running around for nothing.'

There had been quite a few occasions over the years when Sir Philip or one of his colleagues had turned up at Mac's office and killed a case that they'd invested a lot of effort and time in. Mac had always managed to keep his temper during these interviews but only just. However, for some reason he'd gotten quite a liking for Sir Philip. He was a disarming man who seemed to treat everything as if it were some sort of wonderful game.

'No, it's definitely not one of ours or any of our so-called colleagues in the other services. We have our spies there too,' he said with a wink.

Mac wouldn't have been at all surprised.

'So, if it isn't some sort of intelligence led operation then what's going on in there? You've heard nothing at all about it?'

'I wouldn't say that, just nothing that I can tell you about,' he said with a charming smile. 'However, now you've brought the subject up, I think that we'd like to know more about what's going on there too. If you come across anything that I might find interesting then please call this number. Someone will be monitoring it twenty-four hours a day.'

Mac took the card from Sir Philip and thought that this might have been the end of the interview but he continued.

'So, how are you keeping old friend?'

'I'm okay and I'm working which definitely helps. The local Major Crime Unit let me help them out now and then and I do a little private detecting too.'

'Ah, the Home Counties answer to Phillip Marlowe! He always was my favourite character.'

'Not quite,' Mac said with a smile, 'but it keeps me busy.'

'Do you remember that case...'

Sir Philip and Mac then took a pleasant stroll into the past and Mac found out a few things about an old case that he hadn't even guessed at. Then there was a knock at the door.

'I'm sorry Mac but I have to go,' Sir Philip said as he looked at his watch. 'The Prime Minister wants to have a word.'

'What's going on with the Government at the moment?' Mac asked remembering what he'd heard on the radio.

'Let's put it this way. She's drowning not waving. Once De Gray is out of mourning for his sister it's odds on that he'll be the new PM. Unless something happens, of course.'

Sir Philip gave him his best smile, then they shook hands and said goodbye. The muscular young man was waiting for Mac outside the door and he escorted him back to the lobby.

Sir Philip waited for a while after Mac had gone before picking up the phone.

'We might have a situation,' he said.

He explained to the person on the other end what he'd learned from Mac.

'Does this change anything?' he was asked.

Sir Philip gave this some thought.

'It could but, with things being as they are, we might well be able to turn it to our advantage. I suggest that we should let Mr. Maguire get on with his investigation. I think it's time, don't you?'

'And you trust this Maguire to keep us fully in the loop?'

'Yes, yes I do,' Sir Philip said.

'Very well.'

The line went dead.

Sir Philip put the phone down and hoped that he'd done the right thing. Of course, he had total confidence that Mac would update him if there was anything he should know. Even so, he called the muscular young man inside and had a word with him.

As Mac walked back towards the car park he chewed over what Sir Philip had told him. He'd been mildly surprised when he'd learned that the intelligence services weren't involved with the museum. With all the secrecy that surrounded it he'd thought that it was a better than even chance that it was an intelligence led operation.

He could only hope that the British War Museum director might know a little more.

He was lucky and managed to find a disabled space nearby. He walked through the gate and was impressed by the high-domed building that was the museum. It had a Grecian styled stone portico made of white stone that was supported by six substantial columns. He'd never visited the museum before. Nora had liked the Victoria and Albert Museum and they'd gone there a few times and he'd visited the Science Museum once. A museum devoted solely to war had always seemed a little odd to him.

He walked into the huge lobby and asked at the visitor's desk. He'd called earlier and they had a visitor's badge ready for him with his name on it. He was once more escorted to an office but this time by a bright and talkative young girl in her twenties. Sir Joseph Adamson was as unlike Mac's preconceived idea of him as was possible. He was in his fifties and wore glasses but his hair was long and he wore an open neck pink shirt and blue jeans. Mac showed him his warrant card.

'A pleasure to meet you Mr. Maguire,' he said with a strong Northern accent. 'What can I do for you?'

'Sir Joseph, we're working on a case and the Museum of Modern Air Warfare, which is on a site not far from yours at Duxford, has cropped up. It's not central to our investigation as yet but we'd still like to know a little more about it.'

'Oh, please call me Joe. Sir Joseph makes me feel old,' he said with a smile. The smile turned into a frown as he continued, 'That's not something I can really help you with I'm afraid. When I first heard about the museum being mooted, some four or five years ago, I was worried at first that it might be a competitor. However, our marketing team ran some models through the computer and came to the conclusion that more museums in the same area might actually increase our footfall. So, we were all for it in the end. I know it can take some time to get a museum up and running but, as far as I can see, nothing's come of it so far.'

'Your assistant said that you thought it might be something to do with the intelligence services. Is that right?'

'Well, that was one idea that occurred to me,' Sir Joseph replied.

'Your assistant also said that you missed out on some exhibits you were after that went to the Museum of Modern Air Warfare instead.'

'That's right and I must admit that I was as mad as hell. The Harriers are one of the most popular exhibits we've got, people love seeing the vertical take-offs and landings. So, we put in for some of the more modern versions when they were getting decommissioned recently but only got the one. The rest went to them instead.'

'Any ideas why?' Mac asked.

'Not really,' Sir Joseph said with a shrug. 'We normally get most of what we ask for as we're the biggest air museum in the country but not when it came to the Harriers for some reason. I even took it up with Geoffrey Cummings and it was his stonewalling that gave me the idea that the intelligence services were involved.'

'Who's Geoffrey Cummings?' Mac asked.

'He's the Deputy Minister for Defence Procurement,' Sir Joseph replied.

'So, he works under Julian Sangredo then?'

'Yes, that's right.'

Sangredo again, Mac thought. He was beginning to feel that it wasn't a coincidence that his name was cropping up all over the place.

'Was it just the Harriers that went to the museum?' Mac asked.

'Now that I think of it, yes. As far as I know they haven't asked for anything else but, then again, perhaps they have their own ways of procuring exhibits.'

'What do you think is going on at the museum then?'

'Well, if it isn't an intelligence operation of some sort, then my best guess is that they've run out of money,' Sir Joseph replied. 'It happens more often than you'd think with such long-term projects. They get enough money for the first stage and then become over-optimistic about future funding streams. They rarely take into account the political and economic changes that can take place and, when something happens as it always does, they get stuck.'

Mac had learned nothing more from Sir Joseph and, as he walked back to his car, he wondered if it might be as simple as Sir Joseph had suggested. Perhaps there was no mystery after all and the museum had simply run out of money.

He got back into his car and decided to head home. Before he started the engine up, he called and arranged to meet up with Jo and Leigh for a quick debrief at the station. After that he had a date with Tim in the Magnets. As he drove back towards Letchworth, he had plenty of time to think about what he'd learned. He'd managed to hit the rush hour and the traffic was even slower than usual as there were road works on one of the major routes out of the city. Going through Hendon a young woman pushing a pram easily kept pace with him for quite a distance. He looked out of his rear view mirror from time to time and, although he couldn't see anything definite, he had the distinct feeling that he was being followed.

Had Sir Philip been lying to him when he said that the intelligence services weren't involved? he thought.

It wouldn't have been the first time but, in spite of that, Mac was inclined to believe him. So, had Sir Joseph been right when he said that the museum might just have simply run out of money? It certainly sounded plausible enough. Mac only had questions and no answers so he gave up and turned the radio on.

The Prime Minister was being interviewed and, while she was trying to sound confident and controlled, she came over as being even more shrill and desperate than usual. After the interview ended the presenters predicted that she wouldn't see out the month. He sighed and turned the radio off. He found listening to politics profoundly depressing these days.

While he was once again stuck in traffic an idea occurred to him. It was just before six when he eventually pulled up outside Letchworth police station. He sat in the car and made a call before he went inside.

Jo and Leigh were waiting for him in the team's room. Dan was on the phone in his office and Martin was shutting the lid on his laptop as Mac sat down at Jo's desk.

'Coffee?' Jo asked.

'Yes please,' Mac said with real gratitude. He then turned to Leigh. 'So, what have you been up to since Jo called me?'

'We went back to see Elinor, Professor Braithwaite's assistant, to see if we could get any more out of her. You should have seen her face when we told her about what her boss had been getting up to with Professor De Gray every other Wednesday night. She couldn't speak for a good five minutes.'

'Why was that? Was she surprised at the news?'

'Gobsmacked would probably be a better description but there was something else there too, disappointment and perhaps some regret as well,' Leigh replied. 'I guess that Jo might have been right when she said that his assistant might have had a thing for the Professor. Anyway, we'll have to go back and see her again. She was so choked up that we had to stop the interview.'

Leigh was interrupted by Martin who dropped a sheet of paper on the desk.

'That's all I could find,' Martin said.

'Is she nice?' Leigh asked with a mischievous smile.

'Yes, she is,' Martin replied as he returned the smile. 'She's nothing whatsoever to do with the police and, when it comes to technology, she only just about knows her way around her phone. More like perfect actually. See you.'

On seeing Mac's somewhat mystified look Leigh explained, 'It was the after shave. It's really expensive, that plus the fact that it's Friday.'

'Is it really Friday?' Mac said.

'Yes, the week's flown by, hasn't it? He's wise not to be dating anyone in the police though, I've tried it and it turned out to be a disaster every time,' Leigh said with a frown.

'It didn't turn out too badly for Jo though, did it?' Mac observed.

'No but Jo and Gerry are, well different, aren't they? I mean if Gerry had been a bit younger, I might have had a go myself,' Leigh said as the mischievous smile returned.

'Girl, have you got your eyes on my man?' Jo said in a thick Jamaican accent as she handed the coffees out.

'He's quite dishy you know,' Leigh said with a laugh. 'No, I was just saying that dating policemen hasn't worked out well for me.'

'I know what you mean. I tried it a few times myself and it never worked out that well for me either. They seem to think that they've got to be so macho about everything. Thankfully Gerry's not like that at all but he had to do some heavy persuading to get me to go out with him. Luckily for me, persuasion is something that he's very good at,' Jo said with a wink. 'Anyway, I'm meeting him for a desperately needed drink in less than half an hour so back to business. Where are we then?'

Mac told Jo and Leigh what he'd learned at MI5 and the War Museum.

'So, you don't think it's anything to do with MI5 then?' Jo asked.

'I suppose it's always possible that it might be some sort of freelance operation but I'd guess that they'd know about those too. However, this link to the Steeley Boys was still puzzling me so I rang DI Peter Harper, he used to be my sergeant when I last worked with the London Murder Squad. During our time working together we dealt with quite a few cases that were linked to the Steeley Boys' operations and so I wondered if he might know something that could be useful. He told me that he did and he wants me to go and meet him at my old station in London tomorrow morning.'

'And that's all he said?' Leigh asked.

'Yes, he was being a little mysterious but if Peter says he has something then you can be sure that it will be well worth the trip into London.'

'Martin's given me the list of employees that are supposed to be currently working at the museum,' Leigh said as she handed Jo the sheet of paper.

'Just four names. It's not exactly a big operation then, is it?' Jo said as she looked at her watch. 'Okay, shall we meet up Monday morning and decide what our next moves should be then?'

'Sounds good to me,' Mac said. 'You never know, I might have something to report by then.'

Mac drove home and then called his favourite taxi driver and arranged for her to pick him up from his house at seven o'clock. His dog Terry jumped up and down in excitement when he saw Mac pick up his lead. Mac smiled. You'd have thought from his antics that he hadn't been out for days even though he'd been for a long walk earlier in the day with his neighbour Amanda.

As he walked Mac wondered what the 'something' was that his old friend Peter said might be interesting. He was quite hopeful as Peter never was one for overstating things.

He'd just have to wait until tomorrow then.

Chapter Sixteen

Mac had something of a restless night. Even his favoured sleeping position didn't ease the pain. He decided to give up on sleep when he picked up his clock and saw that it was five thirty. He wasn't due to meet Peter until ten thirty so he had some time to kill. After getting himself some breakfast and walking Terry for as far as he could, he found that it was still only seven fifteen. He set off for London anyway. The traffic was relatively light and so he made good time. He followed a route that he'd taken into London at least five or six times a week for many years yet it all seemed strange to him now. As it was a Saturday it didn't take him too long to get to the Central Police Station.

He slowed down as he drove past the place that he'd worked in for some decades. It was an unremarkable grey stone building on a street of grey stone buildings that stood a little way back from the retail madness of one of London's busiest shopping streets. One immediate difference from when he worked there was that he now had to hunt for a parking space. It was lucky that he'd come early as it took him over twenty minutes and several turns around the block before he finally found a disabled space that was free.

He walked around the corner to the front entrance and noticed that he had to go up at least ten steps to enter the building. He sighed and remembered the days when stairs and steps never needed any consideration, they were just things to be walked up without a thought.

This was only the second time he'd been back since he'd been forced to retire because of his pain issues. The first time he'd visited the station everyone had seemed more than happy to see him but he'd found it strained and awkward. He remembered that he'd still been quite bitter at being forced to leave the job he'd loved but now, with a space of time having gone by, he'd come to terms with it. In hindsight, he honestly couldn't see what else they could have done.

He found that he was still a little anxious about meeting his former colleagues again, even Peter if he was honest. Although they'd met up a for drinks a couple of times since he'd retired, he knew that their relationship, forged through many years of working together, could never be the same again.

He took a deep breath and carefully made his way up the steps. He found himself in a familiar space. When he used to work there, he'd just wave to the duty sergeant and make his way upstairs. The sergeant behind the counter was unfamiliar to him and he knew that he was now very much the visitor.

He asked for DI Harper and sat down to wait. He didn't have to wait long. Peter bounded down the stairs and came towards him with a big smile on his face. They shook hands warmly and all of Mac's anxiety evaporated on seeing his old friend once again. He was about the same height as Mac but much stockier. He'd done fourteen years in the army before he'd joined the force and he still kept himself fit.

'Boss, it's been too long,' Peter said.

'Yes, yes it has. How have you been keeping?' Mac asked.

'I've been okay I suppose but we've all missed you. Any chance you could come back?' Peter said with a smile.

'If only I could,' Mac replied.

It had been all he'd wanted when he'd been forced to retire, his old job back heading the team. However, that wanting had dimmed a little over the past few months and, if he was being honest, he wasn't sure that he had the energy for a full-time job anymore.

He followed Peter to the lift. He only remembered having to use the lift in the months before he retired. Looking back, he realised that the writing had been on the wall for him then. The murder team's office was more or less empty but the few detectives who were there all came over and greeted Mac. He was more than happy to see them and the only awkward thing was his realisation that he should have visited again long before now.

Peter still sat at the same desk and Mac glanced over at his old desk which was now covered with stacks of files.

'Who's your boss now?' Mac asked.

Peter gave him a look that said a lot and none of it was any good.

'DCS Bolsover, he came over here from East London.'

'What's he like?' Mac asked.

Peter didn't say anything. He stood up and gestured for Mac to follow him over to what used to be the old stationery store. It now had a frosted glass panel in the door on which the legend 'DCS Bryan Bolsover – Knock and wait' was etched.

Mac gave Peter an unbelieving look.

'I never liked being in an office personally,' Mac said as they returned to Peter's desk. 'I always felt that it cuts you off from the rest of the team. That 'Knock and wait' though, is that for real?'

'Oh yes and he always makes you wait too, even when I'm fairly sure he's doing nothing more than looking out of the window,' Peter replied with a frown. 'He's only been here six months and I'm afraid that he's already pissed off just about everyone on the team. We're now in the position of trying to work around him rather than with him. Luckily, he's so pompous that a bit of soft soaping goes a long way and it usually keeps him off our backs. He also loves his reports and stats so we make sure that he gets plenty of both.'

Mac shook his head. He'd been in that position himself before but thankfully only for a fairly short time. Working with such a boss was sometimes like trying to run with leg irons on.

Mac gave Peter a shrug. It was a problem but, thankfully, it wasn't his problem anymore.

'You said that you might have some information about the Steeley Boys?' Mac asked.

Peter smiled as he said, 'That I do. Follow me.'

They went down in the lift to the lock up in the basement. Peter spoke to the duty sergeant who went ahead of them and opened up one of the cells.

Mac followed Peter inside and he then shut the door behind them.

A young man was sitting on the bed. He was dressed in regulation street clothes; a designer track suit, massive sneakers and a red patterned bandana on his head topped with a baseball cap on back to front. He also wore the regulation scowl on his face. A dark red puffer jacket lay on the bed beside him. As soon as they entered the young man jumped up and sprayed them with a stream of angry invective and street jargon, some of which Mac's untuned ear didn't quite get.

Mac turned to Peter with a look of puzzlement on his face. Peter just smiled widely. When he turned back the young man was standing with his hand out and a big smile on his face.

'DS Dion Best, a pleasure to meet you DCS Maguire,' he said in a northern accent.

Mac shook his hand and then turned back to Peter and laughed.

'A pleasure to meet you DS Best, you're very good. I take it that you're working undercover with the Steeley Boys?'

'Please call me Dion. Yes, that's right, I've been working on the estate for just over four months now. Whenever I have some information that I need to pass on I arrange to get arrested and spend a few nights in the cells.'

Mac nodded. He respected and admired the officers who had the nerve and skills required to carry out such work. He'd never felt happy sending out any of his team undercover because of the risks involved but he also knew that the information such operations provided could be absolutely invaluable. From the outside you could see what a gang might be doing but it was why they were doing it that was the really important thing to know. You could only get that from informers, who could never be totally trusted, or by someone on the inside.

He briefly explained why he was interested in finding out more about the Steeley Boys and especially why they were operating so far away from their patch in North London.

'There's something definitely going on but I'm not sure exactly what just yet,' Dion said. 'Let me explain about my cover. I'm someone who's had to leave Moss Side in Manchester because I'm supposed to have upset a few people there. I'm a wannabee gang member who makes his money from selling knocked-off booze and cigarettes to some of the local shops so they call me 'Boozeboy'. I give it to the gang members for nothing and they think I'm funny so they let me hang around with them. The free drink is a useful tool as they often let a few things slip out once they've had a few.'

'That's clever,' Mac said. 'So, what do you think this 'something' might be?'

'I've no idea as yet,' Dion said with a shrug. 'The members at the top of the gang have been very close-lipped recently but they're excited about something, that I'm sure of. Skank Moussero, who's one of the gang's enforcers, recently let something slip. He said something about a 'Little Jools' and how they'll be running the country soon.'

Mac gave this some thought.

'Was he talking about Julian Sangredo do you think?'

'That's what we think,' Peter replied. 'However, we've had to keep this news to ourselves as we don't have any clear evidence as yet and there's a...well...complication shall we say. DCS Bolsover's wife is one of Sangredo's PR people and the two of them socialise with him a lot.'

Mac frowned on hearing this.

'I can see how that might be something of a problem. So, what would you do if you did find some clear evidence of Sangredo's involvement with the gang?'

Peter shrugged, 'If I'm being honest, I'd be straight on the phone to you to ask for advice.'

This made Mac smile.

'I still don't get it though,' he said. 'Sangredo's fairly young, well-connected and with a bright future in politics from what I'm hearing. Why on earth would he chance all that by getting mixed up with a drugs gang?'

'That's exactly what we thought at first but now I'm beginning to change my mind,' Peter said. 'We've heard other whispers about him too and it's made me want to look at him a bit closer. What you've just told me only adds to that.'

'You'd better tread carefully, Peter. If news gets out that you're investigating one of the star ethnic minority politicians in the government and you've got nothing to back it up then your job will be on the line.'

'We're all too aware of that, believe me Mac,' Peter replied. 'The only people in the team who know anything about this at the moment are Dion here, Manny Ibbotson, who's now my sergeant, and you.'

'Manny's your sergeant now?' Mac asked. 'He's a good choice. So, what did you plan to do next?'

'I've no idea to be honest. Our only reliable source of information is Dion here, so all we can do is wait and see what he comes up with.'

'Well, it may be that the investigations into the deaths of Bernie Bright and Professor Braithwaite have opened up another avenue that we can explore. I think that we should work together on this if that's okay with you.'

'That would be great boss, just like the old days,' Peter said enthusiastically.

'Would you be up for a conference call first thing on Monday morning?' Mac asked.

'You bet,' Peter said with a grin.

Mac shook hands with DS Best and wished him the best of luck. He knew he'd need it. He said his goodbyes to Peter knowing that they'd be seeing each other again soon.

It felt good to be working with his old friend once more.

Before he drove back to Letchworth he first rang Dan Carter and then Jim Ormesby. He explained the situation as best as he could to each of them without bringing Julian Sangredo's name into it. Luckily, they both went along with his suggestion and agreed that the teams should work together for a couple of weeks and that they'd review the situation after that.

So, he had Peter Harper, Manny Ibbotson and Dion Best from the Central London team, Jo and Leigh from the Major Crime Unit and DS Patterson from Bethnal Green.

Not a bad team at all, Mac thought with a smile. He couldn't wait for Monday to come so that he could get back to work.

Chapter Seventeen

It was finally Monday and Mac looked out at the morning while he drank his coffee. The grass in the back garden was still white with frost and all of the shrubs and trees had a dusting of sparkling ice. He went out and filled up the bird feeders. There was a family of robins living in the little privet hedge nearby and he threw a fat ball under the hedge just for them. He was glad to get back into the warmth of the kitchen, it had been so cold outside that it almost took his breath away.

Mac was anxious to get on with it and arrived at the police station early. He was lucky enough to catch Dan Carter before he left on a case. He told Mac that the investigation into Professor De Gray's death was now more or less completed. He seemed relieved that he the team were now investigating a 'normal' case, the suspicious death of a woman in Royston over the weekend. Mac gave him a quick debrief, again without mentioning Julian Sangredo by name, and asked if he could borrow his office for the conference call. He wanted to make sure that what they were about to discuss wouldn't be overheard.

As he sat there waiting for Jo and Leigh to turn up, he went over in his mind what they knew about the case so far, if indeed the deaths of a history Professor in Cambridge and a rough sleeper in Stepney really constituted a case. There was only one recent event that connected the two men and that was their meeting in the pub. He thought over what Baz had told him. Bernie and the Professor obviously hadn't tried to keep their meeting secret, in fact they could even be seen from the street. It seemed to have been a friendly meeting, there had been laughter and then the Professor gave Bernie some money. He guessed that it was just a generous gesture to an old friend who was in dire straits but then he had a thought. He wondered how it might look to someone who didn't know about the past relationship between the two men.

This gave Mac an idea. It was about the money and whether the Professor's kind act might have also been his death sentence. The more he thought about it the more possible it seemed.

Jo and Leigh came in together.

'Good morning Mac,' Jo said cheerily. 'How did your weekend go?'

'It went well, very well I think,' he replied.

He took them into Dan's office and explained what had happened.

'So, we're now going to be working with some of your old team and this DI Patterson from Bethnal Green?' Jo asked.

'Yes, for a while at least. Dan and DI Patterson's boss have agreed that we should give it a couple of weeks and see what we come up with.'

'What about the boss of the Central Team? Hasn't he or she been informed?' Leigh asked.

Mac was impressed with Leigh's quickness of thought.

'Ah well, there's a bit of a complication about that.'

Mac explained about DCS Bolsover and his personal connections to Julian Sangredo.

'So, what happens if we find some evidence that implicates Sangredo in a crime?' Jo asked.

'I'd guess that we might need to go over DCS Bolsover's head but we'll cross that bridge if and when we need to. Okay then, we'll need to collectively take some decisions as to how we handle the investigation going forward. Are you ready?'

'If I'm honest I think that a coffee might help to improve my concentration a bit,' Leigh said.

Both Mac and Jo found that they could fully agree with this sentiment. While Leigh got the drinks, Mac sent out the email with the conference call details and put the phone on speaker. At nine fifteen exactly the phone rang. It was Peter Harper and Manny Ibbotson calling from Central London. DI Patterson from Bethnal Green called in a few seconds later. Mac asked everyone to introduce themselves and, after a little coaxing, he found out that DI Patterson's first name was Jorell. After all the introductions were done Mac kicked the meeting off.

'Before we start looking at the case itself, I thought it might be wise if we started using a code name of some sort for Julian Sangredo. I've two reasons for suggesting this. Firstly, if he is involved in some sort of criminal activity then we don't want to tip him off. He's fairly high up the political ladder and it's always possible that someone in the government or Home Office might get shown our reports or let something slip. Secondly, it's more than possible that he's totally innocent of any wrongdoing and the press would have a field day if they found out that he was under investigation. So, any ideas?'

'What about LJ?' Manny suggested. 'We think that he might be the 'Little Jools' who one of the Steeley Boys said would be running the country soon.'

'Is that okay with everyone?' Mac asked. It seemed that it was. 'Okay then from this point onwards whenever we talk or text or mention Julian Sangredo in a report we'll use 'LJ' instead. So, onto the case, such as it is.'

Mac attempted to summarise the case.

'So, what we have are two deaths, one of which was obviously a murder while the other initially looked like it could be an accident. There's also an attempted murder in the mix. The links between the murder of Bernie Bright and the attempted murder of Alfred Feycourt are fairly obvious. They were both rough sleepers and the MO is exactly the same. We know for a fact that members of the Steeley Boys gang were involved in the second attack as someone helpfully videoed the whole thing and two of the men who took part in the attack ended up in hospital afterwards. We've identified these men as being Steeley Boys from their tattoos. Jorell have we found out anything else about them?'

'Please call me Jay, that's what everyone calls me.'

Mac briefly wondered if Jay had some issues with his name.

'We've been able to identify the two men from their criminal records,' Jay continued. 'They're middle-ranking gang members called Trayvon Edwards and Hosea Wiston both in their mid-twenties. Their criminal records start from around the age of ten and since then they've been done for just about everything you can think of. Neither of them would say anything to us or perhaps I should say that Hosea wouldn't say anything to us. Trayvon can't say anything at all as his jaw's broken in two places and he's lost quite a few teeth as well. With regard to the MO forensics have confirmed that the barbecue lighter fuel used to set fire to Bernie Bright's body was exactly the same as that used in the second attack.'

'Was any DNA found?' Mac asked.

'I think they're still working on that,' Jay replied.

'Okay so the first big question we should ask is what were four members of a North London drugs gang doing so far off their patch? They must have passed through at least two other gang's territories to get to Stepney and that's something that they'd normally avoid like the plague as it's almost a declaration of war,' Mac said.

'That's true. We've had well over thirty 'postcode killings' in the last year in London alone. Killings that took place solely because gang members had strayed from their patches into that of another gang,' Peter chipped in.

'Bearing that in mind I think we can safely assume that the attacks on Bernie Bright and

Alfred Feycourt were not just random incidents. There are plenty of homeless men on their own patch so, if they wanted to carry out such sick acts, why take the risk of going all the way to Stepney? So, if it wasn't random, we have to ask ourselves what connects these two homeless men to the Steeley Boys? The only connection we've come up with so far is LJ. His older brother Brian used to be the gang's leader until he was killed and his seat in Parliament includes the Steeley Boys' patch. He's currently the Minister for Defence Procurement and it's probably no coincidence that Bernie Bright worked in the RAF for most of his life. A tenuous link at best perhaps, however, we do know that not long before he died Bernie came into some money. At around the same time he also visited the Houses of Parliament to attend a debate on the 'Future of the Armed Forces', a debate that was hosted by LJ.'

'We thought that it was possible that Bernie Bright was blackmailing LJ,' Leigh said.

Mac was quiet for a moment.

'I'm not usually in favour of theories that depend on so many assumptions but I think it might be useful in this case in helping us to decide what to do next. Perhaps it might have gone something like this...

Bernie Bright was broke as he was having trouble with his benefits and he was forced to scrounge alcohol from his friends. Even they were starting to get fed up with him so, in desperation, he had an idea. He knew something about LJ, something that he reckoned he could trade for money. He somehow found out about the Armed

Forces debate and headed off to the Houses of Parliament. After the debate he contacted LJ who gave him some money with the promise of more to come. However, LJ knew that he couldn't afford to have whatever Bernie knew made public and so he set the Steeley Boys on him. I don't know if LJ had a working relationship with the gang previously but it's my guess that he must have.'

'From what we're hearing from our source inside the gang it certainly looks that way,' Peter said.

'LJ wanted to know if there was anyone else involved, if there was someone who might have put Bernie up to it. So, the Steeley Boys find Bernie and they follow him for a while. Then they see Bernie talking in a pub to a well-heeled man who gives him some money. Perhaps they also overheard something that made them think that the Professor was either involved in the blackmail or that he was buying information from Bernie. So, they go back to LJ with this information and Bernie is murdered shortly afterwards. It takes them a while to track down the Professor but, as soon as they do, he's murdered too so there are no loose ends.'

'What about Alfred what's-his-name?' Jo asked. 'What's his connection?'

'I don't think there's any connection at all,' Mac replied. 'I think it's probable that the attack on Alfred Feycourt was merely a blind. They must have heard that someone was looking into Bernie's murder and I think that it was an attempt to convince us that it was just some sick madman randomly attacking homeless men.'

'What do you think Bernie had on LJ then?' Jay asked.

'If I'm being honest, I've no idea but it's my guess that it must have something to do with this mysterious museum that Bernie worked in for a while,' Mac replied.

'Your theory makes some sense from what we know so far but it also implies that a sitting Member of Parliament might have conspired in two murders,' Peter said.

'That's why we need to be so careful. We have no real evidence as yet and, until we do, we must make sure that no word of this investigation gets out,' Mac replied.

'So, what do we do next then?' Jo asked.

'Well, there are three areas that we need to look at. There's the air museum, the Steeley Boys and there's Bernie Bright. If he was blackmailing LJ then it must be connected to something in his past.'

'We've managed to get the names and addresses of some of the museum's employees so Leigh and I could follow that up,' Jo suggested.

'And we'll ask around and see if we can find out what the Steeley Boys are getting up to,' Peter said.

'That sounds like a plan,' Mac said with a smile as it was exactly what he was going to suggest. 'Jay, I was wondering if perhaps we might work together on chasing up any leads connected to Bernie Bright?' Mac asked.

'That sounds good to me,' Jay replied.

'Okay then, I'll meet you at Bethnal Green around noon. I'll like to have a word with Bernie

Bright's daughter first just in case there might be something that she hasn't told us yet.'

'And I'll chase up that DNA report,' Jay said.

As soon as the meeting ended Mac rang Marcia Notts and arranged to meet her at her place of work. Mac had his coat on and was halfway out of the door when he had a thought. He went back to Jo's desk. She and Leigh were in the process of putting their coats on too.

'Jo, I was just wondering if you were going to interview Professor Brathwaite's assistant again?' he asked.

'Yes, we were planning on seeing her once we'd finished the interviews with the museum employees,' Jo replied. 'Was there something in particular that you wanted me to ask her?'

'Well, I was just wondering if the Professor was ever politically active. From what you've told me about him he sounds as if he was fairly left wing, at least when it comes to interpreting history. So, I was wondering if he might have had any political connections, especially with any of the opposition parties. If he had then this might have provided LJ with another reason to have him killed.'

'Yes, that's good thinking. I'll check it out,' Jo promised.

An icy blast of air made him gasp as soon as he stepped outside. It had gotten even colder while he'd been inside the police station. He had to carefully pick his way to his car as it was made treacherous by patches of frost and iced-over puddles. He couldn't afford a fall.

The solicitor's office was right in the centre of Welwyn Garden City, just around the corner from the shopping mall. He had to drive around the square several times before he found a parking space. The street was lined with shops and they all seemed to have a big red sign saying 'Sale' in the window. The solicitor's office was above a carpet shop and, like all the rest, it too had a sale on. He carefully climbed up the stairs and asked the young girl in reception for Mrs. Notts.

She appeared wearing a different outfit from the last time that they'd met but it was no more colourful being of muted shades of grey. She ushered him into an empty office.

'Have you found something?' she asked in hope.

'You could say that. Mrs. Notts...'

'Oh, please call me Marcia,' she said.

'Okay then Marcia, the first thing I've got to tell you is that you don't need to worry about paying me as I'm no longer working for you on your father's case.'

Seeing a look of disappointment on her face he quickly hurried on.

'That's because I'm now working with the police. I think it would be fair to say that your father's death has become more of a priority due to certain circumstances.'

'What do you mean?' she asked clearly puzzled.

'The police feel that there's a real possibility that your father's murder might be tied to another death. Have you ever heard your father talk about someone called Eric Braithwaite? He would have known him when he was in the RAF, they worked together for a while,' Mac explained.

'The name sounds vaguely familiar for some reason but I'm afraid that nothing comes to mind,' Marcia replied. 'However, I could have a look through dad's things if you like. He kept a lot of stuff from his time in the RAF and I didn't have the heart to throw any of it out. I was hoping that he'd eventually get settled somewhere and want it all back so it's all up in my loft.'

'I'd be very grateful if you could. We're also looking at this museum he used to work in. Did he ever say anything about what he did there?'

She slowly shook her head.

'Dad was a great talker and he always used to chat to us about his work, until he went there that is. For the first couple of years he was fine but, after that, anytime that Mum and I would ask him how his day went and what he got up to at the museum he'd always change the subject. We stopped asking him in the end as we didn't want to push it, we were both just happy that he was working and doing something he loved.'

'And what was that? The 'something he loved' I mean?' Mac asked.

'Oh, working in the stores again, he said that it reminded him of happier days. Of course, it was nothing like the RAF really, the hours were so odd for one thing.'

'In what way?'

'Well, they paid him whether he worked or not. Sometimes he might not work for weeks and that didn't do him much good as he spent most of that time down the pub. Then he'd start doing twelve hour shifts for several weeks and then nothing again for a while,' Marcia said.

'Was there anything else that was odd besides the hours?'

'Well he said that it was a great big barn of a place and yet only a few of them worked there. I asked him several times when the museum would be open to the public but he only laughed which I found was a bit strange.'

Marcia paused and was thoughtful for a while.

'Dad changed while he worked there, he became more secretive and, perhaps I'm wrong, but I couldn't shake off the feeling that he was disappointed in himself for some reason. I remember him once saying something about 'having fallen so far' but I never found out what he meant by that.'

Mac didn't get anything else of value but those words stuck in his head as he drove towards London. What could Bernie Bright have possibly been doing in a museum that would cause him to say something like that?

Chapter Eighteen

Once again, he was stuck in traffic on his way into London as a lane on one of the main roads into the city was closed. A sign informed him that they were upgrading the gas mains and that the work would take six months. Mac said a prayer of thanks that he no longer had to drive into London every day.

He let his mind wander over the details of the case. The thing that still struck him as being the most bizarre was the fact that members of the Steeley Boys gang had carried out attacks in an area of the city where they had no right to be. He played back the video of the attack on Alfred Feycourt in his mind. The attack was already underway when the video started and this gave Mac an idea.

He met with DI Jay Patterson at Bethnal Green and he too thought that Mac's idea might be worth a shot.

Callum had named the street in his statement but, as it had been dark, he said that he couldn't pinpoint the exact spot where the attack had taken place. Mac knew that the street was quite long so they both watched the video again in the hope of finding some clues.

'There aren't any defining background features as far as I can see,' Jay said. 'It's just some open land with a low fence in front of it.'

'Some open land that has flats with balconies or an open walkway on the other side of the street,' Mac said. 'The angle of the video is downwards so it must have been taken by someone who was at least on the first floor of a building and, as there's no window frame in the shot, it must have been taken from a balcony or walkway.'

'Okay, let's go for a drive and see what we can spot,' Jay said.

They drove up and down the street twice before they found what they were looking for. They found a match for a tree that appeared briefly at the edge of the frame. It was near a street lamp and it was well lit. The tree had been cut back and looked a bit lop-sided. The block of flats opposite the tree was brick-built, four storeys high and each flat had a large balcony that protruded outwards from the building. Mac guessed that the video could have been taken from any of the six balconies on the first floor. He replayed the video once again on his phone. It gave him another idea.

He pointed to one of the middle balconies and said, 'Let's try that flat first.'

They caught the lift up one floor and Mac thought it was the slowest and ricketiest lift he'd ever been in. He breathed a sigh of relief when the doors finally opened and he was able to step out. They walked past the first two doors and then Mac stopped. He rang the doorbell of the third one.

The door was opened by a wide-eyed middle-aged woman in a sari who had no English. She looked scared, said something that neither of the policemen understood and then shut the door on them. It was opened again a couple of minutes later by a bleary-eyed young woman who had obviously just been summoned from her bed. Mac showed her his warrant card.

'Did anyone here witness an attack that took place opposite these flats last Friday early in the morning?'

She shook her head, 'I'm sorry but we know nothing about any attack. I work nights at the hospital at the moment so I wouldn't have been here anyway.'

'What about your parents?'

'They would have told me if anything had happened,' she replied. 'They're very sound sleepers anyway.'

'Can you tell me if there's anyone on this floor who uses a wheelchair?'

'Yes, the lady next door,' she replied pointing to her left.

'Do you know her name?' Mac asked.

The young woman shook her head, 'I'm sorry but we don't really know any of the neighbours.'

Mac took her name and then let her get back to her bed. They went to the flat next door and rang the bell. The door was eventually opened by a woman in a wheelchair. She was in her early thirties. She had long hair that was frizzing and badly needed cutting and wore a shapeless jumper that once might have been pink. A look of frustration and disappointment was etched on a face that otherwise might have been quite pretty. Mac showed her his card.

'You sent us this video, didn't you?' Mac asked as he replayed part of the video on his phone.

'You'd better come in,' she said with some anxiety.

She turned her wheelchair around and they followed her inside. The flat was dingy and dark. It obviously hadn't been decorated for some years. There wasn't any sofa so Mac and Jay pulled out some chairs from under a table that had seen better days. The chairs didn't match but, thankfully, they looked robust enough.

Mac introduced himself and Jay and then asked for her name.

'It's Vicki, Vicki Jackman.'

'Do you live here alone?'

She nodded and a flash of deep sadness crossed her face.

'Tell me about the video,' Mac said.

'Well, as usual I was having trouble sleeping and I got up to get myself a cup of tea when I heard some shouting outside. I had a look out of the kitchen window and saw a group of men surrounding this old man. I could see them quite clearly as they were right underneath a streetlamp. The old man was thin and he looked quite frail. There were four of them and they were taunting him and laughing at him. He looked confused and walked in circles as he tried to get away from them. Then one of them knocked his feet out from under him and he fell to the ground. That's when I went out onto the balcony with my phone and started videoing them. I felt so helpless when they started kicking him. I was going to shout at them but then that other man appeared. When they threatened him with those machetes, I thought they were going to kill him. I almost shouted at him to run but before I could get the words out of my mouth two of the men were already on the ground and the others were running off. Whoever he was, he was very brave.'

'Did you see anything else after you stopped the video?' Mac asked.

'No, not really,' she said with a shrug.

'The two men who ran off, where did they run to?' Jay asked.

'Oh, they went back to their car. They drove off towards Stepney Way.'

'What was the car like?'

'I'm not sure about the make but it was a big black thing, something like a Land Rover,' Vicki replied.

'Could it have been a Mercedes?' Jay asked hopefully.

Vicki thought for a moment.

'Is that the one with a sort of star on the front?'

'Yes, it's a three-pointed star,' Jay replied.

'Yes, it was a Mercedes.'

'What about before you started videoing, did you see or hear anything?' Mac asked.

She gave this some thought.

'When I came out onto the balcony, I heard one of them shout something. It was 'Make sure you get it all' I think.'

'Do you think that you could identify either of the two men who ran away?' Mac asked.

She slowly shook her head as she thought.

'They all had their hoods pulled up so you couldn't see their faces but I got the impression that the one who kicked the old man when he was on the ground might have been a bit younger than the rest.'

'What made you think that?'

'Well, the others were quite big and broad across the shoulders whereas he was quite slim. He had slim hips too, like you see with teenaged boys.'

'Thanks, that might be really important,' Mac said.

They got nothing further from Vicki but on the whole Mac had been quite impressed with her. On his way out, he noticed several large tins of paint and paint brushes still in their packets near the door. They all had a thick layer of dust on them.

'Are you thinking of redecorating?' Mac asked.

'Well that was the idea. I got those in a fit of optimism not long after I moved into this dump. Then, when I realised that my benefits barely covered the rent and food, redecorating became somewhat less of a priority. I'm not so good at stepladders these days so I'd have to hire someone. However, as I like eating, that's not going to happen anytime soon,' she said with some bitterness.

Mac had an idea but he kept it to himself for now. Jay gave her a card in case she remembered anything else.

As they walked to the car Mac asked, 'Why was the make of car so important?'

'The Steeley Boys like to use big black Mercedes four by fours, it's a thing with them,' Jay replied. 'What do you make of what she heard?'

Mac ran what Vicki Jackman had said through his head. 'Make sure you get it all,' one of the gang members had said.

'I can only think that whoever said that was talking to the man who was videoing the attack on his phone,' Mac replied.

He stopped walking and stood deep in thought for quite a while. Jay wasn't quite sure what to do so he just stood there with him.

'Oh, I'm sorry about that,' Mac eventually said with a rueful smile. 'It happens from time to time. Something just occurred to me. Why were they recording the attack in the first place do you think?'

'Well, I know that the gangs sometimes like to put stuff up on social media to show how brutal they are,' Jay replied. 'They want people to be in fear of them.'

'Perhaps but, in this particular case, there might well be another reason,' Mac said. 'We need to go and see Callum McEachan. He's only down the road at the church.'

Jay didn't look all that delighted to be finally meeting the Tiger. Mac surmised that he'd probably seen the video.

It was nearly two o'clock and they were told by the same church warden that Mac had met when he'd first visited the church that Callum would most likely be asleep. When Mac explained that they needed to see him urgently she went off to wake him up.

Callum ambled into the church some ten minutes later looking red-eyed and unkempt.

'So, what do you need?' he asked as he sat on the pew next to Mac.

'I'm sorry for waking you Callum but I've got a question to ask. The men who attacked Alfred, were they wearing balaclavas or ski masks? Anything that might disguise their features?'

Callum thought for a while.

'No, they had their hoods up but their faces were uncovered.'

'Did you get a good look at either the man who was kicking Alfred and then tried to set him on fire or the man who was videoing it all on a phone?'

Callum shook his head as he said, 'No sorry, I was only looking at the two guys with the machetes.'

Mac thought that, while it was unfortunate, it made absolute sense given the circumstances.

'The person who took the video of the attack thought that the man who was kicking Alfred was younger than the rest. Would you agree?'

Again, Callum gave this some thought.

'Yes, they might well be right. The two with the machetes were quite big and obviously worked out. I don't remember much about the one with the phone but the other one was quite slim. Yes, he could have been younger.'

'Thanks Callum,' Mac said. 'I'll let you get back to sleep.'

'Can you thank whoever took that video for me? It really got me off the hook,' Callum said.

Mac remembered his idea and smiled.

'Why don't you thank her yourself? Her flat needs redecorating and she's in a wheelchair.'

'Aye, I'll do just that. I've never tried interior design before but I guess that there's a first time for everything,' Callum said with a smile.

As they walked back to the car Jay asked, 'Why were you asking about balaclavas and ski masks?'

'Well, if the video of the attack was meant to be put up on the internet, they'd hardly show their faces, would they? Not only that but the attack took place right under a streetlamp and I can only think that they did it there to make sure that the scene was well lit. No, I think that this particular video might have been taken for some other reason.'

'Have you any ideas as to what that reason might be?'

'No, not really,' Mac replied, 'but I've got a sneaking feeling that if we knew that then we might be much closer to breaking the case.'

They climbed into the car but Jay didn't start the engine straight away.

He turned to Mac and asked, 'Was that really a good idea? I mean giving Vicki Jackman's address to Callum McEachan?'

'It might sound strange to you but yes, I thought it was a good idea,' Mac replied. 'I know there's no harm in Callum these days and I think she desperately needs cheering up. A redecorated flat might help a bit with that. It certainly seems to work on the television.'

He could see that Jay wasn't totally convinced by him sending a man who had once been a violent criminal to help a woman in a wheelchair. However, Mac knew that he would do her no harm. He would stake his reputation on Callum.

He stopped as the thought struck him that he already had.

Chapter Nineteen

Before Jay could start up the engine his phone pinged. It was a text message saying that the DNA report had arrived. They decided to go straight back to Bethnal Green police station and see what it said. Jay printed off the report and quickly scanned it. Mac could see from his face that there was something in it that interested him.

'Unfortunately, they didn't get anything that might be helpful from Bernie Bright's body but they've also sent in an initial report on the attack on Alfred Feycourt. There were lots of different DNA traces on Alfred and his clothing but nothing that they could specifically link to an attacker, apart from one thing that is. They were able to get some DNA from a spent match that they found stuck to Alfred's overcoat,' Jay said with a smile. 'They said that the overcoat was mostly polyester and the hot matchhead had melted some of the fabric and, luckily for us, it became stuck fast.'

Mac ran back the video in his head. He could see a young man kicking Alfred and then spraying him with barbecue lighter fuel before trying to set him alight by throwing lit matches at him.

'So, we might have the DNA of the youngest of the attackers. Have they been able to identify it yet?'

Jay shook his head, 'Not yet but they're still looking through the databases.'

Mac found that he was getting even more interested in that particular young man.

'Has anyone tried to analyse the video in depth yet?'

'Well, I've had a few people look at it but they haven't managed to spot anything useful,' Jay replied.

'Do you mind if I send it to someone else to have a look at? I've worked with him before, he's very good,' Mac said.

'Yes, of course, if you think it will help.'

Mac sent the video off to Martin Selby, the Major Crime Unit's computer specialist with an accompanying email in which he explained why the video had been taken and his especial interest in identifying the youngest attacker.

'So, what now?' Jay asked.

Mac looked at his watch. It was nearly three o'clock.

'Let's go and visit the pub that Bernie met the Professor in, the Blue Boar I think it's called. Even if they don't remember seeing either of them, they might do a decent lunch.'

As Mac predicted the landlord and bar staff shook their heads when shown photos of Bernie Bright and Professor Braithwaite. The Blue Boar turned out to be one of those many pubs in London that had once been working class locals but which now haughtily regarded themselves as 'gastropubs'. What this usually meant was redecorating the place to make it look even older than it was, charging twice the price for drinks while handing out smaller portions of food on oddly shaped plates.

Mac found a table free right by the window and guessed that this might have been the very one that Bernie and the Professor had sat at when they met. The tables were small with little room between them so it would have been very easy for someone to overhear what they were saying.

Jay went for a simple cheese sandwich but Mac felt quite hungry. He opted for the 'hand-finished Aberdeen Angus steak pie with shallots and Chilean Merlot jus' and afterwards wished he hadn't bothered. It turned out to be a very average steak pie in an enamel pie dish with a bit of puff pastry on the top. He wasn't overly impressed and left most of it.

He pushed his plate away and looked at his watch. It was now four fifteen. There was no point in setting off for home for a while, all he'd do is get stuck in the rush hour.

'What time do you need to finish today?' Mac asked.

Jay shrugged, 'No particular time. The wife's away in Birmingham visiting her mother so I've nothing to rush home for.'

'Do you fancy going back to the station and going through the case file again for an hour or two? You never know, we might get lucky.'

'Might as well. We can check and see if we've gotten anything new from forensics as well.'

As they drove back to the station Mac rang his neighbour Amanda and asked her if she could walk his dog Terry that evening just in case he was back late. As usual she was more than happy to help out. She was an absolute godsend and he made a mental note to send her some flowers when he had more time.

They sat next to each other gazing at the computer screen as they scanned the pages of the case file. Nothing jumped out at them. Still Mac had a question that he'd been meaning to ask for some time.

'You don't like your name, do you? Why's that?'

Jay shook his head and smiled.

'Yeah, I love my dad but it wasn't his finest moment when he decided to call me Jorell.'

'It's an unusual name alright but it also sounds familiar for some reason.'

'Superman,' Jay said with a frown.

Mac got it then.

'That's right, Jor-El was the name of Superman's father, wasn't it?'

'After the original film came out in the late seventies, Jorell became quite a popular name for boys in Jamaica. Unfortunately, my father saw it for the first time quite a while after that, in fact just the month before I was born. For some reason he thought that naming me after Superman's father was a good idea. I've forgiven him since but only just,' Jay said with a smile.

'Yes, it's funny what some parents think is a good name for their offspring. I remember that I once arrested a man, a burglar who'd been involved in scores of break-ins. His surname was Steel and his forenames were Robert Andrew. When asked for his full name during interviews he always used to answer 'Rob And Steel'. I was never quite sure if he used that name because he became a thief or if the name gave him the idea in the first place.'

This made Jay laugh out loud.

'Well, somehow Jorell doesn't sound quite so bad after that...'

Jay stopped talking and pulled his phone out. The ring tone was from a Bob Marley song, 'Don't worry, about a thing...'

After saying 'yes' a few times he ended the call saying, 'We'll be right there.'

He did, however, look very worried as he put his phone away.

'There's been a shooting not far from St. Philips Church and apparently a giant Scotsman's involved.'

'Callum?' Mac said as he stood up. 'Is he alright?'

'Apparently he's fine but there's someone else at the scene who's got five bullet holes in him.'

'Come on, let's go,' Mac said already halfway out of the door.

Jay glanced over at him as they drove. He couldn't help noticing that Mac had his fingers crossed.

Chapter Twenty

Leigh glanced over at Jo as they once again drove towards the History Faculty building in Cambridge. She didn't look happy. Leigh could well understand why, it had been a total waste of a morning. Out of the four men who were supposed to be working at the Museum of Modern Air Warfare they only got to speak to two of them. One didn't appear to be at home while she was fairly sure that the other was in and was hiding behind the curtains. She saw them twitch as they drove away.

'Did you notice that they both said more or less the same thing?' Jo eventually said.

'Well, that might just be because it was true,' Leigh said but without much conviction.

'No, I didn't buy what they said about just maintaining the building structure and not knowing anything about the vans and trucks that came into the site. They conveniently didn't even know who employed them. It was all done via email they told us yet neither of them could show us a single email to back that up. You know, at times it sounded as if they were reading from a script to me.'

In thinking back to the interviews Leigh could see what Jo meant.

'Yes, even some of the phrases they used were the same,' she said.

'I'd bet that they could tell us quite a lot more about what's going on in that museum if they wanted to. We'll just have to think of a way of prising it out of them,' Jo said.

'Shall I dig out the thumbscrews?' Leigh said with a smile.

Jo laughed.

'Please don't, I might be tempted to use them. No, some real evidence would do the trick but God knows where we'll find it. Anyway, let's hope that Ms. Grayem-Weiss has recovered enough to talk to us, otherwise the day's going to be a total washout.'

She met them in the lobby as before and they went up in the lift to the Professor's office. It still had his name on the door. Jo couldn't help noticing that Elinor had changed, instead of the skirt and twin set she now wore ripped jeans and a tight red top. She'd ditched the black rimmed glasses too. She looked about ten years younger than she had the last time they'd met.

'I'm sorry,' Elinor said as they all sat down, 'about the last time I mean. It was all a bit of a shock.'

Jo thought that she still looked quite tearful and more than a little disappointed in life. She decided to tread softly.

'In the light of what we told you about Professor Braithwaite's affair with Professor De Gray we just need to know if you've thought of anything that might help us?'

Elinor shook her head slowly.

'I still can't believe it if I'm being honest. I've talked about it to Jan, Professor De Gray's assistant, and she's finding it hard to take in as well.'

'Yes, the two Professors were very good at keeping secrets, weren't they? When we first spoke to you, I remember that you said that Professor Braithwaite only worked on his history projects. Was there anything that he ever did outside of work? Politics for instance?' Jo asked.

'Yes, I don't know why I never mentioned that,' Elinor said looking puzzled. 'It was a few years ago now and I suppose that was why.'

'Can you tell us about it?' Jo prompted.

'He got to know David Kalinic, who's the local MP for Cambridge, during the last general election. He helped him quite a lot by introducing him around the Cambridge colleges, canvassing and speaking at meetings and so on. It worked too as David won the seat back from the Liberals for the first time in ten years. The Professor was really made up when the result was announced. I was at the victory party with him afterwards and we all got a bit squiffy. It was a really good night.'

'And did the Professor have much contact with Mr. Kalinic after he was elected?' Jo asked.

'No, not really. I think they met in one of the House of Commons bars a couple of times when the Professor was in London but that was about it, I think.'

From her expression Jo could see that something had popped into Elinor's mind. She kept quiet and let her think.

'There was something they discussed now I think of it,' Elinor said. 'The Professor had been talking for some time about putting a book out on the weaponry used during the Civil Wars, not just about the weapons though but the people who made and supplied them too. Some of them supplied arms to both sides and made a lot of money doing it. The publishers had persuaded him to call it 'The Merchants of Death' which he thought was a bit lurid but, as they were giving him a good advance, he said that he wasn't going to quibble about it. I remember he told me that David had agreed to do a foreword for the book.'

Jo looked a bit puzzled at this.

'Did he know much about Civil War weapons then?'

'No, but he does know quite a lot about modern weaponry though and how they're sold. The foreword was going to say that not much has really changed in the three hundred and fifty years or so since the Civil Wars ended.'

'So how does Mr. Kalinic know so much about modern weapons?' Jo asked.

'Well, he is the Shadow Secretary of State for Defence so I'd hope that he'd know something,' Elinor said.

Jo and Leigh exchanged surprised glances. Had they just discovered another motive for the Professor's murder?

As Leigh drove them back to Letchworth Jo tried to get Mac on the phone but he wasn't answering for some reason. She sent him a text instead.

'What are you thinking?' Leigh said after Jo had been silent for some time.

'This David Kalinic must be Dominic De Gray's opposite number in the Labour party. I'm sure that he'd be the last person that LJ would want to get wind of whatever it was he was up to.'

'You're right there plus the fact that they can't stand each other,' Leigh said. 'They were both on Question Time a while back and I thought that they were going to start throwing punches at each other.'

'So, from what we know, it's probable that there was nothing suspicious in the Professor meeting with someone who was going to contribute to his book and then with an old friend who was down on his luck but let's look at it from LJ's point of view,' Jo said. 'What if he saw the Professor talking to Mr. Kalinic in the House of Commons bar? A little later on the Professor is then spotted talking to Bernie Bright who we think was possibly blackmailing LJ. He might regard that as being more than a bit suspicious, don't you think?'

'When you put it like that yes, I think he might, especially as the Professor was seen giving Bernie money as well,' Leigh said. 'Do you think that LJ might have been afraid that Bernie was giving information to the Professor and that he was then going to pass it on to one of his political enemies?'

'That's exactly what I was thinking,' Jo replied. 'So, what on earth did Bernie Bright have on LJ? Whatever it was it must have been dynamite.'

Chapter Twenty-One

Callum went back to bed after speaking to Mac and Jay. However, try as hard as he might, he found that sleep eluded him. He thought about the woman in the wheelchair. He guessed that now would be as good a time as any to pay her a visit. He could always fit in a couple of hours sleep later in the evening if he was feeling tired.

He hadn't known what to expect when he rang her doorbell but he certainly hadn't been expecting her. He thought she'd be older for one thing but there was something about her, something that he couldn't put a finger on.

She found herself looking at his midriff and she had to look right up to see his face.

'Oh, it's you!' she said in surprise.

'A policeman just told me that you might be in need of a painter and decorator. Is that right?' Callum said with a smile.

'Really? I remember saying something to him about it but I never guessed that he'd want to help. You'd better come in,' she said as she turned the wheelchair around.

Callum followed her inside and he immediately saw what Mac had been talking about. The flat was dark and dingy inside. It felt dead and lifeless and as if the walls were closing in on him.

'Look, you really don't have to,' she said looking a little flustered.

'Oh, but I do. That little video you took saved me from spending some time in the police cells,' he replied. 'Anyway, I'd like to help if I can.'

She gave him a measured look and was thoughtful for a while.

'How did you do that? You know, what you did to those two men?' she asked. 'Were you in the army or something?'

'No, I...well, I was a criminal. Violence was what I did, it was my profession.'

'It looks like you were pretty good at it,' she said.

'I was. I was a bad man and I did some bad things.'

'And now?'

'I'm trying really hard not to be that person anymore.'

'What do you do, now that you're not a criminal anymore?' she asked.

'I work at St. Philips, helping out in the soup kitchen and I also do some outreach work with the homeless. I bring them food and help them with their benefits and medicines and so on. The man that was being attacked was one of my clients. He's just a nice harmless old man.'

'How is he?'

'He's still in hospital but he's recovering they tell me.'

'Good, I'm glad he's okay,' she said before she gave him another thoughtful look. 'Am I safe with you?'

'You are,' Callum said.

'For some reason I believe you,' Vicki replied as she gave him a smile. 'Have you done much painting and decorating before?'

'Well, if I'm being honest, no.'

'That's okay, I can show you what to do. I used to have my own business once.'

'Really? You were a painter and decorator?' Callum asked with a surprised expression.

'Well, I wasn't always in this wheelchair you know, I used to be able to get up a ladder with the best of them. We called it 'interior design' back then but basically yes, I was a painter and décorator. In another life,' she said with obvious sadness.

'Well, I've got a couple of hours free. Shall we get started?' Callum said.

Vicki told him where to get some old sheets to cover the floor and then told him to stir the paint first before putting some into a tray. She showed him how to load the roller and the best way of putting the paint on the wall. Callum was a willing pupil and ninety minutes later two walls and the ceiling had been given a thick coat of paint. The flat already looked brighter.

'And there was me worried about not having a stepladder,' she said.

'Aye well, the ceilings aren't all that high in these flats, are they?'

She showed him how to clean the roller and then put it in a plastic bag so it wouldn't dry out.

'Shall I come back again tomorrow?' Callum asked hoping for some reason that her answer would be yes.

'I'll look forward to it,' she said as she gave him a warm smile.

He couldn't get that smile out of his head as he walked back towards the church. It was freezing cold outside but he felt strangely warm inside. He was so deep in thought that he never noticed the black Mercedes four by four slow down and then pull in beside him. He only knew he was in trouble when he felt the barrel of a gun in his back.

He suddenly snapped back into the real world and quickly took in the situation. There was a driver and a passenger in the front seat. The passenger smiled widely at him and showed him his gun. Thankfully the passenger never got out so he only had the one to deal with.

'Get into the car,' a gruff voice from behind ordered.

Callum knew that if he got into the car, he'd be a dead man. Luckily, it looked as if he was dealing with amateurs. The passenger, by keeping to his seat, was basically out of the game while the man behind him was being far too confident just because he was armed. While pushing the gun right into his back might shield it from the view of others, it meant that it was well within his reach too.

He made a step towards the open car door and then another. He put his hand on the car door and turned slightly so that the gun was now sticking in his right side. He then made his move.

He feigned a trip and then he quickly half-turned, grabbing the man's wrist as he did so. He jerked the man's arm forward with all his strength.

The gunman was surprised and was easily thrown off balance. He could do nothing to stop Callum as he held his arm against the door jamb. Callum then slammed the car door on it as hard as he could. He was counting on the man dropping the gun. The plan then was to use him as a human shield so that he could get into the safety of an entryway to his left and then escape into the flats.

However, the effect of the door smashing into the man's forearm caused a different reaction to the one Callum had expected. He didn't drop the gun, instead his hand went into spasm and gripped the gun even tighter. His index finger jerked inwards and pulled the trigger. He kept it pulled as a volley of bullets smashed into the windscreen just after ventilating the man sitting in the passenger seat. The car engine died and the driver decided that he wasn't going to hang around. He jumped out of the car and ran off as quickly as he could.

Callum opened the car door and the man started screaming in a high voice, 'You broke my arm, you broke my fucking arm.'

Indeed, his arm did look somewhat swollen. Callum grabbed him by his coat and lifted him right off his feet. He put his face right into his and gave him the look.

'If you don't shut up, I'll break the other one too,' he said softly and with menace.

He got the message and just whimpered lightly as Callum phoned the police. Two uniformed officers quickly arrived, followed shortly afterwards by two more. They didn't quite know what to make of the situation. Mac and Jay turned up a few minutes later with another car following behind with three of Jay's detective team inside. They only glanced at the man in the front seat through the large hole in the windscreen as they walked by. From the number of bullet holes in his body they could see that he was most sincerely dead.

'Keep the public away from the car until the forensics team get here,' Jay said to the uniformed officers. He then turned to Callum. 'What happened?'

Callum told him.

'I was really surprised at the gun going off like that. I only felt the barrel in my back, I didn't know that it was a machine pistol.'

Mac looked at the gun that was now lying on the floor of the car.

'It's Polish, isn't it?' Mac said. 'I haven't seen one of those for a while.'

'I take it that he was the one who put the gun in your back?' Jay said as he looked down on the man who was sitting on the pavement with this back against the car.

'He broke my fucking arm,' he said feeling intensely sorry for himself.

'Stand up,' Jay ordered the man.

The man gingerly got to his feet. Jay took his arm and felt it up gently and down before pulling down the collar of his jacket down. They could all see the Steeley Boys tattoo on his neck.

'You're a bit off your patch, aren't you?' Jay said.

'I'm not saying nothing,' the man sulkily replied. 'I need a hospital, I know my rights. You've got to take me to see a doctor.'

'We've already gotten two of your lot in Bart's Hospital under armed guard so I guess another one won't hurt,' Jay said as he turned to one of his detectives. 'Get him in the car.'

Jay then turned to Callum.

'A couple of my men will take you to the station and take your statement. I'm afraid that we'll have to keep you there until we get some evidence to support what you've told us.'

'What about Vicki?' Callum asked. 'Er…Miss Jackman I mean? Is she in any danger?'

'That's a good point,' Jay replied. 'I doubt that they'll know about her and the video yet but I'll get someone up to her flat right away just in case.'

Callum nodded and seemed relieved to hear Jay's words. Mac wondered at Callum being so concerned, after all he'd only met her once.

'Come on Mac, let's deliver our man to the hospital,' Jay said as they walked to the car. He stopped and was thoughtful for a while before he continued, 'It would be really nice if we could get some information from our man in the back there, wouldn't it?'

'It would certainly help but I'm not holding my breath,' Mac replied. 'The Steeley Boys we've arrested so far haven't told us anything at all, have they?'

'Let's just wait and see,' Jay replied with an enigmatic smile.

Mac was puzzled. Even though he hadn't been to Stepney for some time, he still knew that Jay was heading in more or less the opposite direction to the hospital. They drove into a working-class housing estate and Jay parked up. He got out of the car and went into a house. A couple of minutes later he came out and got back into the car. A young man appeared in the doorway. He leant against the door jamb and watched the car intently.

'What are we doing here?' the man in the back screeched. 'This ain't no hospital.'

'No, no it's not. Before I take you to the hospital, I want you to tell me why you staged the attack,' Jay said.

'Fuck you, you'll never get anything out of me,' he replied with utter certainty.

'Well, that's a real shame, for you I mean. See that young man over there? He's a well-known member of the local gang here, the A13 Boys, and he really doesn't like other gangs coming on his turf. For some reason he especially dislikes the Steeley Boys and when I told him that you'd been operating on his turf he was quite severely pissed,' Jay said.

The man glanced over at the young man in the doorway. He had a long knife that he was sharpening with a whetstone. His face was hard with hatred.

'And what's that got to do with me? You've got to take me to the hospital, my arm's broke.'

Mac could hear the fear start to creep into his voice.

'No, it isn't. It's just bruised that's all,' Jay replied. 'Well, as you won't talk, you're of no use to me. We're dropping all charges.'

Mac looked over at Jay and wondered where he was going with this. He had an idea but he fervently hoped that he was wrong.

'What do you mean, dropping all charges?' the man asked smelling a rat.

'What I mean is you're free to go,' Jay said.

'So, if I'm free to go then drop me off at a tube station then,' the man said hopefully.

'No, it doesn't work like that,' Jay replied. 'If you're not going to tell us anything then you have to get out of the car. Now!'

'What here?' the man said as he eyed the young man in the doorway who was now on the phone.

Mac could see the whites of his eyes. He was now sweating with fear.

'I'd guess that he's calling for the rest of the gang to come over so they can all say hello to you. A couple of months ago they caught a member of a gang from across the river on their turf. He was never seen again. We never found the body but we were fairly certain he was dead because we found his cock and balls. They'd thoughtfully cut them off and posted them to his family in a little cardboard box. Oh, they'll have some fun with you alright. So, get out, unless you've got something to tell me that is.'

'But I can't, if I say anything the Steeley Boys will kill me,' he said in desperation.

'Okay, in that case I'll let you explain what you're doing here to him and his friends,' Jay said menacingly.

'Can't we cut a deal?' he implored Jay in a shaking voice. 'I don't want to die.'

Jay was thoughtful for a moment.

'I tell you what, if you tell me everything you know right now then I'll take you to the hospital and the police records will show that you told us nothing. I won't record anything and we won't say a word, will we?' Jay said as he glanced over at Mac.

'Not a word,' Mac echoed wondering what he'd just gone along with.

The man gave it a few minutes thought. Jay reckoned that he'd had long enough. He climbed out of the car and opened the rear door.

'That's it! Out!' he shouted.

The young man at the door stood up, smiled and drew the blade of his knife across his throat.

'I'll tell you anything you want, just shut the door,' he pleaded.

Jay shut the door and got back into the car.

'I don't know what this is all about, honestly. We were just told to go out and pick up this big Scottish guy. We knew he lived somewhere near the church but that was all. We were just driving around looking for him, it was bad luck for us that we found him. I should have shot him when I had the chance but we were told not to kill him. They wanted to ask him some questions first.'

'Who are 'they'?' Mac asked.

'I don't know,' he said. When he saw the sceptical expressions of the policemen's faces, he quickly carried on. 'Skank gave us our orders and he said that they came straight from the top. That's it, that's all I know, honest.'

He looked at the two policemen in near despair.

Jay glanced over at Mac who nodded. He believed what he'd been told.

'Right then, let's get you to the hospital,' Jay said as he started up the car.

They handed the man over to the armed police contingent at Bart's Hospital after ensuring that were first brought up to speed. They left after a doctor confirmed Jay's diagnosis. The man's arm was just badly bruised.

As they drove back to Bethnal Green police station Mac couldn't contain himself any longer.

'Was all that back there for real?' he asked.

'Didn't it look real?' Jay asked with a straight face.

'Well, yes it did actually but threatening him like that...'

'It worked though, didn't it? Okay we didn't learn much but we learned something. It was the only way,' Jay said with a serious expression on his face.

'If he'd have called your bluff would you really have turned him over to the local gang?'

'Well, that would have been a bit difficult as the nearest street gang is well over a half a mile away from where we were,' Jay said with a smile. 'That was my mum's house and the young man you saw is my youngest brother. He's a drama student and he was all up for playing a gang banger from the hood.'

Mac laughed out loud, as much with relief as anything.

'Oh, that was good!' he said as the tears rolled down his face. 'No wonder you scared the hell out of him, you had me fooled too.'

'So, at least we know that they needed Callum alive for some reason. Any ideas?' Jay asked.

'I'm not sure, it would have been so much easier to just shoot Callum with the machine pistol as they drove by, wouldn't it? He said that Skank had given him his orders. That name came up in the briefing, Skank Moussero. I'll pass that information on to Peter Harper when we get back to the station. I take it that we haven't told anyone outside of the immediate team about the video?'

'No, the boss thought that it would be best to keep that to ourselves for now,' Jay replied.

'That was good thinking. I'll ask him to keep it that way. So, as far as the Steeley Boys know, Callum was the only witness to the attack.'

Mac was thoughtful for a while.

'Two of the four assailants are in hospital so that only leaves the one who was videoing the attack on his phone and the young man who was trying to set Alfred on fire. I still wonder about that young man and who he is. All I can think is that the Steeley Boys must have wanted to know if Callum had been able to give a description of the two attackers who got away.'

'Did Callum ever have anything to do with the Steeley Boys before he went into jail?' Jay asked.

'We're fairly sure he did, in fact, we think that it was him who killed LJ's older brother and then nailed him to a tree. We heard about that from a member of an Irish gang we arrested who died not long afterwards. However, we found absolutely no evidence to back up what he said and it never came up in any of the court proceedings. So, while it's a possibility that the Steeley Boys found out about this and decided to take revenge, I think it's highly unlikely. If it was just revenge that they were after then why not just shoot him dead on the street? No, that doesn't make any sense at all to me.'

As they pulled up at the station Mac took a look at his phone. It was now six thirty and there was nothing yet from Martin but there was a text from Jo. He read it with great interest.

'Now that's interesting.' Mac said. 'It appears that Professor Braithwaite was friendly with his local MP who also happens to be the Shadow Defence Secretary. Jo thinks it's possible that they might have been spotted by LJ talking together in one of the House of Commons bars.'

'Well, I'd bet that would have started the alarm bells ringing alright,' Jay said. 'I wonder if he thought Bernie was trying to get paid twice for the same information.'

'I'd bet that's exactly what he thought,' Mac said.

Before they joined Callum, who was kicking his heels in an interview room, Jay had a word with one of his detectives. Mac took the chance to call Peter and update him.

'It seems that we've found three witnesses to the attack on Callum,' Jay said. 'Two of them were walking on the street behind Callum and the other one was in one of the flats overlooking the scene.

They all more or less back up Callum's story. They're on their way in now to make a statement,' Jay said.

'Okay, so what do we do next?' Mac asked. 'I take it that you're not thinking of just releasing him?'

'No way, we'll need to get Callum somewhere secure until we figure this whole thing out. For all we know they might try again.'

'And what about Miss Jackman?'

'Well, I'd guess that she might be safe enough for now but, if they ever found out about her, she might be in the same boat too,' Jay replied. 'I think we'll need to keep them both in a safe place.'

Callum stood up as Mac and Jay walked into the interview room. There was a question on his face.

'You're in luck Callum,' Jay said. 'We've found some witnesses who say they saw the attack and they all back up your story. You're free to go.'

'And is Miss Jackman okay?' Callum asked.

'Yes, we've got an officer with her now,' Jay said as he glanced over at Mac. 'We believe that your attempted kidnap today might have been related to the fact that you're the only witness of the attack on Alfred Feycourt, the only witness as far as the Steeley Boys know that is. There is another witness of course, Miss Jackman. We think that she might be in danger too if word of the video she took ever got out. Although I said that you were free to go, we'd prefer it if you stayed somewhere safe and under guard. After killing one gang member and injuring another three I'd guess that they'll be looking for revenge if nothing else.'

'I don't fancy being cooped up,' Callum said, 'I've got my rounds to do as well and I don't want the lads to go hungry. Anyway, I can look after myself.'

Mac had a feeling that he might say something like this but he also knew that if Callum went out on the streets, he'd be far too vulnerable. He didn't think the Steeley Boys would try kidnapping a second time, they'd just shoot him.

Jay was about to say something, probably to argue his case that he should stay under guard, but Mac got in first.

'We're just going to see how Miss Jackman is getting on. Want to come along?' Mac asked.

Jay shot him a questioning look but Mac just shook his head.

'Yes, yes I do,' Callum said already getting to his feet.

Mac smiled at his obvious eagerness. He had an idea about how he might get Callum to agree to stay under guard.

Chapter Twenty-Two

The door to Miss Jackman's flat was opened by one of Jay's detectives, a woman in her late twenties. She was quite tall with broad shoulders. Her black hair was cut just below her ears and she was dressed in a black trouser suit and white blouse. She looked very serious and very professional.

Jay introduced Mac and Callum and then said, 'This is Detective Sergeant Ieva Mielkute.'

She smiled when Jay introduced her and she suddenly looked like someone who would be fun to be with.

'Is that name Eastern European?' Mac asked.

'Sort of, it's Lithuanian,' she replied in a pure London accent.

Mac nodded as if that explained everything. As he knew virtually nothing about Lithuania, he decided not to say anything else. He'd look it up on Google when he had a chance.

'Has anything happened?' Jay asked as they walked inside.

'Nothing to report as yet, boss,' Ieva replied. 'I asked Miss Jackman if she'd like to go to a hotel where she might be a bit safer but she refused. She said that even the adapted rooms in hotels are rubbish and she'd sooner stay in her flat. She's safe enough here for now though, isn't she?'

'Well, we don't think that the Steeley Boys have any idea as yet that she or the video exists,' Jay replied. 'So, I'd guess that she'd be as safe here as anywhere, for now at least.'

'I've been enquiring about the flat next door which is lying empty. Apparently, it's scheduled for refurbishment before they let it out again. I've asked the housing association to send someone around with the keys straight away. I thought that, if she is going to stay in her flat, then we might be able to use next door as a base. If I'm being honest, I think Miss Jackman is getting fed up with us already. There's not much room in here, is there?'

'That's really good thinking. Can you arrange to get some cameras outside as well?' Jay asked.

'They're on their way,' Ieva replied. 'We're planning on putting one downstairs, to give us notice of anyone entering the flats, one that covers the lift and stairs on this floor and one covering Miss Jackman's front door. We can then monitor any movement twenty-four hours a day.'

Jay smiled, 'Thanks Ieva, I wish I had a few more like you. Let's go and see Miss Jackman.'

In the living room another detective was sitting at the table drinking a cup of tea. The small room was now very crowded. Vicki turned and her eyes quickly scanned the new arrivals.

'Callum, you're alright,' she said with obvious relief. 'When they said that you'd been attacked...'

She didn't finish the sentence but the look on her face said enough.

'Miss Jackman, I'm sorry for landing my officers on you without any warning but we believe that, after the attack on Callum this evening, both of your lives may be in some danger. We'd normally move you both to a hotel or something but, as you don't want that, we felt that you might be just as safe here for now,' Jay said. 'With some added precautions of course.'

'Well that's good news,' Vicki replied. 'It might be a dump but at least it's a dump where everything's accessible to someone in a wheelchair. Would Callum be staying here too?'

'He could, if it was okay with you that is?' Jay said. 'From our point of view just having the one location to monitor would make life a bit easier.'

'That's okay with me,' Vicki said quickly. 'I've got a single bed in the second bedroom and it's never been used. If I'm honest I'd feel a lot safer if he were here.'

Mac looked at Callum, six feet four of solid muscle and then glanced over at the detective drinking his tea. He was more like five feet eight and eleven stones dripping wet. There was no contest really.

'I can see that,' Jay said with a little smile. 'Okay, to give you both some privacy we're going to station our men in the empty flat next door. We'll put some cameras up outside and give you both a panic button that you must wear at all times. I'm afraid that you'll also need to keep the curtains drawn at all times too. If you need any groceries or medication one of my men will get them for you. Have you any questions?'

'I could do with some clothes,' Callum said. 'If you ask Francie at the church, she'll show you where I keep everything. Can you tell them that I'll be stuck here for a while? Someone will need to go out in the van and do the rounds.'

Mac smiled at the fact that Callum was suddenly no longer quite so desperate to be out on the streets.

'Okay, we'll do that right now,' Jay said. 'We'll see you later then.'

News of the attack had already reached the church. They had to assure Francie and the Reverend several times that Callum was okay and that he was only being kept out of circulation for his own safety. It was nearly eight by the time they'd picked up some of Callum's clothes and dropped them off at the flat. The keys to the next door flat had arrived, it was a dump but it had a table and some chairs that were usable and the toilet still worked. They'd move in everything else they needed overnight. Someone was already fitting a camera outside the flat as they left.

'So, what are you going to do now?' Jay asked as they walked to the car.

'Go home I suppose,' Mac said with no enthusiasm at all as he thought of the long trip back to Letchworth.

'It's late, why don't you stay at my place tonight? We've got a guest room you can use. It will save you the drive home and the trip back again in the morning. As I said the wife's away so you'd be company anyway.'

'Thanks, that would be good,' Mac replied with a smile.

He'd been pleasantly surprised by Jay's offer especially as it meant that he'd miss the joys of being stuck in a massive traffic jam in the morning due to the gas main works.

'In the meantime, if you fancy a pint we could go to my local. They do some nice food there too,' Jay said hastily adding, 'and it's definitely not a gastro-pub.'

'Now that sounds like a plan to me,' Mac said with some enthusiasm.

It took less than ten minutes before Jay pulled up outside his house. It was a small house but, even so, Mac knew that any type of house in London was expensive these days. The area around it was mostly flats. Not high rise though, just three of four stories. It all looked tidy enough.

'It's only on the corner there. Will you be okay to walk?' Jay asked.

Mac could see the welcoming lights of the pub some hundred yards or so away.

'That's no problem, especially when I know that there's a pint waiting there for me,' Mac said with a smile.

It had turned bitterly cold and Mac had to watch where he walked so as to avoid the icy puddles. He thought of those men sleeping outside and, even with their 'street skin', he wondered how on earth they did it.

The Cordwainer's Arms was an unprepossessing little corner pub being painted a drab green and having no other identification apart from the name above the door. However, as soon as Jay opened the door, the warm air, the smell of beer and the sound of a dominoes game being played with full vigour told him that he was in the right place. The pub was fairly full and almost everyone nodded towards Jay as he looked for a table. They found one in the opposite corner to the dominoes game for which Mac was thankful.

A group of elderly men, black, white and Asian, were gathered around a dominoes board where four men were playing against each other as if their lives depended on it. They slammed down the domino tiles with a smile when they made a winning move and they slammed down the tiles with disgust when they hadn't. All in all, they were making a fair bit of noise.

Mac looked on smiling. The people seated at the tables around him were just normal people having a drink and a chat. They were of all types and ethnicities and he thought that they were a fair reflection of the city that they lived in. He thanked God that not all of the local pubs had been gentrified and turned into some ideal of what a London pub might have looked like years ago.

Jay returned with two pints of beer and a little handwritten menu. Mac gratefully took a sip from his drink before he looked at the menu.

'I think I needed that,' Mac said.

'Yes, it's been a long day, hasn't it?' Jay replied. 'What do you fancy then?'

Mac took a look and decided straight away. He hoped he'd have better luck this time.

'I'll have the steak pie.'

'Are you sure?' Jay asked looking a little puzzled. 'Didn't you have one earlier at the Blue Boar?'

'Yes, I did but it didn't exactly hit the spot somehow. Perhaps it was the 'Chilean Merlot jus' but I didn't really care for it all that much. This looks like the type of place where you'd get a proper pie, not an enamel dish full of 'jus' with a bit of puff pastry on the top.'

Jay smiled as he said, 'Now that you've said that I think I'll try one too.'

While they waited for their food Mac decided to change the subject. He was interested in finding out a bit more about Jay.

'So, how did your family end up here in London?'

'It was mum really. She was a nurse back in Jamaica but she'd always wanted to go and work in England. So, one day she went along to a job fair in Kingston and got an offer of a job at St. Barts Hospital just down the road from here. In fact, she's still working there now but it's just part-time these days. Dad wanted to go to England too but he wasn't too bothered where exactly. He was a mechanic and he thought that he'd be able to get a job wherever they ended up. So, they both moved to London. We lived not too far from the Steele Estate for a while but we moved down here when it really started to go to the dogs. Dad eventually ended up working for London Transport maintaining the buses and he's still doing that too. So, my mum's a nurse and my dad's working on the buses. I'm a bit of a racial stereotype I suppose.'

'My dad worked on the buses too,' Mac said. 'He was an inspector though not a mechanic. He came over from Ireland to Birmingham having only the skills he'd learned on the family farm. Not much use in a big city really. So, he started working in one of the big car factories but he didn't like it much. He told us that, after standing on the same spot for eight hours doing exactly the same thing over and over again, he knew exactly how a battery chicken felt and he hated working shifts anyway. He got lucky when a friend recommended him for a job as a bus conductor. He ended up as an inspector but I was told that he could have rose higher and become a manager if he'd have wanted to. However, when they offered him the promotion, he turned it down because it was an office job. He really loved being out and about all the time.'

'Have you ever wondered what we might have been doing if our parents hadn't been so adventurous and left everything to come to England?' Jay asked.

Mac had to think on that one for a while.

'That's a good question and, if I'm being honest, I've no idea. Probably working on a farm and drinking too much Guinness in the evenings I'd guess.'

'Same here, except insert 'smoking Ganja' for drinking Guinness,' Jay said with a smile. 'Personally, I'm glad that they made the trip, I really like London. I'll be sad if I have to move out.'

'Why would you need to do that?' Mac asked.

'My wife and I have been trying for a child and, if we're successful, we're going to need somewhere bigger. That means we'll have to move outside London unless we win the lottery in the meantime.'

'Yes, London's so expensive these days, isn't it? We used to live here when I first got a job with the Met. We had a flat near Paddington Green and my wife hated it. We eventually moved out to

Hertfordshire, a place called Letchworth. She loved it there. It's more like a large village than a small town, if you know what I mean, but it's still big enough to be interesting.'

'We haven't looked at too many properties that far out yet but I'll bear it in mind…'

Jay was interrupted by the arrival of their pies. It was a simple meal; golden chips with green garden peas and an oblong block of deep golden shortcrust pastry from which the most gorgeous smell emanated. Mac cut into his pie and a rich dark brown gravy, not 'jus', leaked out onto the plate. He sniffed its aroma with great pleasure. He cut off a corner of the pie and placed it in his mouth. It was a proper pie, meaty with a hint of pepper while the pastry was satisfyingly crunchy on the outside and soft on the inside.

All conversation was suspended until the plates were thoroughly cleaned.

'Now that's what I call a pie!' Mac said with great satisfaction as he pushed the plate away.

The dominoes game in the opposite corner had gotten even louder now and had attracted an even larger crowd of onlookers.

'Fancy a game?' Mac asked.

He hadn't played dominoes for some years now but he thought it might be a nice way to while away the evening and to stop himself from thinking about the case for a time. Unfortunately for him Jay was quite good at the game and, even though he tried quite hard to let Mac win now and again, he still ended up getting soundly thrashed. Mac didn't mind though, he thoroughly enjoyed every minute of his evening at the Cordwainer's Arms.

Later, as he lay back in Jay's comfortable guest bed, he mulled over the day's events. It had been a strange day for sure and, as he gratefully drifted off into a deep sleep, he wondered what tomorrow might bring.

He decided that a little less drama would be good.

Chapter Twenty-Three

Ieva could see her breath on the air. It was still chilly in the empty flat even though the heating had been turned on. The flat had been cold for so long that it would take some warming up.

She looked at her watch. It had gone nine. Just under an hour to go before she and her partner Jason handed over to the night team. She couldn't wait. It had been a long day and she was looking forward to getting home to a large glass of wine and then climbing into a nice warm bed for a long sleep. Just a few short weeks ago she'd have also had a nice warm boyfriend to snuggle up to.

She quickly dismissed the thought. He was a waste of space and it wasn't as if she hadn't been warned. Why was she always the last to see things? Thinking about it now she decided that swapping him for a hot water bottle had been the best thing she'd done in ages.

She snapped her attention back to the present. All three cameras were up and working now. Her partner pointed at one of the monitor screens and she saw someone going into the entrance of the flats on the ground floor. He was weaving around and seemed to find it hard to keep on his feet. He leant against the wall and then bent down and threw up on the floor. He wiped his mouth with his sleeve and then staggered back into the street leaving a pool of vomit behind.

'You'd better remember not to step in that on your way out,' Jason said with a smile.

Ieva gave him the briefest of smiles without turning to look at him. Jason Gabriel was a Detective Sergeant in his early thirties and, in Ieva's opinion, he was too sharp for his own good. She knew that if he could get promotion by walking all over someone else, he wouldn't hesitate. She'd also heard some rumours about his wandering hands and worse from a female colleague so she'd decided to keep him at bargepole length.

'Well, it's quiet,' Ieva said, 'and I just hope it stays like that.'

'What's the story anyway?' Jason asked.

'What have they told you?' Ieva asked back.

'Nothing really,' Jason said with a shrug. 'I only pulled this shift because DC Morell was ill and I said that I needed some overtime.'

Ieva liked Alan Morell and hoped that he'd get well soon, especially if this was going to be a long job. For some reason she didn't trust Gabriel.

After a long pause Jason filled it by asking, 'It's some sort of witness protection I take it?'

If they'd hadn't told him anything then Ieva thought that it was probably for a very good reason.

'I've no idea,' she lied. 'They didn't tell me anything either.'

Jason thankfully went quiet for a while and she thought about the couple next door. She wondered how they were getting on. She'd offered to have an officer stay with them overnight but they both seemed quite happy to be left to their own devices.

Taken separately they were a very odd couple, an ex-villain and a woman in a wheelchair who was now the wrong side of thirty and looked it. She'd had a glance at their records at the station before she'd come over.

Callum's record wasn't as long as she'd have thought considering everything that she'd heard about him. He'd been quite busy when he'd been teenager, small-time robbery and violence mostly, but he'd obviously gotten better at it as he'd only been caught once in the years since then. She reminded herself of what had finally got him sent down. He'd been discovered in the act of breaking a man's fingers and kneecaps with a hammer. She once again wondered if she'd been right to leave him alone with a woman in a wheelchair.

Vicki's record had intrigued her most. She'd only ever been charged with one offence. 'Causing death by careless driving when unfit through drink or drugs' it had said at the top of her record sheet. The charge had eventually been dropped without it ever going to trial. She guessed that this was probably due to the severity of the injuries that Vicki herself had sustained in the car crash. She'd had several major operations on her spine afterwards but they'd only been carried out in order to try and stabilise the damage that had already been done. They'd managed to save her from being incontinent but she'd never walk again.

Ieva could fully understand why the charges against Vicki Jackman had been dropped. She was serving a life sentence anyway.

They were an odd couple alright but somehow, when taken together, Ieva thought that they didn't look that odd at all which she found quite strange.

As she was thinking this, in the flat next door, Callum was sitting on a chair in front of a small TV screen. The chair wasn't that comfortable and he'd had his doubts about whether or not it would take his weight for very long. He'd arranged for a second-hand sofa to be delivered in a couple of days from one of the homeless charities he'd been helping out with recently. He'd be glad when it came. Vicki had her wheelchair parked a few feet away to his left. They'd been watching a history programme about the Ancient Greeks and Callum had been fascinated by it, fascinated enough to completely forget about the chair for a while.

'They'd have loved you back then,' Vicki said with only a hint of sarcasm as the credits rolled up. 'They wouldn't have put you in jail but on the side of a vase in some sort of heroic pose holding a spear. They'd have probably written a poem about you too.'

'Well, I don't know about that,' Callum replied looking more than a little embarrassed. 'They lived in violent times too back then, didn't they? They certainly seemed to have had a lot of wars with those Persians.'

'Yes, they did but, in between all those wars, they still managed to create some of the greatest works of literature, science and architecture ever seen. They also invented democracy itself.'

'I never knew that,' Callum said with a shake of the head. 'It looks a beautiful place too.'

'Oh, it is,' Vicki said with a smile. 'I went to the Greek Islands often with...' She suddenly paused and the smile left her face. 'Well, anyway, they're lovely. I loved everything about them, the beaches, the people and the food but I found that I was most fascinated by the colours of the sea. I never knew that there was so many different shades of blues and greens in the world. I had some really happy times there. Have you done much travelling?'

Callum shrugged his shoulders.

'No, I've never been out of the country if I'm being honest.'

Vicki looked at him with near astonishment.

'Haven't you ever wanted to travel, to see different things?'

Callum was thoughtful for quite a while.

'I realise now that I was in a prison of my own making long before I went into prison for real. Being a criminal meant operating mostly at night and always having to watch your back. I only went to pubs where other criminals drank, always looking for a deal, an edge. I lived in a world within a world. I cut myself off from so much that most people take for granted. The last time I went to the cinema was when I was nine years old, after that I felt I was too tough to be seen in such places. I've never been to a theatre, never been on holiday, never sat down and watched a history programme on TV until just now. By the way it was really nice watching it with someone.'

'You've had a bit of a sad life really, haven't you?' Vicki said with some sympathy.

'Yes, I have. And what about you? How did you end up in that?' Callum asked as he gestured at the wheelchair.

Vicki looked at him but said nothing. She seemed to be trying to make a decision of some sort.

'I was in a car crash…I…'

She suddenly stopped and turned her face away. Callum still caught a glimpse of her pain. She then quickly moved her wheelchair towards the kitchen.

'Would you like a cup of tea?' she asked from over her shoulder.

'Yes, that would be nice but let me help you,' Callum said as he rose to his feet.

As they made and then drank their tea, they chatted about this and that and Callum was aware that she was trying to keep it light. He was also aware that the car crash was something that she didn't want to talk about and he could understand that. So, he tried to keep it light too and they successfully managed to talk about nothing until it was time for bed.

'I'm afraid that you'll have to make the bed up yourself but everything's there,' Vicki said. 'There are some scissors there too.'

'Scissors?'

'The plastic cover's still on the mattress,' she explained. 'I bought it in the hope that I might have some friends staying overnight…'

She shrugged and looked a little tearful.

Her sudden sadness pierced his heart. He wanted to pick her up and protect her from all the cruelties of the world. He didn't though. He just muttered his thanks and then she was gone.

Callum lay down on the bed after some minutes spent wrestling with the duvet cover. He'd eventually won but it had been a close thing. His feet hung over the end of the bed but that wasn't what made him feel strange and unsettled. Images flashed into his mind as he tried to sleep; her smile as she talked, her look of rapt concentration as she watched the TV, the way she flicked away a stray strand of hair that kept getting in her eyeline. He'd enjoyed being with her. Of course, he often enjoyed being with Francie or Reverend Tom too but this was different, very different. He felt a warmth run through his body. He suddenly wanted her and it was like nothing he'd ever felt before.

In prison he'd prided himself on being able to turn off his sexuality. He'd looked down on those who were so desperate that they'd have sex with another man even though they weren't gay. He could control it, keep it bottled up until he could do something about it. The strange thing is that, when he came out of prison, he found that he no longer wanted women in the way he'd done before. Before they had just been something to be used to scratch an itch and then discarded as quickly as possible. Since he'd been out, he'd learned to his surprise that women were people too.

He hadn't had sex for many years now. He'd managed to keep his sexuality at bay while he figured out where this new journey he was on might be taking him. In truth no-one he'd met so far had made him feel as if he wanted to break his self-imposed chastity anyway.

Until now.

He sat up and wondered what would happen if he went into her. He pictured himself opening the door and her turning to look at him. It wasn't a smile he saw on her face though, it was a look of horror. Who wouldn't be horrified at seeing a big tattooed monster like himself coming towards them in the night? He lay back on the bed totally convinced that there was no way in the world that she could possibly have any feelings for him and it made him feel sad.

That didn't make the wanting go away though.

Vicki sat in her wheelchair for some time before she attempted the tortuous business of getting into bed. Of course, she could have asked him to help her but for some reason she found that she couldn't. Then she thought of his strong arms lifting her bodily onto the bed and she had a sudden surge of an emotion that she hadn't felt for years. She thought of his big beautiful body lying next to hers, him kissing her, touching her. She looked at the wall. It was all that separated him from her.

She turned the wheel chair around and made towards the door not quite knowing what she was going to do. As she did so she caught sight of herself in the mirror and stopped dead. She looked at her useless legs and the tousled hair around a face that reminded her of her mother's. She looked old, she looked ugly. Who in their right mind would want that?

She went back and slowly got herself into bed. She'd been lonely for years now but that night she felt lonelier than ever.

Chapter Twenty-Four

The next morning, he and Jay talked through the case while they had breakfast in the police canteen. Jay had gone for black coffee, a croissant and yoghurt while Mac couldn't resist a sausage and egg sandwich washed down with an outsize mug of tea.

Mac had arranged a conference call with the rest of the team at nine thirty but, before they made the call, Jay checked in with the team who were covering Vicki Jackman's flat. They thankfully had nothing to report.

Peter and Manny were the first to call in, closely followed by Jo and Leigh. Mac went first and brought everyone up to date with the findings of the forensics reports, the fact that the attack of Alfred Feycourt had been videoed and the attempted kidnapping of Callum.

'Wow! You had a busy day yesterday,' Jo said. 'So, I take it that both witnesses to Mr. Feycourt's attack are now in protection?'

'Yes, we think that we've managed to keep all news of the video under wraps so both witnesses are staying at Miss Jackman's flat for the moment,' Mac replied. 'We've got men in the flat next door and cameras all over the place so they should be safe enough.'

'Well our day was a little more boring,' Jo said.

She then took them through what she'd found out from Professor Braithwaite's assistant and what she hadn't found out from talking to the two museum employees.

'What you've discovered about the Professor being in contact with one of LJ's political opponents could be incredibly important.' Mac said. 'I also think that your theory about LJ looking at the connections that the Professor had with both Bernie Bright and the Labour MP and then thinking that there might be a conspiracy against him could well hold some water too. Jo and Leigh that was really good work. Peter?'

'We've not got much to report except for the fact that our source has told us that the leaders of the Steeley Boys went absolutely ballistic when they heard about what happened yesterday. The failed attempt at snatching Callum McEachan was put together by one of the gang's enforcers called Skank Moussero who I mentioned before. He was the one who said that 'Little Jools' would be running the country soon. Well, our source saw him go into a meeting and then come out badly beaten. He asked our man to call him an ambulance before he collapsed in front of him. A few minutes afterwards Antonio Waynette and Tel Barklay came out and they don't look well pleased. Waynette had a bloodied baseball bat in his hand.'

'Waynette and Barklay are the two who appear to be running the Steeley Boys at the moment,' Manny interjected.

'We think that the main reason that Waynette was so pissed off was because the man who was killed during the botched kidnap happened to be his cousin,' Peter said. 'Our source says that the Steeley Boys are looking out for Callum and they won't be trying to take him alive this time.'

'That's more or less what we figured anyway,' Mac said. 'The question is why did they try to kidnap him in the first place when shooting him would have been so much easier? I take it that DCS Bolsover is none the wiser about all of this?'

'I've managed to keep him out of the loop so far,' Peter confirmed.

Mac then heard a voice that he hadn't been expecting.

'I'm sorry, I was hoping to be here on time for the call but I overslept.'

It was Martin Selby. Mac knew that he must have found something!

'Martin, what have you got?' he asked with some excitement.

'Well, you asked me to have a look at the video you sent over and, while nothing really stood out, something bothered me about it but I just couldn't put my finger on it,' Martin said.

Mac knew that feeling well.

'Then late last night it came to me,' Martin said. 'You asked me to concentrate on the attacker who was throwing matches and, although the video was a bit grainy at high resolution, I could still make out that there a sort of pattern on the sneakers he was wearing. It didn't make much sense to me at first and I thought that the pattern must have been blurred somehow. Then, while I was watching a music video, I saw a pair of sneakers that a rapper was wearing. They were made out of a sort of knitted fabric that seems to be quite fashionable nowadays and it suddenly made sense. I spent most of last night going through hundreds of images of sneakers before I found it.'

Mac could sense of collective holding of breath as Martin paused.

'I'm fairly certain that they're a rare edition of an Adidas sneaker called Red Apple. Only a few hundred pairs were made and they were all sold on the opening day of their new store in New York.'

'New York?' Mac said. 'Do you think that our attacker was American then?'

It was rare to find American street criminals working in the UK but not unheard of.

'No and this is where it gets really interesting. I'd been doing some research on LJ anyway and I realised that I'd seen those sneakers before. It was in a photo posted on Facebook in which a very excited young man could be seen holding a shoebox open displaying the sneakers. You can see the Adidas store front in the background,' Martin said.

'Who is he?' Mac asked feeling somewhat breathless.

'Well, the Facebook account was Sangredo's, sorry, LJ's own account and the young man was his seventeen year old son, Brian.'

The phone went quiet for more than a minute as everyone took this in.

'Hello? Are you still there?' Martin eventually asked.

'What do you know about LJ's son?' Mac asked.

'Not much really,' Martin replied, 'just what I learned from what he's posted on social media. He's currently studying at an expensive private school just outside London. There are the usual photos of him hanging out with his schoolfriends and listing all the music he likes but there were also some photos of him taken on the Steele Estate, some of which were taken with gang members. I'd guess that he's trying to look tough but he doesn't really succeed.'

'Thanks Martin,' Mac said with real sincerity, 'as usual you've come up with a crucial bit of evidence. We now have a narrative that's finally beginning to make some sense. So, here's what I think might have happened. Bernie Bright, broke and desperate, goes to see LJ and asks him for money with the threat that he'll tell what he knows otherwise. LJ realises that Bernie, being an alcoholic, is a liability and can't be trusted to keep his mouth shut when he's had a drink. So, he has him followed. Bernie's then seen in a pub being given money by an obviously well-heeled man and this starts the alarm bells ringing. So, he cooks up a plan and orders the Steeley Boys to kill Bernie and make it look like it's the work of some nutter. Then, some days afterwards, he discovers that the man seen with Bernie in the pub was none other than Professor Braithwaite. He'd already seen the Professor before, in a bar in the Houses of Parliament talking to his number one political enemy, and he must have felt that his secret was very close to being exposed. If the Professor was overheard talking about his proposed book 'The

Merchants of Death' then that might have only made his murder all the more necessary in LJ's eyes. So, the Professor is run over with, I'd bet, a stolen Mercedes SUV and that's mission accomplished as far as LJ is concerned. His secret is still safe.'

Mac paused as an idea occurred to him.

'Are you still there?' Jo eventually asked.

'Yes, I'm sorry about that,' Mac said. 'However, when I appear on the scene asking questions about Bernie, once again LJ feels that he's in danger and that he should do something about it. If he hadn't responded at all he might have been better off but I'd guess that he might be one of those people who, when they feel threatened, just have to react. So, they cooked up a plan to kill another homeless man with exactly the same MO thereby confirming that it was indeed a nutter who killed Bernie Bright in a random act of violence. Thankfully for us things didn't go according to plan as Callum turned up on the scene and spoilt their party. Things had now gotten worse instead of better for LJ as he had yet another threat to face, there was a witness to the attack. He knew that Callum must have talked to the police and that he was the only witness to his son's involvement in the attempted murder of Alfred Feycourt. I reckon that he wanted to know exactly what he'd said to us and how much trouble his son might be in. That's the reason why he didn't want Callum dead.'

'That makes sense,' Peter said, 'but why was his son there at all? As far as we know he isn't a member of the Steeley Boys.'

'Yes, I just had an idea about that. Consider it from the gang's viewpoint, one of their number is really smart and goes to university where he excels and makes connections. He then creates a persona for himself, the poor kid that made good through his own efforts, and enters politics. He ticks a lot of boxes in being from an ethnic minority and also from a desperately poor area. He also talks a lot about how people can pull themselves up by their own bootstraps just as he's done. His party lap it up and he becomes something of a star, in fact I believe that he's currently being touted as the next Home Secretary if Dominic De Gray becomes Prime Minister. A street gang member as Home Secretary and head of the UK police service, can you imagine that! However, the Steeley Boys must have gotten a little nervous about where LJ's allegiances might lie once he got his feet under the Home Secretary's desk. So, they decided that, after all the favours they'd done him, some insurance might be required. Brian Sangredo is just seventeen and he's studying at some expensive private school just outside London. From what Martin's just told us it's my bet that he's a gang wannabe and that he's probably boasted about the Steeley Boys to his rich schoolfriends so that he'd stand out. So, one night the gang give him the opportunity to prove himself and they take him along when they attack Alfred Feycourt ensuring that he's the one seen throwing the matches. Capturing his son on video taking part in a murder would be powerful insurance indeed. Even if he didn't love his son it would totally ruin his political career if it ever got out.'

'Yes, it all holds together,' Jo said, 'but what's the big secret that LJ is trying to keep covered up?'

'Now that's the crucial question,' Mac replied. 'Once we know that then we'll know just about all of it. I'm as certain as I can be that the answer lies in the museum somewhere. Jo and Leigh, you'll need to go back and speak to the people who work at the museum again. Get some help from Dan if you need it. See if you can get them back to the station and pressure them a little. If you get anything out of them let us know.'

'We're on it,' Jo said.

'Peter, can your source keep his ears open, especially about any action the gang might want to take against Callum?' Mac said. 'I'm sure that they're going to try something else before long.'

'Of course. It would be helpful if you could give us the direct number of the team guarding Callum McEachan and Miss Jackman just in case we need to contact them,' Peter said.

'Sure,' Jay said and read out the number to him.

'As for us we'll see what we can find out about the museum from this end. If any of you come up with a lead let me know straight away,' Mac said. 'We'll catch up tomorrow morning if nothing new comes up.'

Mac sat in silence for a few minutes after ending the phone conference. Jay didn't interrupt his thoughts.

'I think that we need to go back to the British War Museum. I'm hoping that someone might have had some second thoughts.'

As they drove Mac was deep in thought. He felt that they were almost there and that only one crucial fact was missing. What was it that Julian Sangredo was so desperately trying to cover up? His thoughts were eventually interrupted by Jay.

'Who's this DCS Bolsover then? Is he Peter Harper's boss?'

'Yes, he took over from me after I retired,' Mac replied.

'Why is he being kept out of the loop then?'

Mac explained Bolsover's links to Sangredo and how both Mac and Peter thought that he might compromise the whole investigation.

'As if it wasn't complicated enough,' Jay said. 'He's taking a chance though, isn't he? Peter Harper, I mean. If it all blows up it could cost him his job.'

Mac said nothing. He was all too well aware of the fact. He knew at some point they'd have to make DCS Bolsover aware of what they'd found but they'd have to make sure that the evidence against Sangredo was overwhelming. It still worried him though.

As they waited in the huge lobby of the museum Mac asked, 'Have you ever been here before?'

'Yes, a long time ago now, when I was at school. It's changed quite a bit since then,' Jay replied as he looked around. 'You said you've spoken to this Sir Joseph Adamson before?'

'Yes, he was under the impression that what was going on at the Museum of Modern Air Warfare was some sort of intelligence led operation although I've been told otherwise by someone who would know. I'm hoping that the interview might have got him thinking.'

The same bright and breezy young girl appeared and escorted them to Sir Joseph's office. He stood up as they walked in and shook hands with both of them. He was dressed somewhat more formally in a dark grey suit and deep red tie. He still had a pink shirt on. Mac introduced Jay.

'How can I help you this time?' Sir Joseph asked as he sat down.

'The case has progressed somewhat and we find that we're even more interested in the Museum of Modern Air Warfare and what they do there. I was hoping that you might have thought of something that could help us.'

Sir Joseph looked thoughtful for a moment.

'I have been thinking about it since we had our last meeting but I'm sorry, I've not come up with anything.'

'This Geoffrey Cummings, Mr. Sangredo's deputy at the Ministry of Defence, how did he suggest that the intelligence services might be involved?'

'Well, nothing he said that's for certain, it's probably more what he didn't say. I'm afraid that I got a bit mad with him stonewalling me and asked him outright if the spooks were running the show but he didn't reply. He just smiled and tapped the side of his nose. I took that as a yes.'

Mac found this very interesting.

'Is there anyone else in the aviation field I could speak to who might know something?'

Sir Joseph sat up and his features became more animated.

'Yes, yes of course. Why didn't I think of him before?'

He got a sheet of paper out of drawer and wrote on it. He passed it over to Mac. He'd written a name, an email address and a website on it.

'So, who's this Marcus Rawlinson then?' Mac asked.

'All I know is that he runs a private newsletter called 'Air Warfare News and Views'. It sounds a bit boring but over the past few years he's become one of the leading authorities on what's going on in the field. I'd guess that just about everyone connected with modern combat aircraft is subscribed to it.'

'And that's all you know about him?' Mac asked.

'Yes, that's it really. We've never met but I contact him from time to time via a messaging form on his website and then he emails me back from that address.'

Mac thanked Sir Joseph and left. As they walked back through the lobby Jay said, 'Well it certainly looks like this Geoffrey Cummings is up to his neck in whatever's going on.'

'It certainly does but, as he's the Deputy Minister, I'd guess that he'd have to be if whatever scam LJ is running was going to work,' Mac said.

Once they'd made it back to the car Mac took his phone out and sent Marcus Rawlinson an email.

'I'm hoping that he'll respond quite quickly but, just in case, can you phone his name in and see if you can get an address?'

Jay took his phone out but it rang before he could do anything. He put the phone to his ear.

Mac saw his face go grey as he listened.

'Christ!' he said softly. 'Christ!'

He put the phone down.

'We need to get over to Vicki Jackman's flat, right now!' he said as he started the car.

'What's happened?' Mac asked fearing the worst.

'The message was a bit garbled but I've just been told that they've got three dead bodies over there.'

Chapter Twenty-Five

Ieva had come on shift at ten that morning and she still had another four hours to go. She gazed at the monitors and the comings and goings in the flats that surrounded them. She was beginning to recognise people and to tune in to the patterns of their movements.

Once again, her partner for the shift was DS Jason Gabriel. Alan Morell was due to be back from sick leave in a couple of days and she couldn't wait. She'd found Jason to be a bit strange to say the least. Yesterday he was really chatty and asking all sorts of questions about the case but today he seemed to be on edge and had hardly said a word. However, this suited her as it gave her some time to think.

Her parents' anniversary was coming up fast and she'd discussed what they were going to do to celebrate it with her younger brother the evening before. Next month they will have been married for thirty years and she wanted to arrange something special for them. She thought that they'd been so brave in coming thousands of miles to a new country in search of a better life. Her mother had been pregnant with her when they'd left Vilnius for London and she'd been determined that her child was going to be born in England. And that's the way it had happened.

She smiled as she thought of the little grey-haired woman who had given birth to her. There was definitely some steel in her.

'Postie,' Jason said in a bored monotone as he pointed at the screen.

A man in a postman's uniform had entered the building and made for the stairs. He emerged onto the first-floor landing and pulled a small parcel from his sack. He looked at the address and then looked at the doors of the flats. He then made his way down the walkway and stopped outside their door. They heard a sharp rapping on the door.

'It must be for the people who used to live here. I'll go and get it,' Ieva said.

Jason shrugged.

Ieva opened the door to find that the postman wasn't holding a parcel but a pistol with a long silencer mounted on it. He shot her in the head and she fell to the floor. He then shot her in the heart twice and once again in the head. He closed the front door behind him and made his way into the living room. Jason Gabriel was cowering and walking backwards away from the postman.

'No, no this wasn't supposed to happen like...'

His words were stopped by the bullet that had entered his head. He also received three more bullets after he'd hit the floor.

The man sat on a chair and smiled as he reloaded the pistol.

'Two down, two to go,' he said softly to himself.

He waited for a moment and then went back outside, closing the door gently behind him. He went to the flat next door and rang the bell. The door opened and he raised the gun and aimed it at a flash of movement. He looked puzzled when he realised that it was the head of a mop he was looking at. It took him a split second to look down and see Callum crouching on the floor. In that split second Callum had inserted a knife into the man's groin just behind his scrotum. The man lowered his arm and tried to aim at Callum but Callum's strong hand had already caught him by the wrist. Callum then stood up keeping the man's arm high above him. Two bullets flew into the ceiling. As he stood up Callum also pulled the knife upwards with all his force. It sliced through the man's scrotum and lower belly. The blood gushed out and Callum knew that he would be dead in matter of seconds. He prised the gun from the man's hand just before he slumped lifeless to the floor.

Callum looked up and down the walkway. He noticed that the door of the flat that the police were using was shut. He guessed that the postman must have paid them a visit first. He closed the door and put the gun into the pocket of his jacket that was hanging near the door. He then pressed the panic button that was hanging around his neck before he went back to Vicki who was in her bedroom. He poked his head around the door so she wouldn't be able to see the blood on his hand.

'It's okay,' Callum told her with a reassuring smile. 'It was just the postman. He had the wrong address as it turned out.'

It took three minutes before the police showed up. Jay and Mac turned up twenty minutes later. It had taken them that long to cross the river from

Lambeth even with the sirens going. One of Jay's detectives, a weary looking man in his late thirties who was introduced as DS Jim Johns, walked them through what had happened.

'We've had a quick look at the CCTV and it seems that the killer came dressed as a postman and first knocked on the door of the flat that we were using as a base,' he said as they walked towards the door. 'Ieva answered it and he shot her four times.'

The door was open and Mac and Jay could see her body lying in the hallway. The four bullet holes were clearly visible.

A very professional hit, Mac thought, while at the same time feeling intensely sad at such a promising young life having been cut short.

'He then went inside and shot DS Gabriel four times too. Forensics are in there now so we'd better leave them to it. The pistol used was American, a Nighthawk, and it was fitted with a silencer.'

They all turned and looked at the body on the floor. It had obviously been moved a few feet to one side as a wide blood track led away from the door of the flat. His lower abdomen had been sliced wide open from his crotch to his belly button. The knife was still deeply embedded in his body. Mac looked at his face. The dead man was in his mid-thirties, slightly balding and intensely anonymous.

Not a bad thing if you're a professional killer, Mac thought.

'Your Mr. McEachan did that to him. It looks like Miss Jackman was right when she said that she'd feel safer with him,' DS Johns said.

'Where have you moved them to?' Jay asked as he looked at the bloody tracks left by a wheelchair.

'McEachan and Miss Jackman should be back at the station by now. We took them in an armoured van with an armed escort,' DS Johns said.

'Do we know exactly what happened here yet?' Mac asked.

'I haven't spoken to McEachan yet in any detail but, from what we could see on the CCTV footage, the postman raised and aimed his gun when the door opened but he found himself looking at a mophead. I'd guess that McEachan was down on his knees and he stabbed the postman from that position. We only see him when he stands up and he's gripping the postman's wrist so that the gun's pointed up and away from at him. McEachan took the gun from the man's hand just before he dropped to the floor. He then looked up and down the walkway before shutting the door. Judging by the time stamp on the video he must have pushed the panic button right after that.'

'Okay I'll leave you to look after the crime scene,' Jay said. 'Call me if forensics come up with anything. Come on Mac, let's go and talk to Callum.'

Mac was pensive as they drove to the station.

'How on earth did they find out about Vicki and where she lived? I thought you said that only the police team knew about Vicki and the video.'

'Only they did know,' Jay said giving Mac a bleak look.

Callum and Vicki were being held in separate secure interview rooms in a section of the station that Mac hadn't visited before. Armed policemen guarded the entrance that led into the area and they also stood outside both interview rooms. Mac guessed that it had originally been designed for holding terrorists. They had a quick word with Vicki Jackman first. She looked pale and agitated.

'Did Callum really kill that man?' she asked as soon as they walked inside the door.

'Yes, yes he did,' Mac said.

He could see a look of intense disappointment on her face.

'He saved your life,' Mac continued. 'We think that the man that Callum killed was a professional assassin. He killed the two police officers who were in the flat next door before he knocked on your door.'

Her hand went to her mouth. Mac could see the shock in her eyes.

'That nice policewoman, she's dead?'

Mac nodded. He turned and glanced at Jay. He looked almost as shocked as Vicki did. He guessed that what had happened to his colleagues was only just sinking in.

'If it hadn't been for Callum's quick thinking, you'd be dead too,' Mac said. 'Did you see or hear anything?'

Vicki shook her head.

'I was having a chat with Callum about a programme we'd been watching on the TV when he suddenly went quiet. He put his finger to his lips, pushed me into the bedroom and closed the door behind me. I heard a few sounds but I couldn't make out what they were. Then Callum poked his head around the door saying that it was just the postman and that he'd gotten the wrong address. A few minutes after that the flat was full of policemen and most of them had guns. Without a word one of them pushed me out of the door past a dead body that was lying in a pool of blood and then we were whizzed off in a van. Now I'm here, still trying to get my head around what's happened.'

'We're going to go next door and talk to Callum now but we won't be too long. Is there anything we can get you while you're waiting?' Mac asked.

'A glass of water would be good, oh and tell Callum...' she stopped obviously unsure of what to say. 'Just tell him thanks.'

Mac nodded noticing that she looked more scared than thankful. Jay arranged for the glass of water and then they opened the door of the interview room that held Callum. He too appeared to be agitated and he was pacing up and down. The memory of the tiger in the zoo came back into Mac's head.

'How is she?' Callum asked with a worried expression.

'She's a little shocked but she's okay. She told me to say thanks for saving her life,' Mac replied. 'Sit down and tell us exactly what happened.'

Callum sat down but he looked uneasy. His left leg moved up and down of its own accord making the table shake slightly. He put his hand on his knee and the shaking stopped.

'Me and Vicki were having a chat about Cyprus. We'd just finished watching a programme and it was all about a war in the seventies that had divided the island. It was really interesting. I was enjoying talking to Vicki about it when I thought I heard something. I'm still not sure exactly what it was but it set the alarms off, if you know what I mean. So, I pushed Vicki into her bedroom and shut the door. Then I heard a rapping on the door.

'Postman' a voice said.

I could see a blurred figure through the frosted glass panel in the door. I thought it was strange that one of the policemen from next door hadn't intercepted him so I didn't take any chances. I took a mop from the cupboard and then pulled a knife that I'd put in the pocket of my jacket near the door. I'd sharpened it and put it there just in case.'

Mac and Jay glanced over at each other.

'I got down on my knees, waved the mophead near the glass and then opened the door. He aimed his gun at the mophead and that was his mistake. I stabbed him in the groin and then caught his arm as it came down so he couldn't aim the gun at me. I stood up and pulled the knife upwards as hard as I could.'

Callum looked down at the table with a despairing look.

'I promised myself that I'd never do that again but I couldn't help it.'

'You did exactly the right thing Callum,' Mac said. 'He'd have killed both you and Vicki if you'd have given him any sort of a chance.'

'Thanks Mac, I needed to hear that. Anyway, I waited for a few seconds knowing that the loss of blood would kill him pretty quickly and then I took the gun and let him fall. I made sure that there wasn't anyone else around and then I shut the door. I put the gun in my jacket pocket, pressed the panic button and then told Vicki that it was the postie and that he'd gotten the wrong address.'

Mac thought that Callum had only been telling the truth when he'd said that.

'I honestly didn't know what else to tell her,' Callum said. 'What about the policewoman next door?'

'He got her and her colleague first,' Jay replied with some bitterness.

Callum didn't look at all surprised.

'I figured that he'd look after them first. He was a professional, wasn't he?'

'Yes, it certainly looks that way,' Mac replied. 'The gun's American and not one we'd normally see over here. I'd guess that the Steeley Boys had brought in someone to do their dirty work for them.'

'Was Vicki really okay though?' Callum asked looking somewhat desperate. 'I'll never forget the look on her face as they wheeled her out of the flat. She looked at the body and then at the blood on my hand. She was scared, scared of me. I could tell.'

'You'll have the chance to ask her yourself soon if you like,' Jay said. 'But first, if I were you, I'd have a shower and wash the blood off. I'll see if I can get you some clean clothes. Just take it easy, we'll be back soon.'

Outside in the hallway Jay said, 'I think he quite likes her, doesn't he?'

'Yes, I think he does too,' Mac said. 'The question is could she ever like him now she's seen exactly what he's capable of?'

Jay could only reply with a shrug before saying, 'I think the Police Rugby Team's kit is kept around here somewhere. It's our only chance of finding anything that'll fit him.'

Mac got himself a much-needed coffee and waited in Jay's office while he hunted for some clothes for Callum. He was enjoying the silence when his phone pinged. He had an email. It was from Marcus Rawlinson. He opened it up. The email was brief, it gave an address in Crouch End and said that he'd be free anytime after four o'clock. It was now three thirty.

'Well, I managed to get him something,' Jay said as he walked in. 'He's in the shower now.'

'I take it that you're going to be busy for a while?' Mac asked.

'You can say that again. I'll need to let Ieva's family know what's happened,' Jay said with a frown. 'I've met her mother and father before, they're a lovely couple so I'm not looking forward to that at all. I'll have to do the same for DS Gabriel's family too.'

Mac showed him the email.

'Would you mind if I chase this up by myself then?' Mac asked. 'It should only take a couple of hours or so. I can meet you back here later and we can discuss where we're up to then.'

'That sounds good to me. However, it might be wise to let some uniforms drive you there,' Jay suggested.

'I'd just as soon get going,' Mac said not wanting to waste any time. 'Crouch End should be safe enough and no-one knows I'm going there anyway apart from this Mr. Rawlinson.'

'Okay, it's your call. It's just as well the wife's away, she wouldn't be seeing much of me anyway,' Jay said with a sigh. 'I'll see you later then.'

The traffic was slow as the rush hour had just begun and it only got slower the closer he got to the Finsbury Park area. He kept looking in the rear-view mirror but he still couldn't pick out who was following him. He was fairly sure that someone was trailing him but, whoever it was, they were good.

Then a green Almera, very like his own, pulled out a little further up in the queue and indicated to turn right. Mac saw a car pull out behind him in his wing mirror before quickly pulling back in. He smiled. He'd been right about being followed.

He was driving north and the thought struck him that he was getting ever closer to the Steele Estate. Luckily, this would be as close as he'd get as he'd soon be heading east towards Crouch End. Even though the traffic eased a little it was after four thirty by the time he pulled up outside a three-storied Victorian villa in Dashwood Street. It was a nice part of the area and Mac guessed that such a house wouldn't come cheap. A long concrete ramp ran up to the front door. He rang the bell and wondered what an aviation expert might look like.

The man who answered the door was slim, quite good looking, in his early thirties and bearded. He looked vaguely familiar and Mac wondered if he'd seen him on TV or something.

'Mr. Rawlinson?' Mac asked.

'Yes?' the man said looking puzzled at first. 'Oh, are you the man that Marcus said was coming? Mr. Maguire isn't it? Come in.'

Mac followed him inside the house and into a wide hallway. It was decorated in keeping with its Victorian heritage being old-fashioned and with years of collected clutter on display. Mac instantly liked it.

'By the way I'm Jonny, Marcus' younger brother. He's in here,' he said as he slid open two large double doors that ran on rollers.

A man in a wheelchair turned around and faced him. He looked as if the two halves of his body belonged to different people. His legs looked thin and lifeless while, in direct contrast, his upper body was muscled and powerful. His hair was fashionably long, blond and tousled, his jaw square and determined. He smiled at Mac and held his hand out as he rolled towards him.

'Mr. Maguire, please sit down,' he said as he pointed towards a sofa. 'How can I help the police?'

'Sir Joseph Adamson at the War Museum gave me your name. I'm helping the police out with a murder case and we're interested in the Museum of Modern Air Warfare in Duxford. Sir Joseph thought that you might be able to tell me something about it,' Mac asked.

His hopes of learning anything new fell when he saw a look of puzzlement on Marcus' face.

'I'm afraid that I can't tell you anything at all about the museum. I first heard about it some years ago and it surprised me that anyone thought it would be a good idea as it was so close to the

British War Museum. I've heard absolutely nothing about it since so I'd guess that I might have been right.'

Mac decided to take a chance and tell him what he knew.

'Okay, here's what we know about the museum and I'd be interested in seeing what you make of it. It only employs a few people, all ex-Harrier mechanics and storemen, but, even then, they're not always there. They seem to work intensely for a few weeks and then not at all for even more weeks. Vans and lorries are seen going in and out and, every now and again, a low-loader with what we think might be an aircraft fuselage on board goes in during the night. Any thoughts?'

Marcus slowly shook his head.

'Any idea what exactly might have been on the low-loaders?'

'Well, Sir Joseph said that the museum had managed to get their hands on some Harriers that were being decommissioned. It most likely would have been those, I'd guess,' Mac replied.

Marcus was thoughtful for quite some time. He then wheeled himself over to a broad L-shaped desk that had a computer keyboard and two monitor screens on it. He looked for something on one of the screens and then gestured for Mac to come over.

'I'm wondering if this might be relevant,' he said pointing to the screen.

It was an article on his website. It was entitled 'The Mystery of the Middle Eastern Harrier

Reliability Envelope' and it was written by 'Tam McNaught and Marcus Rawlinson'.

'Tam McNaught is an old Harrier hand and he was part of the team that did most of the initial reliability analyses for the aircraft. We were having an online chat a few months ago when he said that there was something niggling him. Two Middle-Eastern governments bought quite a few aircraft from us some years ago. We fell out with them when the world found out that they were using the Harriers as mobile gun platforms against their own people when they were out on the streets protesting. The UN voted unanimously for strict arms control sanctions against both countries so, in principle at least, they should be deprived of any spare parts if and when the aircraft broke down. Tam pointed out the fact that, between them, the two countries had fifteen Harriers and to date all of the aircraft were still operational. And that's what had been doing Tam's head in.'

'I take it that some of the planes should have broken down in that time?' Mac said.

'That's right. In fact, according to Tam's calculations, only six of the aircraft should be fit to fly by now and Tam's very proud of his figures. So, either Tam and his whole team were wrong or...'

'Or someone's been supplying them with spare parts in contravention of UN sanctions,' Mac said finishing the point. 'How much could you sell these spare parts for?'

'Well, if you run a car you know that any spare part seems to cost an arm and a leg these days and it's much, much worse in the air sector. However, breaking UN sanctions is a serious business so I'd guess they'd get at least fifty or even a hundred times what the list price would be, maybe more for certain parts.'

'So, it would be well worth it then, if you could get away with it.'

'Yes, that would be the trick, getting away with it,' Marcus said. 'And not having a conscience would help too.'

Mac was thoughtful for a while.

'Do you think it's possible that the museum was getting the Harriers and then stripping them down and selling the parts?'

'From what you've just told me I'd say it was highly likely. Since Tam and I wrote that article, a group of us have been on the look out for any clues to who might have been supplying the parts but we've found nothing so far. Your museum sounds like an excellent candidate to me.'

'Me too,' Mac said suddenly looking serious. 'Can you get on to your group and see if they can come up with anything else that might help?'

'I'll do that right away,' Marcus said.

They were interrupted by the door sliding open. A beautiful young woman in a nurse's uniform came in. At first Mac thought she might be Marcus' carer but he dismissed this notion when he saw his face light up with a smile as she came into the room. She tousled Marcus' hair and then gave him a kiss on the cheek. Mac had the feeling that it would have been much more if he hadn't been there.

'This is my wife, Allie,' Marcus said with a wide smile.

He then introduced Mac.

'Nice to meet you Mr. Maguire. I'll just go and change,' she said leaving them to it.

A thought occurred to Mac as he watched her go into the bedroom.

'Be careful Marcus and tell your group to keep a low profile too. Some of the people involved in this case will stop at nothing.'

'The same thought has occurred to me,' he replied with a frown as he too looked towards the bedroom door. 'Have you got a number I can call if we find anything?'

Mac gave him his mobile number and Jay's as well, just in case. Mac was curious and wanted to know more about Marcus so he thought that he might just as well ask.

'Do you mind me asking how you got to become an aviation expert?'

'Well, I've been mad on aircraft since I was a small child. As soon as I was old enough, I joined the Air Cadets. Being a pilot was all I ever wanted to be,' he said somewhat ruefully.

'So, what happened?'

'Well, at least part of my dream worked out. I joined the RAF and started pilot training but, unfortunately, it didn't last long. A friend of mine, another trainee, had just gotten a new motorbike so we took it out for a spin. We were going too fast, of course, but I didn't tell him to slow down, like him I found speed exhilarating. He didn't really do anything wrong either but you're not exactly well protected when you come off a motorbike. We hit a pool of diesel and the bike slid off the road and right into a tree. Jack, who was driving, was killed instantly and I ended up like this.'

'You must have been devastated,' Mac said.

'I was, it's taken me years to accept what's happened. After the accident I had my ups and downs, probably more downs that ups if I'm honest. In fact, there were times when I was so depressed that I couldn't even get out of bed. I somehow got on with life but it was only when I met Allie that I really turned a corner.'

'She's a nurse?' Mac asked.

'A physiotherapist actually. She's really good too, I should know she was mine for a while,' Marcus said with a rueful smile. 'There was a time that I actually hated her believe it or not. I kept telling her that I couldn't do something while she kept insisting that I could. She used to shout at me and she was a real bitch but, of course, she was right. Then I gradually stopped hating her and started looking forward to our time together. When we had our last session, she asked me why I looked so miserable. For once I gave her a totally honest answer. I said that I'd miss her, you know, that I'd really miss her. She told me that she actually had a life outside of work and suggested that we could always go out somewhere for a drink. So, we did. At first, I just thought that she just pitied me or something but she soon made it clear that it wasn't pity, she actually liked me. That's when I think I really started to heal. She's the best thing that ever happened to me but if I hadn't been for the accident then we'd have never met and, even with working legs, I'd have been the poorer for it.'

'That's a good story,' Mac said with a smile. 'Look after yourself and let me know if you come up with anything.'

Mac let himself out. He was still smiling as he climbed into the car. The smile disappeared though when he thought of what he'd just learned and the serious turn that the case had just taken. He was still thinking about this as he drove off.

Perhaps that's why he didn't notice the big black Mercedes four-by-four pull in right behind him.

Chapter Twenty-Six

Peter Harper was up to his neck in paperwork when he got the call. He absolutely loathed paperwork even though it was mostly done online these days. The Home Office had requested further information about a murder suspect who had fled to the United States, information that he'd already given them at least twice before. He loathed anything to do with extraditions as well, it seemed to be a never-ending process and the paperwork involved felt never-ending too.

In this case a porter had been found dead in a laundry trolley in the basement of a hotel. It was one of London's older and more expensive hotels and it still had a working laundry chute on each floor. It was an easy assumption to make that someone had killed the porter and then dumped his body into the laundry chute from one of the upper floors. The porter had died after he'd received a single blow to the jaw. He'd then fallen onto a hard surface causing the back of his skull to crack. This had been followed by a massive bleed on the brain which had been the actual cause of death. Luckily, some of the assailant's DNA had been recovered from the dead man's body. That, coupled with the porter's last room service request, led them to issue an arrest warrant for one Lou Spangler.

It turned out that Mr. Spangler was a former wrestler and minor celebrity in the United States. He'd been over in the UK doing a bit part in an upcoming superhero movie being filmed at Pinewood Studios. Mr. Spangler, however, was nowhere to be found at the hotel. In fact, at the exact time that the porter's body had been discovered, he'd been climbing the steps of a plane bound for Los Angeles. Luckily, the flight he'd bought at the very last minute had a stopover which gave them some extra time. This meant that the conclusive DNA evidence was in well before the plane reached Los Angeles. As soon as it had landed a detachment from the Airport Police Department boarded the plane and took Mr. Spangler away in handcuffs.

Peter was trying to concentrate and get the form completed so he could get back to some real work when his phone went off. He grumbled to himself as he picked up the phone. The number was unfamiliar as was the voice.

'DI Harper, your friend Mr. Maguire has just been taken away by some armed men in a black Mercedes SUV. It happened just now on Dashwood Road, Crouch End. They bundled him into the SUV and then one of the men got into his car and drove that away too. You'll find it parked on Quernmore Road near the rail station.'

The man rang off without saying anything else. For some reason Peter didn't doubt a word of what he'd just heard. His heart thumping, he found the number of the nearest police station and told them to send a car to Quernmore Road to see if they could find a green Almera and another to Dashwood Road to see if they could find anyone who had witnessed an abduction.

He didn't waste any time waiting for them to call back. He phoned Manny Ibbotson and told him to get back to the station immediately. He then called Specialist Firearms Command and got the ball rolling with them. He was able to quickly arrange a meeting with an Inspector Jenny Kelvin.

By that time the local police had gotten back to him. They'd found Mac's car just where the caller had said it was. The keys were still in the ignition. There was no sign of Mac.

He then rang Jo Dugdale and briefly told her what had happened. He said he'd call her back when the meeting was set up. He next rang Jay Patterson and brought him up to date.

After seeing Ieva's parents Jay had thought that his day just couldn't get any worse. He'd been wrong.

'He was going to see someone called Marcus Rawlinson in Crouch End,' Jay said trying to keep his voice sounding normal. 'He's some sort of aviation expert apparently. I wonder if it was him who called it in?'

'I'll get the uniforms who are on the scene to check him out. We're having a meeting in half an hour or so.' Peter asked. 'Jo and Leigh will be calling in but if you make it over here it might be better.'

'I'll be there,' Jay said.

He was nearly out of the front door of the station when he had a thought. He ran back and went into the room where Callum was waiting. He was wearing a police rugby shirt and shorts and looked as if he was ready to run out at Twickenham.

'Callum, can you come with me? I'll explain in the car,' Jay said with some urgency.

Callum just nodded and followed him out. Jay almost ran but Callum only had to walk a little faster to keep up with him. He had to hang on tight though as the police car, sirens wailing, sped off and then swooped in and out of the traffic.

'The Steeley Boys have Mac,' Jay explained as he swung the car around a corner. 'A black Mercedes SUV full of armed men picked him up in Crouch End a short while ago.'

Callum was quiet while he gave this some thought.

'They must be getting really desperate. Poor Mac, he won't stand a chance if they get him back to the estate.'

'That's why I brought you along. Mac said that you'd once conducted a sort of war against the gang. Is that right?' Jay asked.

'Yes, that's right enough but that was nearly ten years ago.'

'Believe me nothing much has changed on the estate since then, apart from them putting some new cladding on the high rises to make them look less shitty that is. I've absolutely no idea what I can do to help Mac but I was hoping that, as you know the estate, you might be able to come up with something.'

Jay soon had to stop talking and concentrate on trying to make some progress. The traffic was becoming heavier as they neared the Holborn area and Jay decided to take to the back streets in the hope of avoiding the worst of the jams. Unfortunately, so did a lot of other drivers and the going was still slower than Jay would have liked.

Callum was quiet for the rest of the ride. He was trying to remember exactly what the Steele Estate had been like. Unfortunately, it also brought back some sharp memories from his former life, along with some regrets that burnt like acid.

It took them just over a half an hour before they pulled up outside the station and the meeting was already underway when they entered the room. Three people stood around a table. A woman in her late thirties dressed in a smart black uniform and a middle-aged man in a wrinkled suit were listening to another man who was speaking. He was of medium height but he had a stocky muscular build and, from the way he held himself, Jay guessed that he was ex-military.

Jay couldn't help but notice the look of surprise on the face of the man who had been speaking when he laid eyes on Callum. He instinctively took a step back before he regained his composure.

'Sergeant Harper,' Callum said as he stepped forward and offered his hand.

'It's DI Harper now,' he said with an uncertain smile as he shook his hand.

Although Mac had told him about Callum, he realised that he hadn't quite believed him until now. He'd been right though. The Tiger had definitely changed.

'You must be DI Patterson,' Peter said offering him his hand.

'Just call me Jay.'

'Okay Jay and Callum, this is DS Manny Ibbotson from my team,' Peter said pointing to the middle-aged man, 'and this is Inspector Jenny Kelvin from CT-SFO, our firearms team. I've asked her to attend as I'd guess that any plan that we might come up will involve the use of firearm officers. We've got Jo Dugdale and Leigh Marston on the phone and I've also asked our source on the Steele Estate to come in and he should be with us any minute. It'll mean that we might have to blow his cover but that can't be helped.'

'Are you sure that this phone call was for real?' Jay asked.

'I believed it right away,' Peter replied. 'However, the uniforms on the scene have confirmed everything I was told. They've got two witnesses who saw a man using a crutch being taken away in a Mercedes SUV. We tried to follow the SUV by helicopter but they were already on the Steele Estate by the time we caught up with them. It wasn't this Marcus Rawlinson who called it in either. I spoke to him a few minutes ago and what he told me throws a different light on the whole case. The stakes are much higher than we could have dreamt possible.'

Peter took a deep breath and told them what he'd learned. He was about to start off again when one of his team walked in and gave him a message. He read it carefully.

'At last some good news, well I'm hoping it's good news anyway,' Peter said. 'Julian Sangredo is still at the Houses of Parliament as there's a vital vote on an amendment to a bill that he's sponsored. The vote's been delayed so that might give us a little more time.'

Seeing the puzzled look on Jay's face he carried on, 'We're assuming that Sangredo will want to be there when the gang interrogate Mac. I've got some people at the Houses of Parliament who'll follow him once the vote's over. We're hoping that he'll be heading straight for the Steele Estate.'

'And if he doesn't?' Jay asked.

'Well, if he doesn't, we can only assume that Mac's already dead,' Peter replied with a bleak expression.

They all looked at each other and were silent for a while. It was Callum who broke the silence.

'Are you hoping to go in and get him?' he asked.

Peter looked up at him in surprise.

'If I'm honest, I don't know, but I'd only be willing to risk more lives if we had a reasonable chance of success. That may well depend on what DS Best has to tell us. He's been working undercover on the estate for some months now and I'm hoping against hope that he might know where Mac is being kept and whether a rescue attempt is even possible.'

'It might be worth discussing what you'd need from us,' Inspector Kelvin said. 'I can start assembling a team just in case.'

'Well, we know that the gang is likely to be armed and we've got to be sure that, whatever happens, we outgun them. Of course, that needs to be balanced against how many officers we can fit into whatever we're using to transport them into the estate. So, I guess the first thing we'll need to arrange is to get some black Mercedes SUVs. They might provide us with some camouflage while we're on the estate.'

'There's a big Mercedes dealership not far from here,' Manny said. 'I can get someone around there.'

'Good thinking. See to it now,' Peter said.

Manny left the room at surprising speed.

'What is it that your people are using these days?' Peter asked.

'For an operation like this the team would be kitted out with Sig-Sauer MCXs,' Inspector Kelvin replied. 'They're fully automatic and can fire up to nine hundred rounds per minute. The magazine has thirty bullets and each officer will be carrying three spares. If it does come to a firefight, we can guarantee that it won't last long.'

Peter looked suitably impressed. He was about to say something when the door opened and someone who might have just escaped from a rapper's convention walked in. It was Jay's turn to look surprised when Peter introduced him as Detective Sergeant Dion Best.

'What have you got for us?' Peter asked with some urgency.

'Something big is going down alright, the whole gang have been scrambled. From what I can make out they're holding someone in Nightingale Tower. I'd guess that it must be Mac.'

'In the underground car park?' Callum asked.

'Yes, but how could you have known that?' Dion said as he looked up at Callum with a puzzled expression.

'This is Callum McEachan,' Jay said. 'He once waged something of a one-man war against the Steeley Boys some years ago. He knew the estate well so I was hoping that he might be able to help us.'

'That was good thinking,' Peter said.

'There are gang members guarding all the entrances to the car park and some of them are armed,' Dion continued. 'They've also got some spotters on the route that you'd have to take from the main road to the tower.'

'So, what would happen if we just went in there and tried to snatch Mac?' Peter asked hopefully.

His hope disappeared as Dion slowly shook his head before answering.

'They'll be expecting something like that. Even if the spotters didn't see you driving towards the tower, which they would as it's the only way in, they've also got people guarding the entrance to the car park itself. The only other way of getting into the car park is from one of the lifts but they've got that guarded too. So, if anyone spots anything, all they'll need to do is to send a text to whoever is holding Mac and they'll have him straight into that lift. They'll take him up to the top floor and get rid of the evidence by throwing him out of a window. They've done it before.'

'How many floors does the tower have?' Peter asked.

'Twenty-four,' Dion replied.

This was followed by a long silence.

'What if the guards are taken out?' Callum asked.

They all looked at him as if he'd just spoken in a foreign language.

'How could you even do that? They're working in groups and I've heard that they've put out all the guns they can get their hands on. That'll mean that at least one man in each group is likely to be armed,' Dion said. 'You'd have to take all of them out at once and without anyone noticing. How would that even be possible?'

'I've done it before,' Callum said.

Dion turned and looked at Peter with a question on his face.

'He really has,' Peter said in confirmation. 'Let's get a map of the estate up on the screen. Jo and Leigh, I'll screen share it with you. So, Dion, show us where they've placed the guards.'

Dion pointed out exactly where the gang had stationed their lookouts.

'So, we'd need to take out the three spotters here on the road that leads to Nightingale Tower, the two men watching the slip road down to the car park, the four men guarding the vehicle entrance and exit and whoever is guarding the entrance to the lift. Is that it?' Peter asked.

'Yes, and not forgetting that there'll be at least five or six gang members holding Mac as well,' Dion said. 'Some of those will probably be armed too.'

'It sounds like something from Mission Impossible to me,' Jo said glumly.

'It can be done,' Callum said.

Everyone looked up at him in wonder except for Peter.

'Well, we'll see,' Peter said before turning back to Dion. 'You're sure that there's no other way of accessing the car park?'

'No,' Dion replied. 'The council blocked off any access by the two sets of stairs that originally went down there. They also stopped the lifts going down there too but I heard that the gang threatened the lift engineers into giving them a key which means that only they can access the car park.'

'What's the car park like?' Inspector Kelvin asked.

'It's just a big wide-open space with lots of support columns,' Dion replied. 'The council also cut off all electricity but the gang have run an extension lead down there. They've got some lights rigged up at the far end but most of the car park is in darkness.'

'Well, that might be something we can use to our advantage,' Peter said. 'Let's see if we can put a plan together.'

'What about your boss, DCS Bolsover? Won't he want a say in this?' Inspector Kelvin asked.

Peter hesitated slightly before he said, 'He seems to be out of touch at the moment but that's no problem. He's given me full authority to proceed with an operation if I feel that it's required.'

Jay looked up at this. Jenny Kelvin seemed to accept what Peter had said at face value, it wasn't any skin of her nose of course, but he'd also noticed Manny Ibbotson's reaction. He was surprised at his boss's words although he quickly covered it up.

Jay thought back to what Mac had said about DCS Bolsover's connections to Sangredo. He knew that Peter and Mac went back a long way and he could understand why he'd do everything he could to get his old boss back in one piece. He also knew that Peter was gambling his job and his pension if he went ahead with an armed operation without full authority.

They went through all of the various options but Jenny Kelvin still appeared to be quite sceptical.

'The main problem is, of course, those guards. If we could somehow get a squad of my officers into the car park without those inside knowing then I think we'd have a good chance of success. Otherwise it would just be a trap.'

Peter couldn't refute her logic. Getting those guards quietly out of the way was the key. But how?

'I'm going to need to start getting my team together,' Jenny Kelvin said. 'If you can send me the layout of the car park then I'll start taking them through it.'

'Of course,' Peter said. 'We'll start working on a plan for ensuring you get a clear run. However, if we can't come up with anything or if Sangredo doesn't head for the Steele Estate after the Parliamentary vote, I'll let you know so you can stand your team down. By the way, what will the team consist of?'

'I think a sergeant and five officers should do it,' she replied. 'I could send a bigger team but it looks as if your transport will be somewhat limited.'

'That sounds like it should be enough,' Peter said with a smile.

The smile disappeared as soon as Jenny Kelvin left. Peter knew that there was really only one option available to him but, if he took it, he would be taking the biggest gamble of his life. He wasn't that worried about his job. If he did nothing and Mac died then he knew he'd probably quit the force anyway. His heart wouldn't be in it. Even if they saved Mac, he knew that he'd probably be fired shortly afterwards for mounting an armed operation without the authority to do so. He also suspected that, if anything went seriously wrong, he might be seeing the inside of a prison cell.

He knew that he'd also be gambling with the lives of his colleagues but, on the other hand, he knew that he wouldn't be able to live with himself if he didn't at least try to save his friend's life.

He looked up to see that all eyes were on him. He knew that he had a decision to make.

Chapter Twenty-Seven

Mac cursed himself for not seeing this coming. He'd warned Marcus Rawlinson to be careful but, for some reason, he hadn't applied the same logic to himself. It was certainly an audacious move by Sangredo but, then again, that's how he got where he was. He was obviously a gambler and one who wasn't afraid to up the stakes when circumstances required it.

They were driving quite fast but, even so, he knew it would take them at least ten minutes to get to the Steele Estate. He had a little time to think. Thinking wasn't made any easier by the barrel of the pistol that was being painfully shoved into his ribs. Besides the man holding the pistol there was a man in the front-seat who wore a loud yellow, green and black bandana and a tall skinny driver with dreadlocks. They never said a single word as they drove on but they all looked quite pleased with themselves.

By the time he saw Nightingale Tower in the distance Mac concluded that he was a dead man. He guessed that Sangredo himself would want to question him and, if this was the case, he knew that he'd be killed shortly afterwards. There was no way Sangredo could afford to let him live. From what he knew of the estate a rescue appeared more than unlikely as the gang would have guards everywhere. It was their turf after all. In fact, Mac hoped that Peter wouldn't even try.

Then again, the thought struck him that his follower might not have told anyone and Peter might be none the wiser anyway. If that was the case then perhaps it might be for the best. He didn't want anyone else's life being put into danger for his.

Two men appeared from the shadows and waved the SUV onto a slip road. They passed by more men as they disappeared into the darkness of the entrance. The car stopped and Mac was roughly hauled out. He didn't think of his back while this was happening, it was now the least of his problems. Mac had heard of the car park underneath Nightingale Tower and what went on there. It had been dubbed the 'Steeley Boys' Torture Chamber' by some of his colleagues. Now he'd get to find out what went on in here for real.

Only the far end of the car park was lit up. Their footsteps echoed as he was dragged towards the pool of light. As he got closer, he could see that three men were waiting for him. It was freezing cold and Mac could see that their breath was white on the air. Two of the men had pistols in their hands.

Please Peter, don't try it, Mac prayed.

'We got him, Antonio,' the man with the bandana said ingratiatingly as they entered the pool of light.

So, Antonio Waynette, one of the gang's leaders was present. Mac felt honoured.

'He doesn't look much, does he?' a tall muscular man said as he walked towards them and then looked Mac up and down.

He wore a black puffer jacket with a red hoodie underneath. The hood was up and, from underneath it, malevolent eyes weighed Mac up. He guessed that this alpha male must be Waynette.

His captor led him to a seat and forced him down in it. Mac didn't think they were doing this as a favour as he could see that sets of cable ties, several pairs of pliers, a soldering iron and a hammer were close to hand. He guessed that these would be used to get what they wanted from him. They used four of the cable ties to tie his wrists and legs to the chair.

'Where is he?' the skinny driver asked as he looked around.

'He'll be along,' Waynette replied looking annoyed. 'Look after him until he gets here.'

Waynette and his little cloud of attendants made off towards the lift. Mac guessed that they were going to warm themselves up. As they walked away the skinny driver picked up the hammer and smiled to himself.

'I could do with some practice. Just a couple of fingers while I'm waiting perhaps,' he said with a smile.

Waynette stopped and walked back. He grabbed the driver by the throat with one large hand and lightly throttled him.

'He's not to be touched until Jools gets here. That's the deal. Once he's finished you can do what you like with him. Get it?'

The driver rubbed his throat and assured his boss that he had indeed got it. Waynette strode off again and disappeared through the door that led to the lift. The driver was still rubbing his throat when he turned and noticed Mac smiling at him. He picked up the hammer and angrily shoved his face right into Mac's.

'I could kill you right now!' he shouted his spittle covering Mac's face.

'Well, I suppose you could,' Mac said with as much calmness as he could muster. 'But, if you did that, I'd guess that your boss would soon be using that hammer on your balls.'

Mac knew he was playing with fire goading the driver like this. However, he found at that moment that he didn't care. The driver held the hammer as if to swing it at Mac's head.

Go on, Mac said to himself. No more pain and perhaps a chance to see his Nora again. He locked eyes with the driver and smiled.

'Do it,' he said softly.

The driver swung the hammer but stopped short of hitting Mac and let the hammer drop to the floor instead. He walked away and leant against the wall, glaring at Mac from time to time his face a mixture of red-hot anger and respect.

Mac found that he was a little disappointed.

He'd been in some tough spots before but never one quite like this. He closed his eyes and tried to think. His options were extremely limited but he still had some. Waynette had sounded quite angry when he said that 'Jools' was late. He wondered if there might be some friction between the two of them that he could exploit. While he was thinking everything went hazy.

The next thing he knew he was being shook. Someone lightly slapped his face a couple of times.

'He's got some balls,' Mac heard Waynette say.

Mac couldn't quite believe it himself. He'd been tired enough, that was for sure, but being able to actually fall asleep just before having your fingers broken was a surprise. Then again, he'd used sleep to escape from the reality of his wife's death. Perhaps he was doing the same now.

Mac shook his head and looked around. The same crew were back but this time there was some additions. Amongst them was a face that Mac now knew all too well.

Julian Sangredo MP was standing next to Waynette and he was looking at Mac with interest. He was dressed in a smart dark grey business suit, white shirt and blue tie. He had an expensive looking overcoat on.

'Here's what we found in his wallet,' Waynette said as he handed Sangredo a business card.

'You're a private detective?' Sangredo said with some surprise in a cultured voice. 'We know that you were asking questions about Bernie Bright and that you were also seen with that big Scotsman who, I believe, has caused some grief to my colleagues here.'

Sangredo smiled but Waynette didn't look at all happy.

'Then you turn up at Marcus Rawlinson's house. I wasn't sure how much he knew and that's why I had a camera set up across the road so we could check who was visiting him. Who are you working for?' Sangredo asked.

Mac saw a couple of the men suddenly become very watchful.

'Did you hear something?' bandana man asked.

Everyone fell silent. Three guns were raised.

A fat rat came waddling out into the pool of light. It looked up at them, sniffed and then took a quick left turn and disappeared again. They all relaxed again.

'I'm working for Bernie Bright's family,' Mac replied quickly in a voice louder than was strictly required. Just in case he waffled on for a bit longer. 'They want to know who killed him and why. I discovered that he was blackmailing you and so you had your friends here beat him to death and then make it look like the work of some sick nutter. Bernie Bright was killed on your orders though, wasn't he?'

Sangredo scowled at the mention of his name.

'I didn't know he had any family. Anyway, I did them a favour when I had him killed. Bernie was a waste of space. What were you doing talking to Marcus Rawlinson?'

Sangredo looked worried, worried that his little secret was out. Mac decided that his best weapon was the truth.

'I was trying to figure something out and I thought that Mr. Rawlinson might be able to help. As it turned out he did. He provided me with the last piece of the puzzle,' Mac said.

Mac noticed Sangredo glancing warily at Waynette and he wondered if he was in on the MP's little money-making scheme.

'Mr. Waynette, has Little Jools here told you what this is all about? What it's really all about?' Mac asked.

Waynette looked uncertainly over at Sangredo and then back at Mac.

'Of course, I've told him everything,' Sangredo said dismissively.

Mac was going to bet on Sangredo being the greedy type. Gamblers like him usually were.

'The Steeley Boys have provided all the muscle and done all the dirty work but I'd bet that Little Jools here didn't tell you how much his little scam is really worth, did he?'

This got Waynette's attention.

'He told me,' Waynette said as he looked warily over at Sangredo.

'Oh good, so he told you that his scam was making him millions, did he?' Mac persisted.

Even Sangredo could tell that Mac hit the target.

'He's lying Anton. He's just trying to stir it,' Sangredo said defensively.

'Well, breaking international law to sell spare aircraft parts to ruthless dictators means that those parts come at a hefty price. I was told that the parts could be sold at up to a hundred times their list price and they don't come cheap in the first place,' Mac said. 'With several planes having already been stripped I'd guess that the amount that Little Jools here has made would come to many millions.'

'Rawlinson!' Sangredo muttered under his breath.

'I wouldn't think about bothering Mr. Rawlinson if I were you. He'll be under police guard anyway, now that the cat's out of the bag,' Mac said.

'What do you mean? How would the police even know that you're missing?' Sangredo said.

'I'd guess that the man who was following me would have let them know,' Mac replied with a smile.

Sangredo looked over at Waynette who looked over at the skinny driver.

'We didn't see anyone,' the driver said. 'Honest.'

'You wouldn't. The man who was following me wasn't a rank amateur like you lot,' Mac said.

'You're lying,' Sangredo said.

Mac could see that he was worried though. He smiled. He was almost enjoying it.

'I have a contact at MI5, someone who I've known for quite a while...'

'I don't believe you. How could a private detective possibly know anyone at MI5?' Sangredo scoffed.

'I wasn't always a private detective. Until fairly recently I used to be a policeman but I thought you might have known that. You obviously haven't done your homework, look me up on the internet if you like,' Mac replied. 'Put 'DCS Mac Maguire' in as a search term.'

Waynette got out his phone and did just that. He looked at Sangredo with some disdain as he handed him the phone.

'We're in trouble,' he said.

'Christ!' was all Sangredo said before he handed the phone back.

'Anyway, I told my contact at MI5 all about the mystery of the museum that never opened, thinking that it might have been one of his operations but he assured me that it wasn't. At the time we weren't exactly sure what you were up to but I promised that I'd tell him if I found anything that might be of interest to the intelligence agencies. He trusts me as much as he trusts anyone and that's not very much really. I knew that he'd have me followed so he could keep an eye on where the investigation was going, just in case. The man who was following me was good, good enough that I only caught a glimpse of him once by accident. He'll have witnessed my abduction and, after letting his boss know, he'll have called the police. Marcus Rawlinson also knows about your little scam. He's already let some of his online group in on the secret but by now the police will have spoken to him too and so now everyone knows what you've been up to.'

Mac could see that Sangredo believed enough of what he said to look deeply worried. He decided to play his trump card.

'It's just as well that you've got some insurance though, isn't it, Mr. Waynette? My guess is that Little Jools here would blame it all on you otherwise and, after all, he does have some friends in very high places. It was very wise of you to take that video.'

'And what video would that be?' Sangredo asked warily.

'Oh, just the one showing your son trying to kick an old man to death and then set fire to him,' Mac said. 'If that got out, I'd guess that wouldn't do much for your political ambitions, now would it?'

Sangredo paled as he looked angrily over at Waynette.

'I told you not to get Brian involved in this,' he said angrily.

'We didn't have to ask, he wanted to do it. He wanted to be one of the Boys,' Waynette said. 'You were getting so high and mighty with yourself that some of the Boys were saying that you'd turn on us once you'd gotten what you wanted.'

'And they were right,' Mac said. 'I heard that as soon as Dominic De Gray took over as Prime Minister Little Jools here would be appointed as Home Secretary. Imagine a Steeley Boy being in charge of the police, what a joke. However, in the end I'd bet that the joke would be on you, Mr. Waynette. I'd bet that Little Jools here has a purge of the Steele Estate planned. As soon as his feet are safely tucked under the Home Secretary's desk you and the rest of the gang would find yourselves safely tucked away behind bars. Who'd believe anything you said then? Isn't that right, Little Jools?'

Sangredo's face was twisted with anger. He stepped towards Mac and slapped him across the face with all of his might. Mac's vision went blurry and he thought that he'd started hearing things too. He shook his head and then looked up to see Sangredo, Waynette and the rest of his captors peering out into the darkness as the sound of footsteps came ever closer. Three guns were raised again, pointing straight towards the sound.

It was the sound of just one man walking towards them and he didn't sound as if he was in a hurry. Eventually a figure appeared at the very edge of the pool of light. He stopped and looked calmly at the group in front of him.

'Sangredo, I wouldn't do that again if were you,' he said calmly.

'Hello, Peter,' Mac said with an uncertain smile. 'It's nice to see you…I think.'

Chapter Twenty-Eight

They'd had a short break before they got down to business as Dion said that he needed the toilet. Peter noted that Callum had followed him when he left the room.

While they were waiting Peter asked Jo if they'd gotten anywhere with the museum workers.

'We managed to get two of them down to the station and they told us what they knew, eventually. Apparently, they were told that they were involved in a top-secret intelligence operation that was of vital interest to the national security. They were instructed to say nothing about it to anyone, not their families and especially not the police. They bought it.'

'Who told them this?' Peter asked.

'Someone called Cummings, apparently he set the whole thing up. He told them that he works for the Department for Defence,' Jo replied.

'Well, he didn't lie about that. His name's Geoffrey Cummings and he's Sangredo's deputy. Mac thought that he must be in on it,' Peter said. 'I can understand why they believed what they were told but I wonder how Bernie Bright discovered that it was all a scam?'

They were interrupted by the re-appearance of Dion and Callum. Now that everyone was back, Peter looked at the faces gathered around the table in something near desperation.

'Any ideas?' he asked hopefully.

Peter knew that there was only one way that he was going to get Mac out, he also knew that he couldn't order anyone to do it.

'So, a street gang are holding a copper hostage,' Manny said. 'Why don't we just go in there with overwhelming force? Get three or four hundred coppers and take over the whole of the Steele Estate?'

'It's a nice thought but it wouldn't do Mac much good,' Dion said. 'As I said if they spot any police presence at all they'll have Mac up that lift and out of a window on the twentieth floor within a couple of minutes. For all that they're a street gang, they're smart too. You won't find any evidence either and all you'll end up doing is having to scrape Mac off the pavement.'

Manny's face fell as he nodded slowly at the logic of Dion's words.

'As you said the guards are the key to getting Mac out of this alive,' Peter said. 'If he's still alive that is.'

There was a gloomy silence for a while before Dion spoke again.

'What's the chance of me ending up in court with this?' Dion asked.

'Virtually zero, I'd guess,' Peter replied. 'Being an undercover officer, we'd try and keep you totally out of any court case, unless you were a witness to something crucial of course.'

Dion was thoughtful for a while.

'Okay then, I'm going to do my job and keep an eye on the gang members who are guarding

Nightingale Tower. I'm going to suggest that you get the team ready for a raid just in case. You can park the three Mercedes SUVs here,' Dion said pointing to a map of the estate. 'It's a part of the estate that the gang don't normally hang out in and it's also just two minutes away from Nightingale Tower. Text me as soon as you've confirmed that Sangredo is on his way and I'll text you when and if the coast is clear.'

Peter looked at Dion thoughtfully. He was about to say something when Dion stopped him.

'Don't ask me anything. As an undercover officer I sometimes have to work in an unorthodox way and, if you don't know, then you can't tell.'

'Thanks Dion,' Peter said warmly.

'Mac's one of us. Tell me, would he do the same if it was me being held in Nightingale Tower?' Dion asked.

'Yes,' Peter replied without any hesitation.

'So that's okay then,' Dion said as he turned to go.

'Thank you too, Callum,' Peter said.

He'd guessed that Dion and Callum had cooked up a plan while they'd been out of the room.

'I like Mr. Maguire,' Callum simply said as he turned to go.

'And try not to kill anyone,' Peter said to Callum's back.

Callum turned and nodded before he left.

Peter was more than grateful to them both. He would now be able to truthfully deny having any knowledge that such a plan existed and that Callum was a part of it.

He picked up the phone and called Jenny Kelvin. 'It's on,' he said.

There was a lot of planning to do but the latest news on the timing of the vote in Parliament suggested that they still had some breathing space.

Outside Dion asked Callum what he needed. He half expected him to ask for some martial arts weapons of some sort.

'Two rolls of duct tape and some black clothing would be good. I'll stick out a bit wearing this,' Callum replied.

As he was still wearing the police rugby kit Dion could only agree.

Nearly two hours later Peter found himself sitting in a black Mercedes SUV on the Steele Estate accompanied by a police driver, Inspector Jenny Kelvin and two firearms officers. They were all waiting impatiently for a text message. He felt like pinching himself. In a few minutes he might be leading a smash and grab raid on one of the most feared street gangs in the country. He frowned when he remembered that afterwards, no matter how well the raid went, he'd probably be out of a job. He still wouldn't have it any other way though.

Peter wasn't a superstitious man but he found himself crossing his fingers as he waited. After a seeming eternity his phone went off and he answered it with some trepidation. With a grim smile he then sent a text off to Dion and Callum.

'Sangredo is on his way.'

Chapter Twenty-Nine

Dion and Callum were already in position when they got the text. It had been easy to spot the gang members on lookout. They were supposed to be strung out along the length of the road but instead they were all huddled together inside a bus shelter. They'd been watching the men for some time from behind a van parked on the other side of the road.

A cold wind howled across the wide-open spaces around Nightingale Tower and it was obvious that the lookouts were feeling its icy blast. They sat with their hands in their pockets and got up every now and again to stamp their feet on the ground to try and bring some life back into them. Dion suspected that at least one of them might have a gun but, whoever had it, they weren't waving it around.

Their plan, like all good plans, was really simple. Dion had bought a couple of bottles of spiced rum as well as making up some spliffs. He reckoned that, on such a cold night, these should be more than enough inducement to get the guards where they wanted them.

His phone vibrated. Dion pulled it out and looked at it. Callum saw a smile grow on his face as he read the message.

'We're on!' Dion said excitedly.

Callum just nodded. He was beginning to have some real respect for Dion. They were about to walk into a situation where it was just the two of them against a whole street gang, some probably armed with guns, and he was obviously looking forward to it. As for himself he felt somewhat nervous. He was about to set a monster loose and he wasn't totally sure what would happen once he did.

Without another word they started following the plan they'd come up with. Callum walked up the street and away from the bus shelter to a curve in the road. He crossed to the other side at a point where he couldn't be seen from the shelter. On this side of the road there was a narrow grass verge and then the ground dipped down into a deep trench behind which there was a wide grassy space. The trench ran alongside the road and had obviously been put there to stop travellers and others parking vehicles on the grass. It was a godsend to Callum as he could use it to approach the bus shelter from behind while being invisible to the three gang members sheltering inside.

Once he was level with the bus shelter, he climbed up the bank as quietly as he could and then crouched down behind it. Although the back of the shelter was glass it had so many layers of sprayed-on graffiti that it was now more or less opaque. Dion came into sight. He watched him as he walked towards them on the other side of the road.

'Hey, it's Boozy!' he heard a voice from inside the shelter shout. 'Hey Boozy, you got a taste for me?'

He saw Dion wave and smile. He jogged towards the bus shelter and crossed over the road.

'What you doing here?' Dion said. 'It's freezing out.'

'Orders from Antonio,' one of the men said with a glum expression.

'I'll let you get on with it then,' Dion said with a shake of the head. 'That Antonio guy scares me, I don't want to get on the wrong side of him.'

He started to walk off but the man caught his arm.

'Please Boozy, we're freezing our balls off out here. Have you got something in that bag of yours that might warm us up a bit?'

'Well, I've got a little party planned in the tower with this fine woman I met,' Dion said as he smiled suggestively. 'I've only got some spiced rum, oh, and some ganja of course.'

'Spiced rum,' the man said with longing. 'Now a little taste of that would set me up for the rest of the night.'

Dion gave this some deep thought.

'A taste you say? Okay but I don't want Antonio to know. Come behind the shelter where we'll be out of sight.'

The man smiled widely. He ordered one of the men to stay on watch while he and the other man followed Dion behind the shelter.

They both stopped in surprise at seeing a giant in front of them. The surprise didn't last long as Callum cracked their heads together and rolled them down the bank into the trench. Dion had laughed loudly to disguise any sounds. He gave Callum the thumbs up and then went back.

'That was so funny! I'd hurry if you want some rum,' he said to the lone guard. 'Those two look like they're going to finish the bottle.'

The man grumbled to himself and then looked up and down the road before following Dion around the back. He didn't even see Callum or his fist which connected with his jaw the split-second he'd appeared. Callum rolled him down into the ditch too and then followed him down. Both he and Dion made themselves busy taping up the men's mouths and arms and legs.

'That went well,' Dion said with a big grin as they climbed back up the bank.

Callum looked down at the three men. They'd taped them up so securely that they wouldn't be able to move an inch.

'It's going to be a cold night,' Callum said softly.

'Never mind going to be, it already is,' Dion said with a shiver. 'Come on, let's have a look and see what the next lot are up to.'

There was a wide-open space all around the tower with nowhere to hide. They decided to approach the tower as if they were drunk. They wobbled and weaved and Callum even stopped and sang a Scottish ballad for a few seconds. Drunks were two a penny in this area and, as they could often be quite violent, the few people who were around gave them a wide berth. They stopped as they neared the tower and Dion took a lighter out and made as if he was struggling to light a spliff in the stiff wind.

'What do you see?' he asked Callum.

'Two of them. I guess that they're supposed to be guarding the slip road but instead they're huddled in a corner of the building out of the wind. They're also well out of sight of anyone who might be guarding the entrance to the car park.'

'This weather is doing us a real favour,' Dion said with a smile. 'Let's wobble up to them and then you can do your thing.'

Callum crouched down a little so as not to appear to be quite so tall. As they weaved towards the two men one of them came towards them. He was holding something in his pocket and he was about to challenge them when he recognised Dion.

'Boozy, where you going?' he asked with a smile.

'Hi, Arvon! I'm looking for the seventeenth floor, there's a party,' he replied slurring his speech a little.

'Well the door's over there,' Arvon said pointing to the entrance.

It was then that he noticed the outline of the two bottles in Dion's carrier bag.

'What you got there?' he asked his eyes lighting up.

'Just some spiced rum for the party,' Dion replied. 'Some ganja too. Rolled it myself.'

Dion could see the longing in Arvon's eyes. He looked around and then called his partner over. They had a few quiet words together.

Arvon wiped his mouth with his hand as he spoke, 'A taste of that rum would be good. We're freezing to death out here.'

'Rum? Why sure, just let me have a look.'

As Dion rummaged around the two men got closer and looked inside the bag in anticipation. They didn't notice Callum ghosting behind them. Dion looked up when he heard a soft thump to find that the two men were flat on their backs.

'Over there,' Callum said as he pointed to a small landscaped hillock nearby. 'It should provide enough cover for now.'

They dragged the two men into the shadow of the hillock and taped them up so that they couldn't move or make a sound. Callum then crept softly to the corner and looked down the slip road.

'I can't see anyone,' he said softly. 'They must be inside the entrance sheltering from the wind. Any ideas as to how we can flush them out?'

Dion gave this some thought.

'If I go down and tell them that Arvon and his friend here are drunk they'll probably believe me. Everyone knows that Arvon likes his rum. That might get at least one of them up here to have a look. It'll also give me a chance to see how many others are down there and exactly where they're positioned.'

'That sounds good to me,' Callum said.

'Wish me luck,' Dion said with a wide grin.

He walked erratically down the fairly steep slope of the slip road and, as he came nearer, a head poked out of the entrance.

'Boozy, what you doing here?' a man asked.

He was a big man and he looked at Dion with some suspicion.

'Is something going down tonight, Ziggy?' Dion asked in a slurred voice.

'Why you asking?' Ziggy replied giving Dion an even more suspicious look.

Dion glanced down the entrance. Three men were sheltering inside. He knew two of them fairly well so he gave them a wave.

'Sorry, I'm bursting,' Dion said.

He walked a few yards further on and looked down the exit. It was empty.

So just the four guards to deal with, Dion thought.

He spent a minute pissing up against the wall before he went back to Ziggy. He just stood there grinning.

'Well?' Ziggy asked.

'Well what?' Dion said looking mystified.

'You were asking if something was on tonight,' Ziggy said in an angry voice.

Dion could see that he was winding Ziggy up nicely.

'Oh yes, that,' he said with a dramatic pause. 'Well, I just saw Arvon and his friend up there and it looked like they were supposed to be on guard or something.'

'What you mean 'supposed to be?'' Ziggy asked.

'I hate to be a snitch but it looks like they've been keeping a bottle of rum company...'

'That Arvon!' Ziggy growled. 'I told him no drinking.'

He marched up the road but Dion didn't attempt to go after him. He watched as Ziggy turned the corner and a split second later saw him fly out again but horizontally this time. He hit the floor and then an arm emerged and quickly dragged his body out of sight.

'Hi, Ake, hi Tyrone,' Dion said with a smile as he turned to look inside the entrance.

They both smiled back. He got on well with both of them. He was glad that it was them, they trusted him.

'Where's Ziggy gone?' Tyrone asked.

'It's so cold that he's just gone up for a quick taste with Arvon to warm himself up. Join us if you want.'

He pulled a bottle out of the bag so they could see what it was. He went back up the road and turned the corner. Ziggy had already been taped up and hidden behind the hillock.

'At least two more of them will be up in a minute,' Dion predicted.

Sure enough a few seconds later Ake and Tyrone turned up with smiles on the faces as they anticipated a warming drink. A few seconds after that they were both on the ground getting hog tied with tape.

'You've got a nice punch there,' Callum said.

Dion laughed.

'It's nice to know that all that boxing I did as a kid wasn't wasted then. It's a pity that I had to hit Ake though, I quite like him. Okay, so just the one to go. I'll tell him that Ziggy's told me to hold the fort for a while so he can have a drink.'

A minute later a young man with an expectant grin on his face turned the corner only to be met with Callum's fist. A split-second later he too was on the floor. Callum looked up as a car glided by and stopped in front of the tower. The car was large and expensive and looked out of place in its surroundings. It stopped as close to the entrance into the tower as it could. Callum quickly pulled the man's body out of sight and crouched down behind the hillock.

Dion came around the corner and Callum urgently gestured for him to get down. Dion got down on all fours and crawled to the hillock. They watched as a man got out of the car and walked briskly towards the entrance. He was dressed in an expensive looking overcoat and they could see that he had a shirt and tie on underneath. The light improved as he came closer and they could see better.

It was Sangredo.

Dion could see that he was looking at his phone as he walked towards the entrance which was just as well. Ake had been placed on the top of the pile but he'd somehow managed to roll himself down so that his head was now peeking around the side of the mound. Dion and Callum had a few tense seconds. If Sangredo had looked to his left then the whole operation might have been blown. Luckily, he walked straight on and noticed nothing.

Callum pulled Ake back behind the hillock and made sure that none of them could wriggle out again.

'So, is that it?' Callum asked.

'More or less but there's going to be someone guarding the lift,' Dion pointed out. 'We'll need to see to him so that no-one can get out that way.'

'I'll take care of that,' Callum said matter-of-factly.

Dion had no doubt that he would.

'Okay then,' he said with a big smile as he got his phone out. He sent a single word text to Peter.

'Clear.'

Chapter Thirty

Peter had been sitting in a tense silence cradling his phone in his hand. The fact that he kept looking at it every two or three seconds didn't help the time to go by any quicker. His mind was going around in circles. He kept telling himself that, with Callum onboard, there was a good chance that the plan might work and that they might get Mac back alive. A few seconds later, after thinking of all the things that could go wrong, he was utterly convinced that their plan would fail miserably.

If they did fail, he didn't want to think of what would follow. He was just picturing having to hand his warrant card over to DCS Bolsover, Mac's funeral and life as a security guard when his phone vibrated. It was a text from Dion.

'Clear.'

It took him a second or so to take in the fact that they'd actually done it. After the second was up he picked up his walkie-talkie.

'GO, GO, GO,' he shouted.

The engines of the three Mercedes started up and they glided out into the Steele Estate. They drove in convoy and as fast as was safe. Peter reckoned that they may not have needed the camouflage of the SUVs after all as the intensely cold weather had driven everyone from the streets. As they approached the slip road leading to the car park the drivers turned off their lights and engines and all three cars glided noiselessly onto the road before coming to a stop near the entrance.

Jenny Kelvin gave her sergeant the okay sign. He was to be the first to enter the car park and his job was to give them a picture of the situation inside. Peter and Jenny could follow his progress on a large tablet that was streaming directly from the sergeant's bodycam.

They only saw blackness for a while until the sergeant cleared the entrance. Then they saw a pool of light at the far end of the car park. They could make out seven people who were standing and one who was seated in a chair. As the sergeant crept a little closer, they could also hear what was being said.

'Christ!' Peter whispered his heart thumping wildly.

He recognised Sangredo who was standing near a man who was seated in a chair. It was Mac. His eyes were closed and his head was slumped forward as if he was unconscious.

Or dead, Peter thought feeling a moment of panic.

A tall man slapped Mac's face.

'He's got some balls,' he said.

Peter saw Mac wake up. He was alive! Suddenly all his misgivings vanished.

"Here's what we found in his wallet,' he heard a voice say.

The tall man passed something to Sangredo.

'You're a private detective?' Sangredo said looking at Mac with interest. 'We know you were asking questions about Bernie Bright and that you were also seen with that big Scotsman who, I believe, has caused some grief to my colleagues here. Then you turn up at Marcus Rawlinson's house. I wasn't sure how much he knew and that's why I had a camera set up across the road so we could check who was visiting him. Who are you working for?'

'Did you hear something?' one of the men asked.

Peter and Jenny had a tense moment as they all turned and looked directly at the camera. Then a rat appeared in the pool of light. It stopped and then waddled off into the dark. Everyone relaxed.

Mac started talking in a loud voice. Peter wondered if he had an inkling as to what was going on. Then he heard Sangredo say the magic words.

'I didn't know he had any family. Anyway, I did them a favour when I had him killed. Bernie was a waste of space.'

Sangredo had just admitted to being a murderer and it was all on record.

Just keep on talking as loud as you can old friend, Peter said to himself.

He then looked at Jenny Kelvin and pointed to the entrance. They were going in!

Jenny and the five firearms officers silently got out of the SUVs. She motioned for them to follow her inside. Peter gave them a minute to spread out before he too crept inside. He waited just by the entrance. He'd let them keep talking for as long as he could. If they could provide a little more rope to hang themselves with then that was all to the good.

When he saw Sangredo angrily slap Mac, he knew that this was his cue. He took a deep breath and started slowly walking towards them. Three guns were trained on him as he stepped into the pool of light.

'Hello, Peter,' Mac said with a rueful smile. 'It's nice to see you, I think.'

'Well, it's certainly nice to see you,' Peter said managing a smile.

Waynette stepped forward and pulled a gun from his jacket pocket. He pointed it straight at Peter's chest.

So, four guns then, Mac thought and wondered what Peter's plan was. He hoped that it was a good one.

'Okay, as you seem to be in something of a hurry let's get down to business,' Peter said. 'What do you think is going to happen now?'

Mac admired his friend's calmness. His voice was level and he kept body his body completely still.

Sangredo and Waynette looked uncertainly at each other. Neither of them answered the question.

'Okay, I'll tell you then. However, first of all, we must have the formalities,' Peter said as he held his hand up and showed his warrant card. 'We are the police and you're all under arrest. Drop your weapons and get down on the floor face first with your hands behind your head.'

No-one moved.

'No?' Peter asked. 'Just so that you fully understand the situation, you will either be leaving this car park in handcuffs or in a body bag. The choice is entirely yours.'

Again, they all looked at each other and again no-one made a move.

'We're armed,' Waynette said as he brandished his gun.

'Yes, you are,' Peter said in a voice that sounded bored. 'You have four pistols and I have seven officers out there with the latest in automatic rifles, Sig-Sauer MCXs that can fire nine hundred bullets a minute.'

'I don't believe you,' Sangredo said with a look that suggested that he probably did.

'Oh well, if it will help,' Peter said. 'Sound off and then move position.'

'Yo!' Jenny Kelvin said.

She then moved three yards to her right.

Mac counted as six more officers shouted out. His captors' heads twitched from side to side as the shouts seemed to come from every direction.

'If you shoot or even move your gun, they are under orders to fire. They have thirty bullets in each of their magazines, so that's exactly thirty bullets for each one of you and they won't be aiming to wing you. It's your decision.'

The seven men around Mac stood unmoving as if they were playing statues. Only their eyes moved. One of them looked as if he was about to panic. Mac could see him close his eyes and his finger start to put pressure on the trigger but, before he could fire, Peter spoke again.

'You've had enough time to think. You've now got five seconds to throw down your weapons and get down on the floor, face first.' Peter then said in a louder voice, 'I'll count from five down to one.

Anyone who is still standing and who hasn't thrown down their weapon will be shot dead when I reach the count of one. Do you understand?'

From their rictus like expressions Mac reckoned they understood alright. Peter was now in control. He was forcing the issue and wasn't giving them any time to think.

'Five...'

No-one moved a muscle. Everyone glanced nervously at everyone else.

'Four...'

'Antonio we've got to...' bandana man said.

'SHUT UP!' Waynette shouted.

'Three...'

The driver threw himself to the floor. He was quickly followed by bandana man and the sound of a gun scraping across the floor.

'Two...'

Sangredo and two others hastily dropped to the floor followed by the sound of metal on concrete as they threw their guns towards Peter. Only Waynette was left standing. He still had his gun in his hand.

Mac genuinely wondered for a moment if he'd try and take on seven marksmen by himself. He braced himself for the inevitable volley of bullets that would soon be flying over his head.

It seemed like an eternity until Peter spoke again.

'One.'

The number had just left Peter's lips when Waynette casually threw his gun down. He glared at Peter with disdain before he too, slowly and deliberately, lay down on the floor.

The firearms officers rushed forward and, using cable ties, quickly tied their arms behind their backs. Peter took out the walkie-talkie and ordered the three Mercedes to drive into the car park. They came in with headlights full on and pulled up side by side. They took three of the arrested men in each vehicle along with three armed officers. This just left Sangredo.

Peter couldn't put him in the last car as he didn't want him to see Dion and Callum. He needed to keep their part in the rescue a secret.

'Put him in the back on the floor,' Peter said to the officers. 'Sit on him if you have to.'

'Don't you know who I am?' Sangredo shouted.

'Yes, you're a murderer, a thief and a traitor,' Peter said with some venom. 'Get him in.'

The officers bundled Sangredo into the back of the SUV and then the two vehicles shot off. Callum came out of the door leading to the lift.

'Good work!' Peter said with real gratitude. 'Come on get in. Let's get out of here before anyone else knows we've been.'

Jenny Kelvin had cut Mac free and both of them were already inside the car.

'Have you got a knife?' Callum asked.

'A knife?' Peter asked in puzzlement.

'I'd like to set at least one of the men we taped up free so he can release the others. It's freezing tonight and if no-one notices them...'

'Sure,' Peter said seeing his point.

Thankfully no-one had died during the operation and it would be nice to keep it that way. Jenny gave him her knife and Callum bounded out of the entrance and up the slip road.

Peter got in and the car took off. They stopped by Dion who was waiting for them at the top of the road. He got in the back via the tailgate and a few seconds later Callum got in beside Peter.

'My God but we did it!' Dion shouted jubilantly as they drove away from the tower.

'Yes, we did,' Peter said almost to himself.

He still couldn't quite believe that they'd pulled it off. Of course, there was going to be trouble with Bolsover but he found that he didn't care about that in the slightest.

'Can you stop by the bus shelter just up the road there?' Callum asked the driver.

'We've got a few more of them taped up in a gully behind the shelter,' Dion explained.

Callum sped down into the trench and started sawing away at the tape holding one of the men when he heard a sound from behind him. He turned to see a young boy who was no more than ten years old looking at him with a serious expression. He was wearing a hoodie that had a figure of the Black Panther on the front and he had a gun in his hand. It didn't look like a toy.

They'd thought that one of the men must have had a gun. Callum guessed that the gun must have fallen from one of their pockets as they were rolled down into the trench.

'Hi kid, now don't...' was as far as Callum got.

The gun went off. The sound scared the boy who dropped the gun and ran away as fast as he could. Callum teetered slightly as he stood.

'Nice shot, kid,' he said softly.

He held a hand to the left side of his stomach but he couldn't stop the blood flowing out. He attempted to run at the slope and almost made it. He was beginning to topple backwards when two hands caught him and pulled him up. It was Peter and Dion.

'Christ!' Peter muttered. 'Get in the car.'

Together the two policemen helped him towards the car and somehow got him inside. Dion got in the back.

As he climbed in Peter shouted to the driver, 'He's been shot. He needs the hospital as fast as you can. Go!'

As soon as the door was shut the car screeched off. Mac was in the front seat so all he could do was turn around and watch while Peter and Jenny, who were sitting either side of Callum, tried to staunch the gunshot wound. Dion, like Mac, could only look on from behind.

'It was just a kid,' Callum said softly. 'Just a little kid.'

'Open the glove,' the driver told Mac. 'There's a first aid kit in there.'

Mac did and handed it into the back of the car. They used the bandages and gauze strips but they did little good, the flow of blood was just too strong. Callum was now unconscious. Mac wasn't sure how long it would take them to get to the hospital but he was having serious doubts as to whether Callum would make it. He'd seen people bleed out before.

'Where are we going?' Mac asked the driver.

'North Middlesex. I've already called ahead. Someone will be waiting when we get there,' the driver replied.

Mac hadn't even thought of that. He wondered how the driver had managed it until he saw his headset and mic.

'How long?' Mac asked anxiously.

'We're here.'

Mac looked over the driver's shoulder and could see a red 'A & E' sign with an arrow pointing up the street. The driver turned right into an entrance that said 'Ambulances only' and pulled up. A team was waiting with a trolley. With some help from Peter and Dion the medical team managed to manoeuvre Callum out of the car and onto the trolley. A doctor quickly checked him over and then he barked something at his team that Mac couldn't quite pick up. Whatever it was it didn't look good as they pushed the trolley inside at a flat out run.

Mac, Dion, Peter and Jenny all stood there for a moment looking at one another.

'I'll stay with him,' Mac said.

He could do no less. Callum had helped to save his life.

'I'll stay too,' Dion said.

'Thanks Dion, I'd appreciate the company. You'd better get going,' Mac continued as he turned to face Peter and Jenny. 'You've both got a lot of work to do and, anyway, it looks like you could both do with a shower and a change of clothes before you do anything else.'

They looked down at themselves and saw that they were covered in blood, especially Peter whose white shirt was now mostly dark red.

'You're right. Keep in touch and let me know if...if anything happens,' Peter said.

'Oh, and can I just say thanks to the both of you,' Mac said with gratitude.

'No problem but I won't shake hands if that's okay,' Peter said.

He held his hands out. They were as red as his shirt.

'See you later,' Peter said and they climbed back into the SUV.

'I think they went down that way,' Dion said as they walked inside.

He then pointed down a corridor.

It was only just registering with Mac that his back was hurting, really hurting. He leant against the wall to take some of the weight off. He wasn't aware of it but he must have winced audibly.

'Are you okay?' Dion asked noticing that Mac had gone suddenly pale.

'I can't walk,' Mac just managed to get out.

Dion disappeared and came back a minute later with a wheelchair. Mac gave him a grateful smile as he sat down. As he was being wheeled along the worst of the pain receded and he had a distinct feeling of déjà vu. Then he remembered his first case with DC Tommy Nugent and how he'd once done him the same favour.

They were soon stopped by a nurse who told them that they couldn't go any further as only the operating theatres lay ahead. Dion told her what had happened. She nodded and took them back down the corridor and opened a door.

'You can wait in here. Someone will be along in a while,' she said with a smile.

'How is he?' Mac asked.

'The man with the gunshot wounds?' she asked.

They nodded in stereo.

'He's being operated on now but he's lost a lot of blood...' the nurse said leaving the sentence hanging.

They didn't need to ask any more questions as the look on her face told them all they needed to know.

The room contained four armchairs and a low table. Dion wheeled him inside. Mac didn't bother getting out of the wheelchair. He was okay where he was and the angular armchairs didn't look all that comfortable anyway.

Dion sat down and then stood up, walked up and down a few times before sitting down again.

'He's a big lad, he'll be okay,' Dion said hopefully.

Mac wasn't so sure. He'd lost so much blood.

The unfairness of it all burnt his insides like acid. He'd been trying to save lives when he'd been shot. From what Callum said he'd been shot by a child who probably thought the gun was a toy. There are certain things that you just can't plan for.

He desperately didn't want Callum to die, he'd gladly offer his own life in exchange if he could. He felt thoroughly ashamed when he remembered how he'd almost welcomed death when the skinny driver had threatened him with the hammer.

'I'm sure you're right,' Mac eventually replied with no conviction whatsoever. 'How did he get to be part of the operation in the first place?'

Dion told him about the plan that he'd hatched with Callum to get rid of the guards so that the firearms team would have a clear run.

'I've never seen anything like it,' Dion said with a shake of his head. 'He was just like some action hero in the movies. We'd never have gotten you out of there without his help.'

Mac sincerely wished that they hadn't tried but he couldn't tell Dion that. After all he'd put his life on the line too.

It just wasn't right though. Callum was still young, he'd turned his life around and he had so much potential while Mac was old and worn out. He'd had a future while Mac now knew that somewhere in his head there was a genuine wish that death would take him. He felt guilty, after all it had been his own stupid fault that he'd been taken in the first place. There he was telling everyone else to be careful while he was driving around by himself. If only he'd taken a few police officers with him as Jay had suggested then this might never have happened. If only.

He suddenly felt emotional and excused himself. He found a toilet a few doors down. It was for single use only and he was glad of it. He sat on the toilet seat and swore loudly at the wall for several minutes.

Then he prayed.

Chapter Thirty-One

After ten minutes or so Mac felt no better about things but he was at least collected enough to feel that he could face Dion again. It had been unlike him but, after the stress of everything that had just happened, he supposed that it was no wonder that he'd become a little unhinged. He opened the door and tried to read Dion's face. Had he had any news? A shrug told him everything he needed to know.

'Are you okay?' Dion asked with a concerned look. 'You look a bit pale.'

'I've just had a strange few minutes that's all,' Mac said.

'I can't blame you. The whole thing seems strange to me too.' Dion shook his head and smiled. 'It was great working with him though. I felt like I was someone in a comic book, Robin perhaps.'

'Robin?' Mac asked with a puzzled look as he sat back down in the wheelchair.

He was thinking of the little red-breasted birds who he often saw at the feeders in his back garden.

'Yeah, you know, like Batman and Robin. Robin might take down one or two of the minor villains but he basically just watches Batman do his thing, doesn't he? He'd make a good Batman Callum would,' Dion said. 'He's got the six pack and everything…'

He looked up at Mac and shook his head.

'I'm talking total crap, aren't I?'

Before Mac could reply a nurse entered the room. Mac and Dion both stood up and looked at her.

'Oh, I'm not here with any news,' she said hastily seeing the expectant look on their faces. 'I just need some details about a patient that was brought in with a gunshot wound?'

It was then that Mac noticed the clip board in her hand. They all sat down again.

'Just to ensure that we've got the right person the gentleman we're operating on has a large tattoo on his back...'

'It's a tiger, a tiger with its jaws open,' Mac said.

'Yes, that's right. It's very realistic, isn't it?' she said. 'Okay, so I've got some forms here as we need to know as much about the patient as we can.'

Mac went through the forms with her but most of the spaces remained empty. He really didn't know that much about Callum.

'Not to worry,' the nurse said, 'at least we've got a name. We'll let you know when we've got some news.'

Dion and Mac weren't left alone for very long. The door banged open and hit the wall as Vicki Jackman wheeled herself in. She gave Mac a frantic look.

'Well?' she almost shouted.

'He's in the operating theatre now but we've no idea how he's doing,' Mac said. 'He's lost a lot of blood.'

Her hand went to her mouth.

'Is it really bad?' she asked in a near whisper.

No-one answered her which was an answer in itself. Jay walked in and everyone looked up at him. From their expressions he could tell that it wasn't going well. He asked the question anyway.

'How is he?'

'We don't know yet, he's still in the theatre,' Mac replied.

'I gave Vicki a lift here. When I told her about Callum, she was going to try and wheel herself all the way here so I thought…'

Jay was interrupted by a knock on the door. Everyone fell silent and looked at the door but nothing happened. There was another knock. Jay opened the door. Two uniformed officers were standing outside. They both carried an automatic rifle.

'We've been sent to guard a patient. I was told to ask for Mac Maguire,' the older policeman said.

'That's me,' Mac replied as he dug out his warrant card. 'The man you'll be guarding is in the operating theatre at the moment.'

'Do you mind if I ask who he is? We weren't told much,' the older policeman asked.

Everyone looked at Mac as he gave the question some thought.

'He's one of ours. He's been working with us for quite a while, you know deep undercover,' Mac said. 'There was a big operation tonight on the Steele Estate and we arrested some of the leaders of the Steeley Boys gang. Unfortunately, he got shot as we were leaving the estate.'

Mac knew that he was being somewhat economical with the truth but he wanted Callum to get the best treatment from his guards that he could. If he lived that is.

If he lived.

'Don't worry sir, we'll look after him,' the policeman said. 'We'll go and guard the entrance to the operating theatres just in case.'

Mac nodded his thanks and they left. An uncomfortable silence followed that seemed to stretch on and on. It was eventually broken by Jay.

'Would anyone like a coffee?' he asked.

Mac could have kissed him. He smiled and said that he would love a coffee. Dion offered to help. That just left Mac and Vicki in the room.

'Are you okay?' he asked.

'No, I'm not,' she said clearly on the verge of tears. She wiped one away just before she said, 'I'm just being silly, aren't I? I mean I've only known him for the shortest time.'

'You're not being silly. If you have feelings for Callum then don't deny them,' Mac said. 'And as for time, I had feelings for my wife about five minutes after I met her. Time means nothing in some cases.'

'He saved my life,' she said, 'but it isn't gratitude I feel. We watched TV together, history programmes mostly, and it was fun. I haven't had much fun since the crash. It was just so nice being with someone but it was more than that. He's very special and I thought...well, I thought that I might be having some luck at last.'

'You've had some bad luck alright,' Mac said.

She fell silent and was thoughtful for a while.

'The crash wasn't down to bad luck though, that was all my fault. I'd been with Jem since we met at

Art School and, at first, we were just business partners. We called ourselves 'Bespoke Interior Designers' but we mostly did basic painting and decorating for a while. He was such a lovely man and I started to get feelings for him. Luckily, he felt the same.'

A small smile came to her mouth and then quickly disappeared.

'We got offered this big contract and, to our surprise, we won it,' she continued. 'It would have made our little company. After we signed the contract we were invited to a party. It was my turn to drive so Jem got a bit drunk. He had every right, he'd worked so hard to get that contract. I was supposed to be staying off the alcohol but I was so happy and they kept bringing around these big glasses of Prosecco. So, I had one and another one after that and perhaps even some more after that. We had a fair way to go to get back home and we didn't have enough money for a taxi so I decided to drive anyway. That was the worst decision I ever made in my life.'

She gave Mac an intensely sad look.

'I lost it on a bend, one I'd driven around a hundred times. We hit the side of a bridge. Jem was killed instantly and I ended up like this. In that one instant I lost my partner, my business and my legs. I lost even more than that. I've no family of my own and his mom and dad and sisters had adopted me as it were. They never spoke to me again after the crash, not a single word. Since then I've been living in hell.'

Mac couldn't think of anything to say.

'Then Callum turns up. You know I must have watched that video I took of him fifty times. I know what he did to those two men was terrible but it was so beautiful, the way he moved and then the tenderness he showed when he picked up that poor man. Then I met him for real and he was...I don't know...overwhelming I think is the word. I started hoping, I started hoping and now...'

The tears came full flood. Mac got up and went over to her and held her as best he could. Her whole body shuddered with the force of her emotion.

They were interrupted by the arrival of the coffees. Jay and Dion diplomatically looked away as Vicki dried her eyes. Then followed the longest five minutes of Mac's life. No-one could think of anything to say and the longer the silence went on the harder it was to break. Then the door opened and a young man in a white doctor's coat walked in.

'How is he?' Mac quickly asked.

'Hello, I'm Doctor Eastman. Are you all here for Mr. McEachan?' the doctor asked with a puzzled expression.

'Yes, we're all police officers except for Miss Jackman here who is...,' Mac almost hesitated as he thought of what to say, '...who is Mr. McEachan's partner. He was shot while taking part in a police operation this evening, he's been working undercover for us on a very important case.'

Vicki gave Mac a grateful smile.

'Oh, I see,' the doctor said as his expression softened. 'I thought that he might have been a criminal or something when I saw the policemen.'

'No, the two policemen are there to guard him just in case the criminals come looking for him,' Mac said.

He realised that the doctor hadn't answered his question. He hoped that wasn't because he had bad news.

'How is he?' Mac asked again.

'Well, he lost a lot of blood, an amazing amount really. That gunshot wound would have killed most people...'

'Then he's alive?' Vicki asked breathlessly.

'Oh yes, he went in haemorrhagic shock due to losing so much blood but, luckily for him, our top trauma surgeon was on duty. It was a sort of balancing act, trying to keep his blood volume up while closing up the hole that the bullet had left. He's still being topped up with blood products and he'll need another major operation soon but we believe that he's through the worst.'

For the first time the doctor smiled. Mac felt as though a ten-ton weight had been lifted from his heart.

'He'll be alright then?' Mac asked just to be sure.

'Yes, we think so,' the doctor said as he turned to face Vicki. 'We should be bringing him down to the emergency department in an hour or two. He'll be unconscious for quite a while but you can sit with him there if you'd like.'

'Yes, I'd like that very much,' Vicki said as she wiped more tears away.

Chapter Thirty-Two

It was morning and Mac was comfortably seated in the police canteen at the Central Station having just put away a much-needed sausage and egg sandwich. He felt a bit tired but on top of the world too.

'So, tell me what happened next,' Peter asked.

Mac had already told him most of the story.

'They let us know when they'd finished operating and he was then sent up to the emergency department. They managed to put him in a sort of side room so that the police guards wouldn't be visible from the main ward. Vicki and I sat with him for quite a while. We talked and she told me quite a bit about herself. I think she's a remarkable young woman really. Life's not done her any favours recently but I'm hoping that might change.'

'Why is that?' Peter asked.

When Callum had woken up for the first time it had only been for a minute or so. He'd been so heavily sedated that he could barely keep his eyes open. Vicki was holding his hand in both of hers. He turned his head, looked up at her and smiled. She bent over and planted the tenderest of kisses on his lips. He then said in a near whisper, 'Now that was worth getting shot for.' Then sleep took him again. Vicki looked quite beautiful at that moment. Hope suited her.

'Oh, just a hunch,' Mac said with a smile. 'When are you seeing Bolsover?'

Peter looked at his watch and sighed.

'In just over an hour. Oh well, I always liked being a sergeant.'

'Do you think it'll be that bad?' Mac asked.

'Probably worse from what I'm hearing, after all he'd be within his rights to kick me out of the force altogether. I'd guess that he's embarrassed about his connection to Sangredo and that he'd like to bury the case and me with it.'

'My God!' Mac said in astonishment.

'What is it?' Peter asked as he turned around.

A very well-dressed man approached their table and sat down. They'd both met him before. He smiled widely at them both.

'Sir Philip, this is a surprise,' Mac said only speaking the truth.

While he'd been waiting for Callum to wake up, he'd thought about the case and what might happen next. One of the more likely scenarios that had entered Mac's mind had been Sir Philip Suskind or one of his colleagues turning up and stopping the case in its tracks. As it involved the delicate matter of a British Minister breaking UN sanctions, he'd reckoned that it might well be on the cards.

'So, is the case being stopped in the interests of National Security?' Mac asked.

Sir Philip looked offended by Mac's question.

'Absolutely not, indeed we want you to prosecute the case against Mr. Sangredo and his associates with the full vigour of the law,' he replied with a playful smile. 'I've managed to have a word with Mr. Sangredo and he is truly repentant and willing to tell all.'

'How did you do that?' Peter asked.

'What was it they said in that film?' Sir Philip asked himself. 'Oh yes, I made him an offer that he couldn't refuse.'

Mac knew that Sir Philip was up to something and was trying to figure out what it might be.

'Old friend you look a little puzzled,' Sir Philip said. 'I've checked this one with the PM herself and, although it's a little embarrassing for the country, she wants the case to be treated no differently to any other.'

'Really?' Peter couldn't help saying in something like wonder. 'You want everything to come out?'

'Oh yes, of course,' Sir Philip said.

'What about Cummings?' Mac asked. 'Are you sure you want him to tell us everything he knows?'

'That's very astute of you, old friend,' Sir Philip said with a smile. 'In his case it will be almost everything.'

'He was one of your men, wasn't he?'

Sir Philip nodded slowly.

'An unfortunate case of a gamekeeper turned poacher I'm afraid. It will never come out in court, of course, but I can tell you that we never trusted Sangredo. We were quite frankly stunned that De Gray could even think of putting a man like him in such a senior position.'

'Why did he do that? Do you know?' Mac asked.

'Well, he's unmarried and a confirmed bachelor by all accounts. I think you can guess why,' Sir

Philip replied. 'The love that dare not speak its name.'

It all made sense to Mac now. Julian Sangredo was charismatic and handsome and love makes people do the craziest things. Even fusty politicians like De Gray weren't exempt from its madness.

'From what we've learned Sangredo was…well leading him on shall we say. So, we got our man in as his deputy to ensure that nothing too untoward happened,' Sir Philip continued. 'Unfortunately for us Sangredo's money appears to have turned his head and the reports he's been sending us have turned out to be total fabrications.'

He gave them a sad look before he glanced at his watch.

'Anyway, I'm sorry to say that I can't stay to sample the culinary delights of the police canteen as I have a short meeting with a DCS Bolsover in a few minutes.'

Sir Philip stood up, said his goodbyes and started to walk away but then he stopped and turned back.

'Dearie me, I was nearly forgetting. Detective Inspector Harper, the PM was so grateful for your bravery in weeding out this nest of vipers that she's nominated you for a gong, an MBE I should think. You'll be getting a letter before long.'

He smiled and left them.

Mac and Peter looked at each other in total amazement.

'Now that wasn't what I was expecting at all,' Peter said.

'The same here. Oh, and congratulations on your impending honour. Peter Harper MBE, that sounds pretty good,' Mac said. 'Unlike a lot of people who get these awards you really deserve it and Grace will absolutely love it.'

Mac knew that Peter's wife Grace had applied to attend many royal events in the past and had always failed. With luck she'd be meeting the Queen herself before long.

'Thanks Mac,' Peter said looking a little embarrassed. 'Yes, she'll love that alright. It all seems a bit surreal though, doesn't it?'

Mac couldn't help but agree. In fact, the whole case had seemed surreal ever since he'd first met Tiger McEachan outside St. Philips Church. Callum's criminal nickname seemed strange to him now.

The time for the meeting with DCS Bolsover drew near. Mac had been thinking about Sir Philip's visit and what lay behind it. He was beginning to have an inkling of what might be really going on when Peter interrupted his thoughts.

'It's nearly time. Are you sure you're okay to come in with me?'

'Of course, if it's a disciplinary matter you have the right to have someone go in with you,' Mac said. 'Anyway, I have an idea that this meeting might turn out a little differently to what we've been expecting.'

In that Mac was proved absolutely right. DCS Bolsover smiled as they entered the room, stood up and shook their hands. He then congratulated

Peter on the success of the operation before handing him a sheet of paper.

'I'm sorry but I forgot to give you a copy of this earlier. It's the letter detailing my recusal from the Sangredo case. As I knew the man socially I, of course, felt that I shouldn't be involved in the case in any way. The letter also gave you total authority to proceed with the case as you saw fit,' Bolsover said with a patently false smile. 'You remember that we talked about it when you raised the matter a while ago?'

Peter looked puzzled for a second until he cottoned on.

'Oh yes, of course I remember,' he said taking the letter.

'Good, then we need say no more,' DCS Bolsover said with some relief. 'You may go.'

Bolsover pretended to be looking at a case file as Peter got up and left the office. Mac got up to go, then he stopped and turned back.

'You were very wise to do that. Those politicians would have torn you to pieces if you'd done what you really wanted to do.'

Bolsover's face went red but he said nothing and so Mac left him to his pretend reading. Peter was waiting for him outside.

'This case gets even more bizarre, doesn't it?' he said in amazement. 'I should at least get a demotion and instead I end up with a medal and a trip to see the Queen. Have you any idea of what's really going on?'

'I just might,' Mac said, 'but not here. Let's go and find a quiet corner of a pub. We'll have a pint and I'll tell you what I think.'

They did just that. They sat there in silence for a while as they let the quietness wash over them.

'Okay, I'm going to tell you a story. I'm not going to insist that it's all true but, well, I'll let you make up your own mind about that.

So, two Middle Eastern countries get a bad press for shooting down hundreds of peaceful protesters who don't like the way their governments run their countries. The bad news for us is that they're using airplanes that we sold them to help them to do this. So, our government successfully leads the call for tough UN sanctions thus showing the world our horror at such actions. Sangredo sees his chance to make a killing by selling these governments spare parts to keep their planes flying and somehow manages to get his deputy, Geoffrey Cummings, on board. Sangredo can be very persuasive and I suppose that the sums of money involved were enormous.

While all this is going on the Prime Minister is fighting for her political life. Dominic de Gray is waiting in the wings to take over at the first opportunity and a good chunk of her party are desperate for him to do so whatever happens. However, I'd guess that the intelligence services, including Sir Philip, might be on the PM's side in all this.'

'Why do you think that?' Peter asked.

'I read up on it during the investigation, especially when I thought that the operation at the museum might have been directly run by Sir Philip's lot. The PM used to work for the intelligence services at GCHQ when she was younger so she has a soft spot for them and, while other departments have recently had their budgets cut, the intelligence services have had theirs increased. De Gray wasn't happy about this and he's called the intelligence services a 'state within a state' and said that they should be 'brought to heel'. I doubt that using that metaphor did him any favours with Sir Philip either.'

'Okay then, I think I can see why Sir Philip would be on the PM's side in all this,' Peter said.

'I guess that's why both he and the PM are so happy to make everything public now, well, almost everything. De Gray was Sangredo's mentor and boss and it was solely his decision to give such him a senior post in the Ministry of Defence. We now have an inkling as to why. I think that Sir Philip must have been delighted when I approached him about Sangredo and, of course, an investigation carried out by the police would carry far more weight with the press than one carried out by the intelligence services who De Gray had so publicly criticised. So, by allowing everything to come out, the government might be slightly embarrassed for a while internationally but it means that Sangredo will be very publicly going down in court and he'll be very publicly dragging De Gray down with him too.'

'Yes, I can just see the headlines now,' Peter said. 'He'll have to resign, won't he?'

'That's my bet. And so, the insurrection against the Prime Minister will be crushed and anyone else wanting to have a go in the future will think twice about it.'

'I think I'd sooner deal with criminals than politicians any day,' Peter said. 'At least you know where you are with them.'

'Yes, they may be crooks but they're usually honest about the fact,' Mac said. 'Anyway, the good thing is that Sangredo will get what he deserves and the Steeley Boys have been dealt a blow that they might never recover from.'

'Yes, but I'll bet that some of the surrounding gangs are already circling like vultures and ready to take over. Of course, that'll mean more violence on the streets and more work for us.'

'Yes, it never stops does it?' Mac said with a sigh.

Chapter Thirty-Three

As the weeks went by Mac kept an eye on the fall-out from the case and also on whether the Post-Traumatic Stress Disorder symptoms he'd experienced after the explosive events in Northern Ireland late the previous year might re-emerge. He was lucky. Even though the kidnapping had been a seriously stressful event he didn't seem to suffer from any flashbacks or bad dreams.

The Steeley Boys as a force more or less ceased to exist shortly after the raid. Tel Barklay, the only remaining leader of the gang, had been stabbed to death some days later. They never found out who by. A short but bitter turf war ensued between two of the neighbouring gangs until they finally came to a working arrangement. The same drugs were still being sold on the Steele estate and mostly by the same people. The money now went into someone else's pockets though.

As time went by, Mac found that he became less convinced by Sir Philip's protestations about Geoffrey Cummings and his 'fabricated' reports. He felt that it was highly unlikely that Sir Philip would take his, or anyone else's word come to that, without verifying it first. He began to wonder whether it was Sangredo who had persuaded Cummings to come in on the plan or the other way around. After all it was Cummings who had seemed to have done most of the work in making the scam succeed. He'd read somewhere that, if the two Middle Eastern governments fell, then the ensuing chaos might mean that oil prices would have to rise dramatically. That outcome would have gotten everyone's backs up and made the Prime Minister's position even more untenable.

He finally came to the conclusion that Cummings might not have gone rogue after all. If he was right, it was a win-win scenario for Sir Philip. If the scam succeeded the planes would keep flying and so help keep oil prices stable and the Prime Minister in a job. He also had 'plausible deniability' when and if it failed. However, the scheme had added value in that, if De Gray started to look like he was a real threat, then Sir Philip could simply pull the rug from under his feet at any time by exposing Sangredo's activities. Which is exactly what had happened.

It was Machiavellian in the extreme and just about what he'd expect from Sir Philip. He had to stop thinking about it though as he knew that he'd never be able to prove anything and his head was starting to hurt.

Marcia Notts came to see him a week or so later.

'I've just come to thank you Mr. Maguire,' she said. 'I'd be grateful if you could pass my thanks on to all your colleagues too.'

Mac promised that he would.

'How have you been?' he asked noticing that she looked quite a lot calmer than the last time he'd seen her.

'When I heard that you'd got the men who'd killed my father I cried. They were tears of relief really, I'd been feeling so stressed out about it all that I thought I might break in two. I'm a lot better now, thanks to you,' she said pausing for a moment. 'Do you remember me telling you that my father had kept some things from his RAF days?'

'Yes, I remember. Did you find something that might help the case?' he asked.

He was hoping that she might have found out how her father had rumbled Sangredo's scam. It really didn't matter much in terms of the case but he was still curious.

'No, I'm sorry I didn't. It was mostly just photos from his RAF days. However, I did find this,' she said as she passed him a photograph. 'I thought that you might want to keep it, to remind you of the case.'

Mac looked closely at the photograph. It was a small square black and white print that had creases on its corners. However, he could clearly see its two subjects. Two young men in uniform were standing outside a military building and they had their arms draped over each other's shoulders. They held a drink up in their other hand as they both looked straight into the camera with big smiles on their faces.

Bernie Bright and Eric Brathwaite.

'This is how I want to remember my father,' she said as she got up to go.

'Thank you,' Mac said knowing that he couldn't have asked for a better souvenir. 'I'll keep it safe.'

The trials took hardly any time to complete at all. Sangredo pleaded guilty as Sir Philip had predicted. He'd told all and had also provided evidence against all the others too. His son, Brian, hadn't been mentioned in the proceedings and was never charged with any offence. Mac guessed that this might have been part of the deal that Sir Philip had made with him.

Waynette and the rest of the Steeley Boys turned on each other as well, now that there was no gang left to wreak revenge on them for snitching. Skank Moussero was arrested while he was still in hospital. He was charged with the murder of Bernie Bright.

The judge went hard on them. Sangredo, and all those implicated in the murders, got life sentences while the rest got between ten to fifteen years in jail. The day after the trial ended the newspaper headlines simply read 'Traitor' in their largest type below a photo of Sangredo.

Mac noticed that the trial of Geoffrey Cummings took place separately some weeks later and hardly got a mention in the press. It finished quietly and in record time which didn't help to allay any of his suspicions.

Dominic De Gray, as predicted, resigned a few days after Sangredo's arrest. He'd cited his sister's death as the main reason and said that he wished to retire from public life to once again take up his research into early nineteenth century political history. His role in the whole affair did not go unnoticed in the press and it wasn't only Sangredo who was tarred as a traitor in the headlines.

Dion Best went back to his life in Manchester where he could once again watch his beloved United play at home. Jay eventually moved to the

Hatfield area after he found that his wife was expecting. Mac did his best to kept in touch with them both.

It was some weeks after Sangredo's arrest that the mystery as to how the Steeley Boys had managed to set up the hit on Callum and Vicki was solved. Jay's team had heard some rumours about Jason Gabriel and his gambling habit and had decided to search his flat. There they found over thirty thousand pounds in used notes under a floorboard. Mac guessed that Gabriel hadn't been told what the gang were going to do with the information he supplied but, even so, the fact that any copper could be capable of selling out his own colleagues in such a way left a sour taste in Mac's mouth.

Even though the Steeley Boys had more or less ceased to exist as a force Callum and Vicki were still put into the witness protection programme as a precaution. For some time even Mac didn't know where they'd gone or what they were doing.

He found himself thinking of them from time to time. He usually said a little prayer for them both when he did.

Ten months later...

He'd been excited when he'd first gotten the invitation and he'd talked it over with his friend Tim. It was Tim's idea to make it a bit of a holiday for the two of them. He was especially keen on fitting in a visit to one or two of the local whisky distilleries.

Mac had arranged for Amanda to pick his dog Terry up for the week. He'd also given her two tickets for a new musical in the West End that was opening in a couple of weeks. She'd been talking enthusiastically to him about it for a while. He'd included a meal and a night in a hotel in the package too. After all she'd done in looking after Terry, and usually at short notice too, it was the very least he could do.

The house was empty as he gave it a final check before he left. He remembered that Nora had always left a little light on in the living room when they were going away.

'To fool the burglars,' she'd always say.

He turned and could almost see her sitting in her spot on the sofa, feet up and reading one of her beloved books. He remembered that she'd always left a light on when he was working late too. She always said that she didn't want him coming home to a dark house.

Before he went, he turned the lamp on.

Even with them both taking turns driving Mac was glad that they'd decided to stop for the night along the way. It was a longer drive than he'd remembered. He and Nora had driven to Stranraer once to get the ferry to Belfast but that had been many years ago, not long after Bridget had been born. Where they were going was even further away than that.

They arrived in Oban just after four on a November afternoon and it was already getting dark. They booked themselves into the two-bedroomed apartment that was to be their home for the next week. The apartment was on the esplanade overlooking the sea and, through their living room window, Mac could see a huge illuminated Calmac ferry heading for the port which was just down the road. The apartment was comfortable and they each had their own room which was a bonus. Mac had discovered when they'd been on holiday in Cyprus earlier in the year that Tim sometimes talked in his sleep. He didn't even say anything interesting which had made it all the more annoying. Nonetheless they'd had a great time and Mac would go back at the drop of a hat.

Another thing that had recommended the flat to Mac when he'd looked it up on the internet was the fact that a pub was handily situated just next door. After a meal and a couple of pints they both found that they were wilting and decided on an early night. Mac thought it was just as well as he had to be in church at eleven the next morning for the rehearsals.

The church, or more correctly the cathedral, was an impressive stone pile just a short walk away from the apartment. They were early so Mac and

Tim took their time walking there, stopping every now and then to lean against the railings and look at the sea. The inside of the cathedral was even more impressive than the outside. Huge stone columns rose up to a high wooden roof but, somehow, they didn't interrupt the space. Rows of arched windows on either side flooded the interior with light. A red carpet ran up the aisle to the altar in the distance.

It brought St. Philips Church back into Mac's mind and took him right back to the beginning of the story. As if he'd just jumped straight out of his memory Callum McEachan came bounding down the red carpet to meet him. Mac had to remind himself that it was Callum Tulloch now. He gave Mac a big hug and then shook Tim's hand.

'I'm sorry we couldn't meet you yesterday,' Callum said. 'We were finishing off a job over in Connel.'

'I take it that the business is doing well then?' Mac asked.

'Oh aye, too well in a way. When we get back, we'll have to take someone on to help us out. Come on, Vicki is dying to see you.'

They followed Callum up the aisle and Mac wondered at the change in him. He was dressed casually in jeans and a blue Arran jumper but the ponytail had gone and so had all the angst. He looked relaxed and happy.

Vicki was waiting for them at the altar. She held her arms wide open so that Mac could bend down and give her a hug. Mac thought that she looked wonderful. The furrowed lines of disappointment that he'd seen etched in her face had gone, indeed she looked like her own younger sister. Mac introduced her to Tim.

'I'm so glad you could come,' Vicki enthused.

'Well, I couldn't turn down an opportunity to give the bride away, now could I?' Mac said with a smile. 'It looks like life has been really good to you two since we last met.'

'It has,' Vicki said as she beamed up at her husband-to-be. 'The interior design business has taken off and now we've got this to look forward to.'

As she said this, she held her hands over her lower stomach.

'When's the baby due?' Mac asked.

'It'll be a Spring baby,' she replied.

Mac looked up at Callum and, while he was smiling, he noticed that there was an uneasiness there too. He wondered if Callum was as happy about the baby as Vicki was. He decided to have a chat with him when they'd finished.

'And is Father Andrew still going to be best man?' Mac asked changing the subject.

'Oh aye, but he can't get down here until tomorrow so he'll have to wing it,' Callum replied. 'Then again I suppose this won't be the first wedding he's been to.'

Mac was looking forward to meeting the man who had helped to change the angriest, most violent criminal that he'd ever met into the huge puppy dog that he now stood in front of.

After the rehearsals had finished Mac asked Tim if he wouldn't mind meeting him at the pub in about half an hour as he needed to have a private word with Callum. He said his goodbyes to Vicki and nodded to Callum to come and join him outside. It was a fine, if chilly, day and Mac leant against the railing and gazed out at the sea and the island just across the narrow strait. He'd spent half of his holiday in Cyprus staring at the sea. He'd found it hypnotic and, somehow, deeply satisfying.

Callum came and stood beside him.

'Since we came here, I find that I do a lot of this too. You know, just looking at the sea. On a day like today, when it's calm, it's really soothing, which is great, but I also like it when the weather's up and the waves are crashing. It can be really exciting.'

'Why did you choose Oban, Callum? When you and Vicki were put into witness protection you could have gone anywhere.'

'I'd been here once before, when I was a wean. I must have been about six when me and my mother caught the train here from Glasgow. I remember us sitting on a wall and eating chips while we watched the boats come in and out. We were only here for the day but that visit has always stayed in my mind. She died not long after that. I suppose it was the last place I was really happy in.'

'How did Vicki feel about it?' Mac asked.

'I don't think that she was convinced about a move this far north until she came and had a look at the place. She loves Oban now, it's our home.'

'Did you have to cook up a cover story of some sort?'

Callum shook his head and smiled.

'No, we both decided that we wouldn't lie to anyone about our past but, obviously, we couldn't tell them the truth either. However, people seemed to have quickly decided what our past was for themselves. Apparently, I'm an ex-army man and, because I never mention the fact, everyone takes it that I must have been in some top-secret SAS unit or something. Then someone else decided that we came to Oban because of Vicki's car crash and that we wanted to forget all about the past and start afresh. People think they know about us now so that's okay.'

'Do you miss London at all?'

'No, all I miss is Francie and the Rev and I'll be seeing them both tomorrow,' Callum replied. 'I do miss the men too, if I'm being honest. I think about them now that winter's coming again.'

'Well, at least one of them should be warm enough,' Mac said.

'What do you mean?'

'Remember Baz?'

'Oh aye, he was the one who identified the Professor from your photograph, wasn't he?' Callum said.

'Yes, that's him. He had this thing about the Professor's coat and that kind of stuck in my mind. When I saw the Professor's sister, I asked her and she was okay about it. So, one evening, a month or so after you left, I took the Professor's coat down to the Old Beetroot and presented it to Baz. He was so made up about it,' Mac said with a wide grin. 'He reckoned he'd even be able to get a drink in the Blue Boar wearing that coat. I made sure and put some drinking money for the lads in one of the pockets.'

'That was kind of you,' Callum said.

'Not really, they'd all helped me with the case in one way or another. So how have you been, really?'

'Good, I mean being shot and nearly dying was bad but not as bad as you might think. While I was working at St. Philips, I wasn't sure where I was going or what I wanted to do. I suppose I was in a sort of limbo really. Coming around after the operation was like being reborn. Knowing that Vicki cared about me made all the difference. It felt as though the old Callum, the Tiger, had finally been laid to rest.' Callum paused and looked out over the sea. 'I still dream about it sometimes though and, in my worst nightmares, I've somehow gone back to the old life. Then I wake up and Vicki's lying next to me. I just lie still and listen to her breathing and everything's alright again.'

Mac knew exactly what he meant. There was a silence and Mac decided that now was the time to ask the question.

'How do you feel about the baby?'

Callum was thoughtful for quite a while.

'If you want to know the truth, I'm scared shitless.'

Mac almost laughed. So that was it.

'And that's all?'

'Oh aye, I mean I love the idea but...'

'But you're afraid that you'll be a bad dad, do all the wrong things and drop the baby on its head several times a day,' Mac said finishing off Callum's sentence.

Callum smiled.

'That's it exactly.'

'Callum just about everyone who's about to become a dad feels like that.'

'They do?'

'God, the sleepless nights I had before my daughter was born. I read up on the whole thing and went to as many pre-natal sessions with my wife as I could but, if I'm honest, I only seemed to pick up on all the things that could go wrong. Do you want to know what was the worst thought I had though?'

'Aye, I do.'

'I was scared that when my daughter finally came that I might not love her. That was the one that really kept me awake at night,' Mac said.

'Aye, that's been on my mind a lot too,' Callum said softly.

'I wouldn't worry about that if I were you. About a second after they handed me the little scrap of life that was my beautiful daughter, I fell instantly and totally in love with her. Believe me, you will too.'

Callum stood up and smiled widely.

'Thanks for that Mac, really thanks. I'd better get back. I'll see you tomorrow.'

They shook hands firmly and then Mac watched him as be bounded back into the church. He then turned and gazed out at the sea again. He still had a few minutes left before he had to go and meet Tim.

Why do we like looking at the sea so much? Mac idly asked himself. He was mildly surprised when he answered his own question.

Because it's the nearest thing to eternity that we'll ever directly experience. Those waves were slapping up against the land millions of years ago and they'll be doing just the same millions of years from now.

Life, though, is short.

Mac still regretted the moment when he'd almost prayed for death. Death is easy, anyone can kill but creating and sustaining a life is difficult. It requires love and hard work.

He was thinking of nothing at all when he heard a voice in his head. It was Nora, his wife.

'Don't worry, I'll wait for you,' she said.

He knew that it was probably just wishful thinking but he didn't care.

'Keep the light on for me, love,' he said softly.

THE END

I hope you've enjoyed this story. If you have then please post a review and let me know what you think. PCW

You can find out more at my author website - https://patrickcwalshauthor.wordpress.com/

Printed in Great Britain
by Amazon